ALIEN HORROR

Unconsciously, Freedman held his breath. Serous fluid welled out of the ruptured cyst on the sleeping girl's arm in small, irregular pulses. And through the yellow fluid, hesitantly, came a head—triangular, alien.

Freedman reached for a pair of forceps.
It had to be now. . . .

With a swift, stabbing motion, Freedman struck, grasping the parasite around the body. He lifted it clear of the girl's arm. It remained rigid, tail arched, legs splayed. He failed to observe the slight movement, the adjustment of the tail as the creature centered it down its line of sight. He saw the tail pulsate and half guessed the reason, but he was far too late. Something splashed on the left lens of his glasses. He felt a tiny warm spot on one side of his nose—warmth that grew to intense heat, blinding pain. Then darkness fell.

EARTH HAS BEEN FOUND

•

a novel by
D.F. JONES

A
DELL
BOOK

Published by
Dell Publishing Co., Inc.
1 Dag Hammarskjold Plaza
New York, New York 10017

FOR M.G. JACOBY

*All people, names, and events
are entirely fictitious.*

Dell ® TM 681510, Dell Publishing Co., Inc.

ISBN: 0-440-12217-1

Printed in the United States of America
First printing—February 1979

· Prologue ·

Last in, Julius Pechall shut the airlock and spun the ancient wheel. He felt the bars slide home; one light in the array changed from red to green. Even as he turned, his companions were lost to sight in the comforting swirl of hydrocyanic gas as it filled the compartment.

This was the best moment: relaxed, free of fear, cocooned in friendly death; a respite from tension, a brief period of solitude, of no-thought.

All too soon the shower, then the drying wind. He and the rest rotated slowly, arms raised, grotesque marionettes performing the prescribed choreography. They stopped, waiting.

All lights green: airlock opening. Beyond, the secure warmth of the Library of Congress. . . .

·I·

1984 . . .

The mere thought of that year filled many people with anxiety, yet their apprehension had no logical basis: All the ingredients for Orwell's nightmarish vision had existed in 1955, but Orwell had chosen 1984, and logic could go to hell.

Not since the 1660s, when half of Europe had similar fears for 1666, had there been so much quiet disquiet. For astrologers, seldom unemployed since the fourth century B.C., the early 1980s were golden years; and when someone announced the existence of a new comet, and predicted it would cast its ill-omen radiance in the spring sky of Orwell's year, a variety of natural disasters was effortlessly added to the catalog of woes to come. Of course, most folks denied any real belief in the predictions; it was "fun," no more. Perhaps; but those who claimed to be able to read the future continued to prosper. The human mind, it would seem, had made minimal progress since the seventeenth century.

But 1983 came first, a year that brought with it a castastrophe so awful, so earthshaking, it made any atrocity man had ever inflicted on man seem absurdly insubstantial.

Many had done their best to shut their minds to it,

had refused to think about it—until it was upon them, taking their children, shattering their lives.

1983 was not the year the world grew up, but it was the year humanity lost its last shred of innocence.

·II·

Even when it began cannot be known. The chronology is virtually meaningless, but it is improbable that anything could have happened earlier than 1916. Beyond question the largest concentration of Events occurred in the 1970s—the largest so far, that is. The first Event, well documented and attested, occurred in 1974.

On April 12, at 0800 Pacific Standard Time, a USAF F-4, crewed by a pilot and an observer, took off from a California air base on a test flight. It climbed to forty thousand meters and, after various checks and tests, was cleared to climb another seven thousand meters and head seaward for two Mach 1 plus runs. At 0825 the ground control radar lost the aircraft's blip. Urgent calls 0826 thru 0835 produced no answer from the plane. Consequently, full emergency procedure was initiated at 0837. At 0841 two more F-4's screamed into the air, followed ten minutes later by specialized search aircraft.

The Combined Services Search and Rescue organization is very impressive, the net it spreads fine mesh. Lives cannot always be saved, but seldom does the SAR fail to come up with an answer. This was one such occasion.

After seventy-two hours of intensive effort, SAR

headquarters reluctantly reported the F-4 lost at sea without a trace, cause unknown.

One of the few areas of genuine international cooperation is the distress communications set-up for ships and aircraft. Code words, procedures, and frequencies are the same worldwide. For aircraft there are two radio links, one HF, one VHF; both are monitored continuously by ground stations around the globe. Rarely does an aircraft in trouble go unheard.

At 1403 (local) on August 7, 1974, a radio man at the USAF base in Guam intercepted a Mayday distress call on VHF. He took a bearing and reported it to the station command post, where it was tied in with an unidentified radar contact that, noted at 1401, had already puzzled the duty officer enough for him to call the station commander.

While the chances of the unidentified airplane being hostile were minimal, no officer stuck with the responsibility dared treat this sort of situation lightly—not after Pearl Harbor. In this case, too many details were wrong: the plane's radar was not transmitting the distress pattern, and when interrogated by ground radar the pilot gave a USAF-type response—but the wrong one. That was enough. The duty officer had automatically brought the base to yellow alert at 1401; at 1405 the sirens wailed for condition red. One minute later three fighters took off under full afterburner thrust and vectored to intercept the stranger, now six hundred kilometers out. At the same time the point defense SAM sites went fully operational. In case it was a genuine distress call, two Grumman HU-6 amphibians were rolling from their hangars before the howling of the sirens had died.

Events moved equally fast in the underground command post. The station commander, Colonel Marvin L. Buckner, a veteran of Korea and Vietnam, arrived on the run. A call had been put out to the stranger and an unintelligible answer heard; a second radar challenge evoked the correct response, the distress mode. The time was 1409.

By then Buckner had a microphone in his hand, buttoned to a transmitter on the distress frequency. He spared fifteen seconds to take in the radar plot: the intruder was five-fifty kilometers distant, tracking south at two thousand meters, estimated speed five hundred knots. On that course he'd never make the base. Buckner thought quickly, only dimly aware of the duty officer talking quietly into another mike, vectoring the fighters.

If this was a suicide mission, maybe the pilot was crazy enough to assume the USAF would oblige and home him onto his target! On the other hand, if the guy was in real trouble, that plane had to be turned in the right direction fast. The fighters would not be up with him for another two or three minutes. That could be a long, long time. . . .

Buckner called the intruder, demanding identification, beginning a sequence of events he would never forget.

Again the answer was slow in coming, the distant, lonely voice slurred, unsure; listening, Buckner had time to read a teletype thrust before him.

NO REPEAT NO USAF MISSION A/B THIS TIME WITHIN ONE THOUSAND KM YOUR LOCATION

"This—this is Mission AF 2419—uh, no . . . Correction, Mission 2194. What's going on? The sun's all wrong—all wrong!" The voice climbed hysterically. "I'm lost! For Chrissake, help me!"

"Check that number," snapped Buckner in a swift and unnecessary aside; his master sergeant was already pounding the Intercommand teletype. "Cool it, man!" The commander said sharply to the distant plane. "Report type of aircraft, nature of distress, and fuel state. Over."

What the hell did he mean, the sun's wrong? The basic aim of military discipline is not heel-clicking and salutes; it is to give a soldier the inner strength to obey when his whole being, his instincts, tell him to run like hell. It is no disgrace for a fighting man to foul his trousers so long as he obeys; and this is true of all armed forces, whatever their political color.

The tough discipline of the USAF got through to the pilot's whirling, chaotic mind: For him the world was standing on its head, but the cold voice in his headset cut through the confusion.

"I'm riding an F-4, sir—fuel state, sixty percent remaining. . . . My distress is . . ." There he broke. "The sun's gone haywire! My gyro's crazy!"

Everyone in the command post froze, staring dumbly at Colonel Buckner. No less staggered than his staff, Buckner gazed unseeingly at the radar scan for several seconds, then slowly depressed the transmit button.

"Say again type of aircraft. Over."

They heard a half-strangled sob. Silence. Then the pilot spoke, his voice high-pitched, teetering on hysteria. "This is an F-4 . . . Christ! Foxtrot figure four! One, two, three, four! You read me!" The man was screaming.

Buckner's mind reeled. In his time he'd hit some sticky problems, but nothing like this. Without in-flight refueling, no F-4 could be that far from land, and certainly no USAF tanker was airborne.

The anguished voice returned. "For Chrissake gimme a heading!"

"Wait! Out." Now another voice, calm and business-like, came in on the fighter channel.

"This is Bantam One. Target held. Closing."

Buckner switched microphones. "Roger, Bantam One. Ed, this is Marvin. Watch your step. Hold your section off at strike range, close, and identify the target yourself. Be careful—suspect the pilot has blown. Out." He switched mikes again. "Mission 2194. Take it easy, don't panic. We hold you and your fuel state's good. Assistance will be with you in two minutes. Maintain present speed, height, and heading."

"Sure glad to hear that, sir!" The lost pilot's relief was obvious. "I can't figure—" he broke off. "Hey—I see a ship!" Again the voice climbed dangerously. "Great—oh, God! What a beautiful sight—"

The colonel cut in sharply. "Mission 2194! Maintain circuit discipline—" The master sergeant, his face pallid, thrust another flimsy before him.

IMMEDIATE. NO MISSION 2194 CURRENT THIS THEATER. NUMBER LAST USED FOR F-4 TEST FLIGHT EX CALIF AIR-BASE EVALUATED LOST AT SEA APRIL 12. PD VERIFY MISSION NUMBER AND REPORT PD

Before Buckner had time to fully absorb this incredible news, Ed's voice filled the room.

"Base, this is Bantam One." The speaker struggled to retain his professional calm. "I'm alongside the plane." He hesitated, then threw away his official voice. "You're not gonna believe this, Marvin, but it *is* an F-4! I'm not seeing things: here are details . . ." He gave tail number and squadron markings, ending with, ". . . aircraft has no, repeat no, external weapon pack."

Although outwardly calm, Buckner had to give himself five seconds to get his mind in gear. "Okay Ed, I've got that. Will instruct the stranger to take station two kilometers astern and one thousand meters below

11

you—" The utter impossibility of it all overwhelmed him. "Ed—you *sure* this is an F-4?"

"Marvin, I know how ya feel. I'm staring at the bastard right now, and I don't believe it! But it's still an F-4!"

"Okay, Ed. Keep your section back at engagement range—you copy that Bantam Two and Three?—If the guy even coughs, take him. Otherwise, come down to four hundred knots and bring him in. His reported fuel state is good. Will keep him on distress channel until he chops to approach control. Right now he needs things nice and simple. Acknowledge."

As Bantam One answered, Buckner called the stranger. In short, clipped sentences he passed along his instructions, adding, ". . . and report name, rank, and number." He glanced meaningfully at the duty officer, pencil poised over his clipboard.

In seconds the Intercommand teletype was chattering with the F-4's answer. Sweating, Buckner spoke as casually as he could, trying to ease the tense atmosphere. "If that dope fits, coronaries will be two-a-penny in Omaha!"

The swift reply wiped out his weak attempt at humor. FLASH. ALL DETAILS MATCH PROFILE OF MISSING AIRCRAFT. IMPOUND PLANE AND CREW IN MAXIMUM SECURITY PENDING FULL INVESTIGATION BY TEAM FROM THIS COMMAND. TAKE ALL PRECAUTIONS.

As he read the last sentence, his face twisted in a sour grin: that put the weight firmly on his back. He concentrated on the first part, still trying to comprehend this incredible string of events. Suppose—somehow—the plane and crew had been captured and brainwashed? Instinctively he rejected that—the pilot was as much a Texan as he was. Suppose it had a nuclear device aboard and was hell-bent on a latter-day Kamikazi attack? What could he do? Again he rejected the notion; maybe the pilot was the best actor since Barrymore, but he didn't believe that, either. Only one thing was certain—the man was terrified, lost; and again, why that weird bit about the sun being wrong?

He looked quickly at the radar plot; time was racing past, the formation barely a hundred kilometers out. He turned to the duty officer. "Chop 2194 to Channel Ten for final approach, Bantam One to cover him until he stops rolling. I want fire trucks and an armed guard to meet the plane, and once he's in the circuit recall the HU-16's." He reached for his cap; this was one visitor he'd meet personally.

He never made it to the door. The duty officer chopped the plane to Channel Ten on loudspeaker. On the fighter channel Bantam One confirmed that the stranger was following orders. The duty officer cued the control tower.

"Mission 2194, this is Guam Control. QNH setting one zero zero six; reduce speed to two zero zero knots at one zero zero zero meters. You are cleared for runway two six, wind two four zero, ten knots, visibility unlimited. Approaching outer marker now. Over."

They heard a series of clicks, a microphone cutting in, then out again, as if the pilot had trouble switching from intercom to radio. He spoke slowly, incoherently, his breathing heavy, irregular. He sounded drunk. "You . . . you say *Guam?*"

"That is affirmative. Check your speed—"

It was more than the pilot could take; fifteen seconds earlier he might have had time to react, to absorb the shock. "*Guam!* That's impossible!"

They were his last words.

The tower held the aircraft visually; it was over the inner marker, on the runway threshold, but not descending. It was too high, too slow.

"Abort!" screamed the controller. "Go round

again—boost—" The rest died in his throat. Nothing could be done.

The fighter seemed to hesitate, the port wing dropped as it stalled disastrously. The watchers in the tower hunched instinctively, each man mentally in the plane. Sunlight glinted on its upper surfaces, then the wing touched the ground; the plane cartwheeled, belching orange flame and black smoke as it careened down the runway: a wheel of fire spinning furiously, trailing black streamers, fragments arching upwards, sharply etched against the sun.

Four months late and five thousand miles off course, Mission 2194 had reached earth and died, its orisons the haunting wail of fire trucks and useless ambulances.

•III•

When the investigation team arrived twenty hours later, preliminary inquiries had been completed.

The sad, obscene mess of torn and burned flesh had undergone postmortem examination by the station doctors. Faced with such appalling evidence, there was little they could say except that the man had died instantaneously at impact. Physical identification was impossible—he was identified by his dog tag.

After extensive aerial and ground photography, the wreckage had been moved to a hangar. Airframe and engine numbers were recovered, and a fuel sample taken from a tank which had, fantastically, survived.

At the same time, statements were taken from all duty personnel and from anyone who had witnessed the accident. The taped records of radio links were impounded and sealed, and the film that had been shot from the control tower was processed.

The investigation team consisted of a brigadier general, a full colonel, and a major. Brigadier Hal Kelly, USAF—"Bull" to a few close friends—a large, balding man with a slab of ribbons on his chest, wasted no time. Hardly out of his plane, he was firing questions at Colonel Buckner, checking arrangements, steno services, waving aside the suggestion that he might care to shower or eat. No, the investigation would begin right now; coffee and sandwiches in the office would be fine.

In any crash, the investigators have to determine what happened and who was responsible. Marvin Buckner's conscience was clear, but he appreciated that his command's part in the tragedy would be worked over in every detail. It occurred to him that the brigadier might be leaning on him, flexing his muscles. Twenty hours back Bull Kelly had been doing something else in Washington, D.C. Since then he'd gotten his team together and flown eight thousand miles, and he still wouldn't take time out to change his shirt before starting in on the job.

By the time he had the team in its temporary office, Marvin Buckner had concluded two things: Someone a lot higher up was leaning on Kelly, and this case looked as incredible from the top as it did from his restricted viewpoint.

Even before he unlocked his bulky dispatch case, Kelly fired off another order: All personnel who had been involved were to muster as soon as convenient— like now. Kelly had never been sweet tempered, and being dragged off a vital investigation into fatigue failure in an experimental plane had done nothing to soften him.

Fifteen minutes later Bull Kelly was on his feet, addressing a crowded room.

"Gentlemen," he said in a rasping voice, "I was an aviator for fifteen years, and I've had seven years in accident investigation. I have to tell you that in all my time there's never been a case like this one." He paused, staring at his audience. "Never. And that goes for Air Force records, too.

"You may wonder why I'm telling you this. I'll tell you. You know there's something mighty strange about this accident. You'll want to talk about it; you'll have your chance in this room—and *nowhere else*!" He let that sink in, his hard gaze resting briefly on the young faces in front of him. "This matter, on orders from the Pentagon, is classified Top Secret, and before we go any further, I'll spell out what *that* means." He did so, and ten minutes later he had a watertight document with all their signatures on it to prove the fact.

"Right," he continued, "you'll all be interviewed— some of you several times. Until you get my permission, all personnel remain at five minutes notice to report to this room, day or night!" He looked at Buckner, "Okay, Colonel."

"Dismiss!" said Buckner, his face impassive, but he was still chewing on that "day or night" remark. He considered it good luck that in a long career he'd never met Kelly before, but he knew his reputation. The man did not kid.

When the room cleared and the stenographer sent for coffee and sandwiches, Kelly relaxed, running a beefy hand across his face. "Joe, how's the documentation look?"

Colonel Joe Grauber was a slightly built man whose nondescript features concealed a sharp analytical brain, wide experience, and the ability to sense when a witness was dodging the truth.

16

"From my angle, first class." He looked inquiringly at the major.

Franklin Arcasso was at first sight no gift to Air Force public relations. He was a lousy dresser, and at thirty-five he had a weight problem. Even in his cadet days he had been unable to achieve a smart, soldierly appearance. He was one of those men who could look badly dressed in swimtrunks. But there were other features. More than one senior officer, meeting him for the first time, had held back harsh comment on his appearance after viewing his ribbons: Although rumpled and crooked, they were of an exceedingly high grade. And an examination of his personnel file revealed more. He had majored in aerospace engineering at the Academy and become a combat pilot of outstanding ability and courage. He'd somehow found time to take a master's degree in his specialty, and moved on to test flying. He was in this assignment now because his left arm was artificial, a souvenir of his last flight as a pilot. One of his better ribbons was also a memento of that flight: He had brought back an experimental ship under impossible conditions and landed it safely after ignoring repeated orders to bail out. He later claimed a radio malfunction.

"The technical data looks good, General, very good." A cigar ash fell on his slacks. "The guy who put this documentation together knew his stuff."

For half an hour the men worked, reading the reports, making notes, eating and drinking. Kelly nodded the stenographer out of the room. As the door closed, he spoke.

"This looks like a pretty fair statement to me."

"Comment?"

"Agreed," said Grauber, "but . . ." He left it there. "Nothing jumps out and bites me, General—apart from the whole goddam business. Of course, we have to be stone-cold certain this is the same aircraft reported lost off California."

"You have doubts, Major?"

"No sir. Dog tags, airframe and engine numbers, tail number and squadron markings all match, but this is such a crazy case I have to see them with my own eyes. This whole thing's fantastic. I'm not inclined to take anything on trust."

Kelly nodded and sighed, letting his thoughts wander. "Fantastic," he said at last, softly. "You have the right approach, Frank, but this is the same plane, let's not kid ourselves." He leaned back, belched. "As I see it, we have two different problems. The first is to decide—if we can—what happened to the F-4 between 0825 on April twelfth and 1401 August seventh. The second is to establish the reason or reasons for the crash. For my money the second's easiest. We'll take that first."

They worked for seven hours, reading, inspecting the wreckage, interviewing witnesses, listening to tapes, and wearing out two stenographers on the side. The verdict was unanimous: pilot error, due to fatigue, shock, and unknown circumstances.

Hal Kelly slammed his file shut, glanced at his watch, then at his colleagues, his eyes red-rimmed. "For local consumption, I'm telling the station commander he may let it be known that the F-4 was on an experimental flight, missed its rendezvous with a tanker due to a faulty compass, and ended up here." He glared at his audience. "So it's thin—but can you do better? At least it'll satisfy most people around this base—okay, I know, not the operations team or the aviators—but they don't worry me. They'll keep their mouths shut.

"That's all, gentlemen. We start on the really tough questions in precisely eight hours."

For three eighteen-hour days they stuck at it; for much of three nights they lay awake in restless thought. On the fourth morning Brigadier Kelly began the session without preamble.

"Before we go over the possibilities one more time, I've just received a dispatch from Washington which will save time. Based on a full fuel load—more than the plane could have had at the time it disappeared—Washington allowed a generous ferry range of two thousand miles. Within that range, every airfield with a runway even remotely long enough to handle an F-4 has been checked out. They're satisfied the plane didn't land anyplace from Alaska down to and including Mexico. Nor did it land in the Hawaiian Islands, or cross the Aleutian chain to Soviet Siberia—just supposing it had a lot of luck and a hundred knot tail wind all the way, which the met boys rule out. And finally—" he paused, anticipating their reaction "—the analysis of the fuel sample is in. It was one hundred percent honest-to-God USAF standard mix."

Frank Arcasso's metal fist crashed on the table. He knew, as they all did, that trace elements were added to Air Force fuel to deter thieves.

"Exactly, Major."

Grauber spoke. "That news, General, also goes a long way toward discrediting the enemy seduction theory. I fail to believe that someone could have provided a tanker aircraft at the right spot at the right time and with the right fuel. And even if I could swallow that, I can't accept that the F-4 crew had already been subverted, and took the plane to a secret RV with the tanker, and then, after all that, took the trouble to return the plane here! No weapon load of any sort—unless the disoriented pilot was the weapon. No, for my part I rule out that theory." They had covered this ground repeatedly and they knew it, but they continued to do so in the hope that something new would occur to them.

"So the plane flew straight up its own ass and stayed there for four months?" Kelly asked sardonically.

"Look, General," said Frank Arcasso, who had made up his mind and would stick to it, "as the junior member of this team, I give my verdict first—right?"

"Go ahead, Frank."

"Sir, my view is based chiefly on the tapes. We're all pilots; we know the man wasn't kidding—he *was* lost. I accept that that is not hard evidence, but there's little of that around. He had a lot of hours in fighters; it's against all probability that this was the first emergency he'd met. His record shows no suspicion of combat fatigue. But he *was* lost and completely thrown by whatever happened. 'The sun's wrong' and 'the sun's gone haywire' are at the root of this accident. I've calculated there'd be a forty degree difference in the elevation of the sun between the two material times. And there's the evidence of their watches: Both stopped at 0846 on the twelfth."

"I accept that last item is very curious," replied Kelly, "but what does it mean? Maybe whatever happened, happened at that time. That still doesn't get us very far."

"That's true—if you think that was the only time the watches stopped."

Both senior men stared at Arcasso. Grauber said, "You ask us to believe that both watches stopped sometime after 0825 on April twelfth, started again, and stopped for the last time on impact?"

"I hadn't finished, Colonel. The watches *possibly* showed twenty-one minutes elapsed time from the original disappearance. There were twenty minutes between the first radar contact at 1401 and the crash at 1421. In my theory, only one minute is unaccounted for."

"That's way-out stuff, Arcasso."

The major kept going. "My guess is the watches restarted around 1400—along with everything else in the plane. I believe the pilot was rocked on his heels by the fact that the last time he saw the sun it was in a totally different place, and he was *not aware* of the passage of time. Sure, it's a way-out theory, but it *fits!* Nothing else I can think of accounts for the pilot's report that the fuel state was sixty percent. Okay, so he may have gotten it wrong, but I doubt it, and," he said grimly, "watching that movie of the crash, and looking at the wreckage, I'd say he still had quite a lot on board at impact."

"You're prepared to say that this plane went out of time, into . . . suspended animation, for the better part of four months?"

Arcasso took a deep breath. "Unless you or Colonel Grauber can spot a fault—given my original premise— yes. If necessary, I'll sign a minority report."

"Grauber?"

"Much as I dislike it, I agree that Frank's theory is the only one that fits. In this case the unbelievable is the only logical answer."

Brigadier Kelly rubbed his face, walked over to the window, and stared out. "Right. Frank, get that steno in here. Christ! Washington's going to love this!"

Brigadier Hal Kelly got it right, first time. After a major confrontation between him and his incredulous boss, the report was released to other, select departments. Their reaction was much the same, but all the top brass who read it appreciated two points: no other theory fit, and however crazy the answer, it was even crazier to suppose that three professional officers would wish to toss their careers down the drain for fun. Every attempt was made to tear the report to shreds, but always the detractors came back to the same problem—what other explanation fitted?

So the ostrich syndrome came into play. Men accustomed to taking decisive action were baffled by the report. It read like science fiction, but no one could fault it as a possible answer. Many took the only road out, treating it as a joke. As the file circulated, thickening all the while, snide comments appeared: "Call Mars" and "Bring back the UFO Committee!" Predictably, there were references to little green men.

Around the world, airplanes were being lost almost every week, and as the months passed, interest waned. By early 1975 the report had orbited the Pentagon twice. Someone added a note—"Not the Marie Celeste again!"—speeding it on its way to Central Registry and oblivion. The incident was forgotten, just one of those inexplicable events.

There are committees for everything in the defense world. Some give their all to the intricacies of female personnel's dress. At the other end of the scale, tight-lipped men brood over Soviet intentions and capabilities.

One such committee, of middle grade, dealt with air intelligence. To it came reports from many sources on widely differing matters, but all had some bearing on its subject. It might be the redeployment of a Soviet air group, the strange acquisition of a sophisticated air defense system by a bankrupt banana republic, or the abstruse scribblings of an astrophysicist in a foreign university. The committee members coordinated, evaluated, and disseminated; to those in the know they were "the jigsaw boys." They met three times a week, more often if necessary.

A regular meeting took place on a bleak morning in February, 1977. From the conference-room window the Potomac could be seen, slate-gray between white banks of snow; to imagine the cherry trees would ever blossom again required a major act of faith.

But the view got scant attention. In the previous two days items had poured in, and the session proved long and tiring. By late afternoon, the jigsaw boys were anxious to get away; still more paper would be piling up in their offices.

"One final item, gentlemen." The chairman looked down the long table. "A quickie. You may think it humorous."

No one looked too hopeful.

"Back in March of last year, we had an item reporting the disappearance of an Aeroflot *Ilyushin* IL-14P—yeah, a real oldie—on an internal flight from Moscow to Irkutsk. Following usual Soviet practice for internal losses, no public announcement was made. Now—and this is the strange part—a previously reliable source says the plane has turned up again, at Vorkuta, North Russia."

Heads turned to study the wall map.

"As you see, that's way off the Moscow-Irkutsk flight line. In fact it's about fifteen hundred kilometers north. Collateral intelligence suggests great Soviet concern; a plane load of high-power KGB men are known to have left Moscow in a hurry, destination maybe Vorkuta." He shrugged. "What that adds up to, you tell me."

Lieutenant Colonel Frank Arcasso, section head of AI (Tech) 4, and Major Chester Holmes, an old friend from Academy days and a top-drawer intelligence man, exchanged meaningful glances; the latter shook his head almost imperceptibly. Neither took part in the short discussion. The item would be kept on file; supplementary intelligence might clarify the matter.

The meeting broke up, but the two men did not leave. Arcasso got up and stared at the bleak scene out the window, while Holmes took his time packing up his papers. The room finally empty, Arcasso turned to his friend.

"Well?"

Holmes hesitated, fiddling nervously with the handle of his dispatch case. "I only saw the report. An awful lot's happened since—since whenever it was—"

"August '74."

"August '74. It's not surprising we're the only ones who remember it. Chances are no one else even heard of it."

Arcasso gestured impatiently. "That's not what I mean, Chet."

"Give me a chance. I was going to say that the angle that really bugs me is the absence of the F-4 report. It should be tied to this item. That in itself is strange—never mind the item itself."

"Could be a foul-up—the computer failed to spit out the F-4 papers."

"I don't think so," said Holmes. He looked up accusingly. "And neither do you."

Lieutenant Colonel Arcasso (to his surprise but no one else's, he'd been promoted) clicked his artificial hand on his case. "We can't walk away from it. It could be a hang-up in the computer."

"How about a private word with the chairman?"

Arcasso shook his head. "I'll do a little checking first. Joe Grauber is now the boss of my old outfit. We were together on the F-4 case."

"Watch where you put your feet, Frank."

"You can bet on it. This is the scariest thing I've ever heard, and I have a shrewd suspicion I'm not alone in that opinion."

Arcasso flopped in his office chair, lit a cigar and examined the ceiling as if it were a hostile sky. The cigar was half gone before he lifted the phone.

"Joe? Frank Arcasso. How would it be if I dropped by for a few minutes?" He sounded casual, but both men knew that "dropping by" involved a good fifteen-minute walk. The Pentagon is, after all, the largest office building in the world.

"Thought I might hear from you, Frank."

Arcasso sat up in his chair. "Oh—why?"

"The tom-toms can be heard quite clearly up here," Grauber said evasively. "Frank, I've got a stack of paper to clear before I leave for a duty cocktail party. Meet me at the east door in half an hour. We can talk on the way to my car; I'll deliver you to yours."

Arcasso replaced the receiver as if it were a sweaty stick of gelignite. Old Joe had not said so many things.

*　*　*

They met on time, for—as Arcasso knew—Grauber was a fanatically punctual man. But he was not prepared for the way his old colonel chose to play it.

"Frank—nice to see you!" A warm handshake, a firm grip on his arm, steering him to one side, out of the mainstream of workers flooding homeward. They went out slowly, down the steps into the bitter cold evening, Grauber talking genially, saying nothing.

Once clear of the building, his manner changed abruptly. "Okay, Frank. Talk."

His strange conduct shook Arcasso, but not enough to stop him from taking a chance. Even to mention AI Committee affairs broke the rules in a big way. Grauber might be cleared for that grade of intelligence, or he might not; but it was not Arcasso's business to tell him. Yet Grauber's behavior indicated he knew something. Arcasso went beyond his original intentions, telling Grauber all. Grauber took it in silence.

"So why no F-4 file?"

Grauber's answer stopped him dead.

"What F-4 file?"

Arcasso froze, then grabbed Grauber's arm, their feet grating on the frosty tarmac. He stared open mouthed, his breath white vapor under the cold potassium lighting, while Grauber, unmoved, fiddled with a bunch of keys.

Grauber spoke softly, face turned downward. "No questions, and don't talk to *anyone*. I'll tell you this much: The real foul-up was in releasing that Soviet item to your committee. You—personally—will hear more. This is not just a Defense Department matter. Not any longer."

· V ·

Next morning, Arcasso's section found him unusually difficult to deal with, and they did their best to stay out of his way.

He tried to concentrate, but his mind soon wandered; he signed letters and initialed files without the slightest idea of their content.

Grauber had said it was no longer a Defense Department matter; he saw that, but where did it all end up—the State Department?—the President? If the Russian report was correct, the problem touched all humanity.

Grauber rang. Arcasso was expected at the State Department in thirty minutes, Room 439. That was all.

Arcasso's puzzlement increased when he reached Room 439. The tablet on the door read Interdepartmental Liaison Section. That he had never heard of the outfit came as no surprise; he'd been around long enough to recognize an intentionally vague title when he saw one.

Room 439 contained a frosty female, her desk, and four chairs for visitors, arranged along one wall under her cold eye. In spite of his preoccupation, Frank was struck by the bareness of the room. On the desk was a typewriter, a phone, a notebook, and a small cactus which resembled a sea urchin, including spines.

"Oh, Colonel. Please sit down." The secretary abruptly returned to the typewriter.

Arcasso dug out a cigar. The secretary said nothing, just looked. He compromised, chewing on it, unlit.

Suddenly she said, "You can go in now, Colonel," her nod indicating an inner door. He wondered vaguely how the trick was done; maybe there was a cue light hidden in the cactus.

The inner room confirmed his suspicions. He'd seen it before. Nylon net curtains did nothing to conceal the fine wire mesh over the window. One wall was curtained from floor to ceiling, and six gray filing cabinets of the latest pattern took up another wall. On four of them, red lights glowed, indication that they were unlocked.

The greeting was warmer than the decor: A tall man in his mid-thirties got up from his desk. "Glad you could make it on such short notice, Colonel." The Ivy League voice matched his suit. He waved Arcasso to an armchair, pushing a cigarette box and ashtray in his direction.

Sitting down, Arcasso noticed something else: His host had no telephone—a sure sign of a high security area. There could be one in a drawer, but Frank doubted it. A tape recorder, yes, very likely, but no phone. He lit a cigar and waited.

His host smiled unconvincingly. "Call me Smith," he said. "This desk is manned 'round the clock; the name goes with the job. First, read this."

"This" was a letter assigning Frank to "additional duties with the State Department" and signed by his commanding general. Smith smiled encouragingly. "It regularizes your position." Arcasso was thinking more about the "additional duties," and Smith knew it. "A major—he's worked in your section before—is being assigned as your assistant in AI (Tech)."

"Ah," said Frank guardedly. "But why me?"

"There's an urgent need for an experienced aviator with a good technical background and with some knowledge of intelligence." Smith might have been reading from an official handout.

"I could name a half-dozen better, right here in Washington."

"I doubt it. Grauber recommended you, and he's regarded as a good judge. He said you had the moral courage to stick your neck out with the F-4 report."

"We all did that."

"Yes—but you did it first. There's another, very important qualification. You already know more than most, and a high-level directive restricts access to this case to a minimum. I won't waste your time, Colonel. Sorry if you feel railroaded"—Smith's tone suggested he could live with it—"but that's the way it is. As of now you're on Case ICARUS—and even the name's Topsec."

"Icarus? That's a dandy name! His wings dropped off."

Smith waved that aside. "You're booked on the Pan Am night flight to London tonight. You'll be met."

"London! What in hell for?"

"The Soviet government's just as keen to talk as we are: Their man's flying in right now." He smiled again. "Ironically, this desk apart, he's the only person with whom you may openly discuss the F-4 incident. In turn, we have their assurance he'll fill you in on their problem."

"How did all this come about?"

"A remarkably direct approach by a senior embassy official to someone of importance." Clearly he gave nothing for free. "He said they had 'indications' of the F-4, and also appreciated we had word of the Ilyushin. In the exceptional circumstances, his government felt a frank but very confidential exchange of information would be beneficial to both parties." He was quoting again. "You represent the U.S."

"In which case," said Frank, "may I see the F-4 file? I'd like to refresh my memory."

Smith crossed to a cabinet and produced the file, now in an unfamiliar folder. He opened it at the AIB report.

Five minutes was enough. Handing it back, Frank said, "There's one other member of the committee who knows both items." He named him.

"Thanks, Colonel. I'll contact him." Smith stood up, offering his hand. "My secretary has your transportation documents. Good luck, Arcasso—and be quick."

Arcasso had no choice. An embassy official met the plane. By 8:30 A.M. they were in a Heathrow hotel drinking coffee.

"You meet in the British Museum. The Soviets have a soft spot for the place," the embassy man said chattily, "no doubt because Karl Marx wrote a good deal of *Das Kapital* in the reading room."

"When?" Frank was in no mood for chat.

"Ten o'clock—when it opens. I'll drop you off at the main entrance. Inside, you'll find a king-size staircase on your left. Go up one floor, at the top of the stairs there's a Roman mosaic floor. That's the pickup point."

"Identification?"

"You'll both have a copy of the London *Times* sticking out of your left-hand pocket—here's yours. D'you know the museum?"

"No."

"Well, he does, and he'll lead. When you've finished, go back to the point where I'll have dropped you. I'll be waiting. How long do you expect to be?"

Frank shrugged. "Hour, hour and a half."

"Okay, I'll take your grip. Not that you'll be needing it. We've got a seat reserved for you on every

Washington flight between four o'clock and midnight. You're really getting the treatment." He added an afterthought. "If you have to give a name, make it Smith."

The contact went smoothly. "What do I call you?" The accent was by no means perfect, but the Russian spoke fluent English.

"Smith," said Arcasso, with no conviction.

"Ah yes," the Russian smiled faintly. "A ver' popular name, Smit. I am Lebedev." With a polite inclination of his hand, Lebedev, a short, thick-set man in a bulky overcoat, led the way. They paused at the entrance to a long gallery for a quick inspection by the Russian, then sauntered in, passing an aged custodian, who after one brief glance resumed his contemplation of the infinite.

"I often wonder what they think about, day after day. There is remarkably little interest in early Islamic pottery." He stopped beside a glass case, through which they had a commanding view of the empty gallery.

"First," Lebedev spoke softly, "it has been agreed that you tell me of the F-4, then I give you the—er—lowdown on our Ilyushin, yes? One moment—" He fumbled in an inside pocket. "My recorder . . ." His tone changed. "Case ICARUS"—he smiled slightly at Arcasso's expression—"Statement by U.S. official Smit." He raised an eloquent eyebrow.

As Arcasso talked, the Russian's mouth hardened. The account completed, he moved slowly to another display, hands deep in his overcoat pockets, thinking.

"You permit one or two questions, Mr. Smit?" His chief interest lay in the time relation of the disappearance and reappearance on radar and radio contact.

Other questions about the fuel state and the fatal stall revealed he had a considerable knowledge of the F-4. Switching off his recorder, he confirmed Arcasso's hunch. "I have not, of course, anything like your experience, Mr. Smit, but I have some hours in a F-4. It is a fine machine: I feel your pilot must have been, how you say, out of his mind."

"I told you the inquiry found the accident due to his error," said Frank shortly.

"I do not mean to be offensive," replied Lebedev soothingly. "Your aviators are superbly trained, the plane handles well and this man had combat experience, and yet—" He shrugged. "One wonders if he was injured."

"As I said, he reported only a compass failure. I don't thing he was injured—he was scared, confused. The bodies were too badly mutilated to reveal anything."

"Yes." They moved on; the gallery was still empty. "Now if you are ready, I talk."

The aircraft, he said, an old feeder-line machine hauling freight, had been lost in March, 1976. It returned in mid-January, 1977, suddenly appearing over the Arctic Ocean west of Novaya Zemla, height three thousand meters heading east. Intercepting fighters escorted it to Vorkuta, where it landed safely. Here Lebedev gave his view of the difference in pilot reaction. Because of the higher latitude at appearance—and roughly at the same time of day on the same base course—the Soviet pilot did not have the traumatic experience of the sun's relocation. And he was not alone on the flight deck; he had a copilot, could see and touch another human. The American flyer had faced a much more urgent situation, alone in his cockpit, his observer only a voice.

He resumed his narrative. The crew was promptly

detained by the KGB for interrogation—he made no bones about that; they were still in custody. Although both had been questioned repeatedly, nothing of substance had been discovered. The pilot's only contribution of possible significance concerned the quality of light: he had had an "impression" that for a fraction of a second, about two hours into the flight, the sky had seemed to darken. Until questioned he had given it no thought, for within seconds he had realized the plane was ten degrees off course, and about five hundred meters above the current flight level. Startled, he had immediately cut out the auto, assumed manual control, and corrected course and level. It didn't make much sense, but he could only conclude he had dozed off and there had been a malfunction in the autopilot—what else?

The second pilot had nothing to offer, admitting he had had his eyes shut at the vital moment. Neither had observed anything remarkable outside the plane: unbroken cloud a thousand meters below, clear sky above. Both said they'd been practically dumbstruck at the appearance of the fighters and the order to shift frequency to Vorkuta approach control for landing instructions. Although they'd had thirty minutes to adjust, the landing they made had been far from steady.

The airplane had been examined exhaustively, including the landing wheels; traces of tarmac that had been recovered matched the surface of the Moscow runway from which the plane had taken off; no unidentified material had been found.

The scant evidence was not conclusive, but there were no signs to suggest the plane had landed anywhere. In another incredible way the story was the same as the F-4's. Fuel and oil consumption fitted a correct flight, and the aircraft clock and the men's watches were wrong, both having the same error.

But there were two other features which could not have been noted in the F-4 case. Neither pilot nor co-pilot needed a shave or a haircut. And something else. Seven holes, each about two millimeters in diameter, had been found in the flight deck section of the fuselage. Distribution appeared to be random, their cause unknown; but two possibilities could be eliminated. In no case could any two holes be related as entry and exit points; all were uniform in diameter. Neither man had any injury, and no foreign matter had been found. That, concluded the Russian, ruled out any theories of cosmic particles or micrometeorites.

Red-eyed, exhausted, Arcasso sat sleepless on the return night flight, staring unseeingly out his window. Out there, beyond this tiny man-made capsule, something inexplicable had happened. . . .

Abruptly he drew the shade, gulped the lukewarm drink he'd clutched for an hour, and ordered another. It wouldn't do much good, but—

It was as if the stopper had been pulled from Sinbad's flask. Black, formless clouds filled his imagination, clouds from which he feared, to the very depths of his being, a baleful genie would emerge. . . .

For Arcasso, the stopper in the flask was the seven tiny holes, circular and perfectly smooth in the dural skin, insulation, and plastic cladding of the Ilyushin's cabin. That they existed at all was bad enough, but the fact that they had been found only in that area— not in the freight deck, the wings, tail plane, or engine cowlings—was significant.

Significant and very sinister.

The staggering news of the Russian plane made surprisingly little impact in Washington, for one very simple reason: ICARUS had the tightest security wrap in history.

Only ten Americans knew the details of both Events, and four of them were members of the ICARUS committee. The committee was chaired by Joseph Langbaum, a top CIA man, and included one representative from the State Department and one from the FBI, plus Arcasso. Their directive: to evaluate Case ICARUS material, and to report their findings and recommendations directly to the President.

They met the day Arcasso returned from London. The first question was whether they believed the Soviet report; they did. They also knew that neither the U.S. nor NATO had any hand in the Ilyushin incident, and believed the Soviets had nothing to do with the F-4—even supposing either side had the ability to engineer such bizarre and pointless action. That agreed, the similarities of the two Events were all too evident. Whatever agency had been responsible for the F-4 had to be responsible for the Ilyushin affair also. At that point progress ceased. The four men stared at one another blankly. Among them, they had access to all the intelligence of the Western world, plus that of the KGB, and no one had even the ghost of a rational explanation. Arcasso, who had lived the nightmare longer than anyone, urged they forget that for the moment. What had happened twice could happen again—if so, what action should be taken?

Late into the night the four men hammered at the

problem; the more they thought about it, the worse it got. An Event might occur anyplace, anytime; but even if they came up with a contingency plan, security would not permit its implementation until the Event happened. And so they shelved that one, too, and with a sense of relief got down to organizing themselves.

It was agreed that all intelligence on any missing plane would be flashed to Arcasso. From his seat in Air Intelligence he could easily cover all U.S. and NATO aircraft, civil and military. The CIA would report all it learned of other nationalities; Langbaum would establish mouth-to-mouth contact with the KGB and seek its cooperation. And on the side, Alvin Malin for the FBI offered anything the bureau might turn up. There the meeting broke up.

Next morning, Langbaum flew to Vienna, meeting by arrangement Arcasso's London contact. Naturally, both covered their true identities, not wishing to cause a major flutter in the international intelligence hen house.

Joseph Langbaum, known on the committee as "CIA Joe," became "Smith"; the Russian remained "Lebedev." They met in a cafe on the Ringstrasse, and "Smith" had a hard time concealing his surprise. He knew a great deal about the KGB organization, and he recognized Lebedev—a relatively new star in the uncertain KGB firmament, but already rated among its ten most powerful men. He had risen with extraordinary speed to the very top of an outfit numbered not in thousands but in hundreds of thousands. Lebedev was first chief directorate, responsible for KGB interests in North America—and he had dropped everything and come running for this meeting with no notice at all. It was obvious that the Russians weren't playing games.

They exchanged amenities. Waiting for coffee, both men glanced casually about them. Smith knew very well that the cafe was as good as Soviet territory, but this was no time for protocol. At least he was certain that the table the Russian had selected was unbugged. He noted too that while the cafe was only half full, large men predominated, and no table in their immediate vicinity was occupied. Of course, some of the men were his, just as others were certainly Lebedev's.

The Russian caught his gaze and smiled. "Satisfactory, Mr. Smit?"

"Sure," said Smith. "Look . . ." He explained what he wanted.

Stirring his coffee, Lebedev listened. He said, "You are prepared to reciprocate?"

Smith smiled gently. "We are wide open—but if you need it . . ."

Lebedev smiled back, revealing some gold-filled teeth. "It would save time."

Smith nodded. "Okay. We're treating ICARUS as Top Secret plus; I imagine it's the same with you. To give you an idea what that means to us, only ten people in the U.S.A. are cleared for this material."

"So many?" replied Lebedev politely. "For us it is seven."

"Democracy has its faults."

Both men laughed unconvincingly. Smith said, "I suggest we pass material through our stations right here in Vienna. Prefixed ICARUS it will reach me in a matter of—well, very quickly."

Lebedev nodded. "Agreed."

Smith was impressed. In his experience a Soviet man, no matter how high up the tree, usually needed time to refer back to home base.

For all intents and purposes, the meeting was over, but Lebedev snapped his fingers and brandy was served. Smith sensed the Russian had something on his mind, but failed to prompt him, and the moment passed. They drank a formal toast and parted.

Intent upon the details of ICARUS, he had not been sufficiently receptive. Lebedev had wanted to say something, but he had needed encouragement, understanding. He was desperate to talk to someone out of the Soviet orbit, to say things that if discovered would inevitably ruin his life, land him in a KGB mental hospital, classified instantly as "schizophrenic."

In the long run it would not matter, but at that point CIA Joe had certainly missed a trick.

After ten days of intensive work, the committee came up with a plan, and it was quickly approved by the President. It included instructions for air traffic controllers, airport managers, and all government agencies, civil and military, in every state in the Union. The orders were sealed in containers that were not to be opened, under any circumstances, without an OK from the Oval Office.

Those who held the containers knew that in certain undisclosed circumstances they would receive a code word and a telephone number. They were to call the number immediately, acknowledging receipt of the code word. Once the container was unsealed, Envelope One was to be opened. This gave the recipient general instructions that varied according to his job. It added that detailed orders would be obtained by calling the same telephone number. There were also Envelopes Two, Three, and Four, none to be opened without additional authority. The beauty of the system was this: Up to and including the opening of Envelope One, neither the recipients nor the telephone control would know more than the simple fact that an air emergency existed. Should it turn out to be a false alarm, no great damage would be done.

Control was a small operations room manned continuously by ranking Air Force officers responsible to the ICARUS committee—on whose orders they would originate the code word, relay instructions, and update the file of missing planes. Hooked into the air defense teletype network, they would know at once if a missing aircraft turned up, and would promptly alert the ICARUS committee. This was all Control knew and they were not encouraged to speculate.

Arcasso and his fellow members set up a four-day roster. On a duty day the committee member kept close contact with the duty officer. For the other three days he was free to move wherever he liked or needed to be—provided he maintained communications and could be back in the Pentagon within three hours. In their different ways, all four men prayed it would never happen. It would have surprised the others, had they known, that tough old Arcasso—the sloppiest dresser ever to make lieutenant-colonel—had taken to saying his prayers in church.

· VII ·

The twentieth century has seen the gradual erosion of the importance of the family in America. A weds B, both leave their parents, set up home, raise kids—who repeat the pattern, leaving A and B to their own devices, free to visit their children's families, but preferably not too often. Then A or B dies. The survivor is left alone, often with no function or purpose in life.

Which is why parts of Florida are the way they are, and why Social Circles are so popular, especially with widowed grandmothers, deprived of their ancient right to boss the family from the fireside while keeping an eye on the stew pot.

The Social Circle of Abdera Hollow, New York, was a lot more than a geriatric get-together: Imbued with the good old American spirit of get-up-and-go, it took full advantage of cheap globe-trotting packages for organized groups, and traveled as often as possible.

Seventy-two Circle members had organized a European tour ("Five Countries and Four Capitals in Ten Days") in September, 1982. The last stop was Roissy-Charles de Gaulle Airport, Paris, France.

Forty were widows or footloose wives; fourteen retired couples, two adventurous widowers, and two single females—who ruined the average age—completed the party. One of the younger women, thirty and newly divorced, came because she couldn't think of anything better to do. The other, twenty, was the niece of one of the widows; she went along, all expenses paid, in return for a little light donkey-work. It was better than staying home and mulling over a disastrous love affair. These two apart, the age scale began at forty-seven and ended at an energetic eighty-two. Most were in their early seventies.

The party had at last been corralled for the return flight by that modern cowboy, the courier. Practically dead on his feet, he was sustained by the thought of the small wad of heavily-scented dollar bills in his jeans—there's always one or two on any tour prepared to pay for a little synthetic romance. He waited, eager to be gone, sadly eyeing the young blonde. He'd gladly have obliged her free.

He glanced at his watch. They were late boarding, but he couldn't go—left to their own devices, some would get themselves locked in lavatories, and one or two were quite capable of winding up back in a Parisian nightclub, on top of the Eiffel Tower, anyplace.

Some of his untrustworthy flock were also casting calculating glances around, noting nontour passengers—and a dull lot they were. A family of five, the kids an authentic pain in the ass before they even got aboard. Half a dozen glum businessmen, nursing bags stuffed with dirty shirts, and no doubt ulcers as well. These were a familiar and unattractive sight to many a widowed eye.

The courier checked the airline desk. Autumnal fog had clamped down across half of Europe; connecting flights were late. Fog was approaching de Gaulle, but the plane would be cleared before conditions got marginal. That cheered him.

Two hours late and four-fifths empty, the giant plane, call sign *Papa Kilo*, took off. At dawn the pilot reported he was on course, ten minutes behind revised schedule due to head winds.

And after that, nothing.

Few people outside of New York State, and not many in it, had ever heard of Abdera Hollow. Legend held that a congressman, desperate for reelection, honored the township with a visit back in the 1890s, and there had been a nasty boardinghouse fire in the twenties. That was about all the excitement this hamlet had seen.

Abdera began in a shallow hollow or dip, a natural resting place after the long haul uphill from the east. Pallid New Yorkers came for their annual vacations, enjoying a brief bucolic retreat on the edge of the

Catskills. By the mid-twenties Abdera had overflowed its hollow; Main Street included a livery stable-cum-gas station, a saloon, three stores, three modest hotels, Mom's Diner, and a chapel. In the last golden year before the '29 crash two more stores, a post office, a barber shop, a mortician's parlor, and a discreet whorehouse had been added—the latter operating, of course, solely for the convenience of the summer visitors. Those were indeed the days.

And then the bad times. After the Wall Street debacle, the Depression had sunk its teeth into Abdera, and half the town had gone up for sale. The slow recovery, NRA, and the drift toward war had barely touched the town. And another adversity was making itself felt—air travel. New Yorkers discovered Florida, and as flying became cheaper more and more of them headed south. By 1945, Abdera Hollow's population was half of what it had been at the turn of the century, and much of Main Street lay derelict. With the departure of the younger folk, only the mortician thrived; and with the closing of the wartime army camp, the whorehouse folded. Abdera eked out a shaky existence from a few faithful vacationers, adulterous weekenders, and agriculture.

But the wheel turned; someone discovered the Catskills had from time to time a great deal of snow. Winter sports arrived on the New Yorkers' doorstep and Abdera was back in business.

One thing did happen in the lean years. There had been a doctor around, a relic of the horse-and-buggy days. The locals got by with him, knowing no better, but it was generally agreed that Abdera was no place to get sick. The old man died, and for a time Abdera did without. Then Mark Freedman, M.D., hung up his shingle.

Laymen are seldom competent to judge a professional in his specialty—not that it stops them, especially in a community like Abdera. Freedman was totally unlike his predecessor. He was not strong on goose grease and similar homely remedies, nor did he use bourbon as a perfume. But—grudgingly at first—the locals had to admit he knew his stuff. He was a strangely birdlike figure, quick of movement and even quicker of mind. Many wondered why he had chosen Abdera over the richer pastures around Central Park. But after ten years of globe-trotting his wife had been ready for a rural life, and so, in fact, had he.

He soon proved to be a first-class physician, and when the winter sports craze took hold, he was particularly busy with splints and plaster. His practice expanded well beyond the town, and in the late 1970s he took on a young assistant, James Scott. Twenty years after his arrival, Freedman was a leading citizen, visiting physician and psychiatrist at the county hospital, a noted authority on local wildlife—and a deadly poker player.

His first twenty years in Abdera Hollow ended in 1982, the year the town rocketed from total obscurity to world notoriety in a matter of weeks.

Since the population of Abdera was no more than fifteen hundred, the loss of seventy-two people in a single "accident" was felt by practically everyone in town. Many were related to at least one of the victims; others had been friends or neighbors. For a week a sense of shock hung over the town. Every encounter, in street or store, occasioned a sharp evaluation of the loss—a mother?—a wife? The media, quick to grasp the drama of the tragedy, did nothing to improve matters.

Freedman and Scott felt the loss as keenly as did most blood relations. Death was no novelty to them, but the majority of the victims had been patients, and they caught the backlash of the bereaved.

Some were truly desolate: husbands who realized, far too late, the emptiness of the lives their lost wives had left behind. Others were delighted; Freedman knew of these men through his poker school or his more gossipy friends. Not that he sought dirt. But his respect for any confidence quite naturally attracted secrets. Freedman mentally filed all that he heard, adding to his knowledge of human psychology.

In the weeks following the "accident" he learned a great deal. Many citizens, lacking lawyers, approached Freedman for advice on possible claims against the airline. Some of them he found sickening, appallingly eager to cash in on the death of a friend or relative. Within a month of *Papa Kilo*'s disappearance, several promising lawsuits were in progress. The victims would have been astounded at the value their next of kin placed upon them.

Some were indeed astounded, but that came later. First came the shattering astonishment, the helpless incredulity of their nearest and dearest—and of the world.

· VIII ·

In the first year of the committee's life nothing remarkable happened. A few small planes, all foreign, were unaccountably lost and stayed lost. But no one can hold his breath forever; tension gradually eased among the ICARUS people.

The committee tidied up its contingency plan for a third Event, then turned to other aspects of ICARUS. They had done all they could to get a plane safely and discreetly back, but what then? Suppose the news broke, what would the reaction be? Obviously, air travel would suffer a terrible blow. But what else—shock? panic?

They drafted several scenarios. If a U.S. military plane returned in U.S. controlled airspace, there was a fair chance it could be hushed up. They'd already dealt with that; Case One, Alfa, as it was designated, was pushed aside.

Case One, Bravo, envisaged a military plane materializing in non-U.S. airspace. The mere idea made them sweat. But Soviet reaction was not the highest priority; the Top Seven would quickly appreciate that it was an Event, not an attack. Or would they? Wouldn't even those top men suspect a ruse, an attempt to take advantage of ICARUS? And whatever their view might be, was their control tight enough to prevent someone in Soviet Air Defense hacking the plane out of the sky? On balance, though, Soviet response was not a serious problem; whatever happened, the KGB net would cover every Soviet citizen: where he worked, wherever he traveled, whatever he read or said. No, the Western world posed a far greater threat to security. Suppose a lost bomber were to reappear in the Middle East? A nasty hypothesis. Case Two, which dealt with civil aircraft, was only fractionally better.

To meet the demands of these cases, hundreds of letters outlining the first two Events were produced, each signed personally by the President, each exhorting the recipient to play the matter down, even if the secret could not be contained. The one secretary cleared by ICARUS had the novel experience of seeing Arcasso and the deputy heads of the CIA and FBI working like office juniors, sealing envelopes, making up Top Secret mail packs. Each state governor got his own pack, not to be opened until a code word was received; he was then responsible for the immediate distribution of his letters. With the help of the recipients, he was to muzzle the press, TV, anyone likely to blow the story.

Similar packs went to all ambassadors for similar action abroad. An info copy went to the Soviet ICARUS committee.

It was only when the last pack was gone and the secretary and her office juniors were relaxing over coffee that CIA Joe had his idea.

Sucking a thumb which had tangled with an electric stapler, he suddenly froze, thumb in mouth, a blank expression on his face.

"Joe," Malin, the FBI man, said caustically, "hold it while I fetch a camera, my boys 'd pay ten bucks a print."

"I wonder . . ." Joe abandoned his thumb and looked at his colleagues. "I think I've got an idea. . . . Of course, it's a downright lie, but . . ." He drifted away in thought again.

"Come on, Joe!"

He refused to be hurried. "It's based on one simple fact of life. If I say I've never stepped out of line sexwise in my life, I don't expect folks would bank on it." His manner stopped any wise cracks. "On the other hand, if I state I'm mighty fond of small boys—" He shrugged. "I know which would be believed."

"So?"

"Suppose the U.S. owns up?"

"Owns up to what?"

"Suppose we say the Event is due to a malfunction in a new and untested defense system?" CIA Joe feigned interest in his thumb.

"Don't tell me; we have a time-warp device of wide range but uncertain accuracy?" asked Malin sardonically.

"Well, yes."

Arcasso broke the silence. "But that's pure *Star Trek* stuff! Who'd fall for that?"

"A helluva lot of people, I'd say," said Malin. "My guess is a whole heap believed in that Martian guy—and we'd have hard evidence—the Event—as collateral."

"It'd cost a few million in compensation," Joe argued, "but what's that compared to the collapse of aviation transportation, the panic and confusion? There's a lot to be said for the idea—the system's not offensive, the masses aren't threatened, no bombs dropped on cities." He smiled as his mind explored the possibilities. "Certain parties who figure the nuclear deterrent is hamstrung, and that they can pull our noses with impunity, would certainly be forced to think again."

"One thing's for sure," observed Arcasso somberly, "it's less fantastic than the real answer."

Sarah, the secretary, was no longer able to contain her curiosity. "Yes! What *is* the answer?"

Arcasso looked at her swiftly. So did Joe. Her voice was pitched a fraction too high. "Slow down, Sarah," growled Joe warningly.

But she had gone too far to turn back; she lit a rare cigarette, her hands trembling slightly. "Look, maybe I'm out of line, but I handle all ICARUS material and keep the records, and that's one thing I never hear about—the cause! I'm not dumb; you *must* discuss it—yet I don't know a thing!" Her voice climbed. "I'm not a machine, I'm one of the ten people in on this frightening case, but I'm excluded from the very center of ICARUS! Think of me knowing so much, but left out on my own. I can't talk with anyone!" She looked wildly at her companions. "Okay, I'm damned sure you don't have a solid answer, but what do you suspect?" She hesitated, turning her head away from their gaze. "Don't leave me out in the cold. . . ." She faced them once more, defiant, unsure, and forced a tight smile. "Silly, but when I'm alone, I sometimes think ICARUS is . . ."—Her voice sank to a whisper —"is God."

Arcasso stared at her strained face. She seemed so different now, hardly the same woman he had first met in "Smith's" outer office. Up to now, she'd been part of the furniture.

"Sarah," he said gently, "you know as much as we do; your guess is as good as ours."

Sarah stared at him, her mouth trembling. In the same low whisper she asked, "Then I'm not going crazy? It could be—God?"

Frank felt great sympathy. He'd had the same thought—they all had—but what man in the late twentieth century, especially a high government official, dared to start talking about God in relation to a hard, factual case? Woolly generalities were one thing, especially from politicians around election time, but . . . He could only repeat, "Sarah, we don't know. For my part, I don't rule anything out."

Alvin Malin of the FBI was silent, impassive. If this was the reaction of a switched-on person who knew all the facts . . . Joe's thoughts followed a different path. He'd happily settle for God—but suppose it was the Devil?

Two days later Jumbo *Papa Kilo* was missing, and a twenty-four hour intensive search produced nothing. On the committee's advice, the President ordered an all-out combined operation by Navy, Air Force, and Coast Guard. A score of ships, dozens of planes, fixed-wing and helos, scoured every likely square meter of ocean.

Conditions were nearly perfect: low sea state, good visibility; yet nothing was found. On the fourth day the committee gave the President its unanimous opinion: A third Event was in progress.

· IX ·

The twenty-four hour chore of Duty ICARUS started at 9 A.M. daily. On Wednesday, December 15, 1982, at 8:45 A.M., Colonel Frank Arcasso lumbered into the ICARUS operations room, already in a gray mood from another breakfast hassle with his wife. They fought with increasing frequency these days. She said he'd changed. She said she was tired of this four-day rotation. Okay, he might have become a bird colonel faster than he'd expected, but what good was that if he was chained to his desk day in, day out?

Arcasso had no satisfactory answer. He *had* changed, physically as well as temperamentally. Without trying, he'd lost weight. His suits and uniforms disgraced not just the USAF but the entire Armed Forces. ICARUS nagged his mind like a bad tooth.

He'd taken to dropping in on Sarah partly to keep an eye on her for security's sake, partly for a little female company where the very word ICARUS was not off limits. God knew, he had no sexual ambitions; sex hardly figured in his life these days. A toothache of any sort dampens libido.

The duty officer made his usual report. The wreckage of a light aircraft missing for a week had been located in the Brazilian rain forest; that was all.

Arcasso glanced at the Missing Aircraft stateboard; the light plane had been crossed out. His gaze rested on *Papa Kilo*. That was the one . . .

"Okay, I've got the con. I'll be in my office."

By nine-thirty he was well into his second cigar, his third mug of coffee, and his first file. He hunched over it, trying to concentrate, but by the time he got to the bottom of the page he realized he hadn't absorbed a word. Wearily, he started again.

For the first time—testing apart—the direct phone to the ops room buzzed: a harmless sound, yet it sent shock waves tingling through him.

"Arcasso." As he listened, fine beads of sweat appeared on his bloodless face. "Say again!" he croaked. The cigar slipped unheeded from his fingers onto the desk. "Okay—I'm coming." Unnoticed, the receiver clattered on the desk.

Arcasso charged down the corridor like a ball in a bowling alley, knowing he should walk but unable to control himself. Clerks and officers stared after him or swerved to avoid him.

The duty officer was sweating, suffering from his first taste of ICARUS shock. Arcasso slumped in a chair, panting. "Okay—give it to me!"

"Omaha came through at one zero zero four with an unidentified, located south of Des Moines, tracking west at eleven thousand meters, out of controlled airspace. There'd been nothing till then; then, suddenly—bang! There it was!"

Arcasso felt sick. This had to be it.

"At 1006, a Mayday from *Papa Kilo*"—the officer's eyes strayed to the state board, his head shaking slowly—"it equates to that Jumbo!" He lost his grip. "Frank—what the hell's going on?"

"Jesus H. Christ," murmured Arcasso.

The officer straightened up. "Fighters scrambled at 1008 to identify. At 1009 I called you." A teletype started hammering.

Arcasso forced himself to sit still while his junior darted to the machine.

"Fighters have positively identified *Papa Kilo*."

"It's *Papa Kilo* all right," growled Arcasso. The plot was rolling, and he felt curiously calm: no more thought, only action. "Make a flash to Omaha: code word and open Envelope One."

Thankful for endless practice in dreary night duty, the lieutenant colonel pounded the keyboard. "Leave that," commanded Arcasso. The man stopped. "Call the committee—emergency procedure." That will bring them running, he thought. He didn't fear responsibility, but there'd be plenty to do, and he'd be glad to have CIA Joe around.

He crossed to the phone bank, and studied the wall map. South of Des Moines, tracking west . . .

A phone rang. "Omaha? This is Control." Frank's voice was dispassionate. "You have understood Envelope One? I authenticate." He gave the codeword. "Satisfied? Okay, listen, get *Papa Kilo* off the distress frequency, put him on any free channel, and pipe it to me on Pentagon 5850—I'll use your transmitter, got it? . . . Yeah—one other thing. Don't listen, and you take damned good care no one else does! What's your name and rank? . . . Got it, Major—let's hope I don't have to call you!" Arcasso clamped the phone down, staring again at the map. Without looking away, he called the duty officer. "Make a flash to the governor, Colorado. Codeword—he's to open his envelope and deliver only the communication for Denver Air Traffic Control."

A lot happened at once. The frantic duty officer was on a teletype, getting a line to Denver. An Air Force phone rang as CIA Joe streaked into the room.

Arcasso paused as he moved to take the call. "This is it, Joe. The Jumbo's back." He took the phone.

"Omaha? . . . Yeah, I'm ready. Stand by for switching check." He depressed the switch on the handset, then released it. "Okay? Put me on."

He waited, heard the faint mush of static. "Papa Kilo, Papa Kilo, this is Control, how do you read me? Over."

Joe glanced at him in surprise: Frank's voice was so level, so calm. He had no idea how hard Frank was working to keep it that way.

"Papa Kilo, this is Control; read you loud and clear also." He paused, wiping his face with his free hand, then resumed, struggling to inject a genial quality into his voice. "Right now you're kinda worried; you don't know what the hell's happened, right?" He paused, listening to the stumbling words of a man fighting to keep his sanity, ten thousand meters up, responsible for eighty-odd lives, including his own. He listened, trying to gauge the pilot's state of mind.

"Okay, Papa Kilo, you've got problems, let me tell you this—right now we've only got one major problem—you. You're not seeing things. There's nothing wrong with you or your ship except you've gotten snarled up in an experiment. I can't say more over the air, okay? . . . Yeah, I know it sounds crazy, but we're going to bring you in at Denver. . . . Never mind why, you just focus on how. What's your fuel status?"

The pilot grew calmer; he reported a fuel remainder of fifty percent. Arcasso was staggered but kept his level tone. "Okay, so you have to burn off some before you're down to landing weight." He made it sound like the most ordinary situation in the world. "You keep hauling west. Soon I'll clear you to Denver approach, but there's time, plenty of time. Tell me, have you checked how the cash customers are making out?"

He listened, sweat pouring down his face.

"Okay, Papa Kilo, that's fine! Give 'em another movie for free—and a highball too. Charge it to Uncle Sam—hell, it's his fault!" Arcasso was playing for time. The pilot knew he was way off course, but he couldn't know about the time factor. "Look, Papa Kilo, I understand your problem. Denver is going to give you approach steerage, QNH, and the rest. You may be surprised at the ground temperature. Okay, be surprised, but believe the man! Another thing—don't worry about airspace restrictions. . . . What? You mean the fighters are still bugging you? . . . . Sure, I'll call them off. Wait—" He shouted across to the duty officer. "Get those goddam interceptors off the guy's tail." In a calmer voice he continued. "Papa Kilo, this is Control. I'll pass you to Denver as soon as those Air Force ships peel off—you tell me." He rested, wiping his face on his sleeve.

Joe sat immobile, a teletype message in his hand.

Arcasso shouted at the duty officer. "Call Denver! Release letters to the FBI and police department—and alert Denver airport for an emergency landing, passengers and crew to be quarantined on arrival, positively no press or TV allowed—and fix a fast ship for me from here to Denver—now!

"Yeah, Papa Kilo, I read you. They've gone? Fine! Stick around, buddy, I have to transfer you to Denver. . . . It may take a couple minutes. . . . You just sit there burning off some weight. They'll call you on this freq! Have a nice day!" Trembling, he released the switch. Forcing himself to another AF phone, he got Omaha and gave his orders, his tone very different from what the Jumbo pilot had heard.

He sank into a chair; the lieutenant colonel was hovering nervously. "Yeah—what?"

"Sir, there'll be a plane ready at Dulles as soon as you get there."

Arcasso nodded, looked at the CIA man. "What's your score, Joe?"

"The President's been told." He stopped.

The two men were eyeball to eyeball. Cold water raced through Arcasso's veins. Of all the members of the committee, CIA Joe was closest, the one he understood best. "And?"

Joe waved the teletype in his hand. "From Moscow. A flash: the Ilyushin pilot's died suddenly; the other's hospitalized."

·✕·

At 1248 Jumbo *Papa Kilo* touched down at Stapleton Field, Denver, Colorado. It was directed to an isolated corner of the airport and immediately surrounded by police, who—thinking it a hijack operation—were ready at the drop of a hat to start shooting. When the initial excitement had passed, they huddled deeper into their coats. The west wind off the Rockies was icy cold, and the thin sunlight gave little comfort.

The ICARUS committee, and Frank in particular, had been frantically busy. While his police escort broke every traffic regulation in the capital, CIA Joe got a line to Denver Tower, ordering delaying tactics until Arcasso took over. He also briefed the city's FBI chief, letting him know that the deputy head of the bureau was on his way and could be highly critical if local cooperation was less than one hundred percent.

The mobile boarding steps appeared, crawling toward the giant plane. Denver Tower instructed the pilot not to open the door until transportation arrived, citing the bitter cold temperature outside. By the time the buses began to move slowly around the perimeter,

Arcasso, after a Mach 2 flight aided by absolute priority in the airways, was in the landing circuit. Still in his flying suit, he stood near the Jumbo, talking urgently to the governor, before the crawling buses had reached the plane.

He quickly convinced the governor to stay calm, not query presidential action, and get back to his office, where the President might conveniently call him. Curious, and impressed with the speed at which Washington was moving, the governor left; maybe the President would fill him in.

Watching the passengers stumble out, his mind closed to anything but the job at hand, Arcasso fired orders at his tiny knot of officials. Passengers and crew were to go to the VIP lounge and be given food and drink—served by the FBI. Accommodations for the night were to be arranged, preferably on one floor, under FBI guard. An FBI approved doctor was to report at once. No telephone facilities were to be available to crew or passengers until further orders. And the plane was to have a police guard until a team of investigators from Arcasso's department, already on its way, arrived. They alone could board the plane.

A police car got him to the VIP lounge first. Stripping off his flying suit, Arcasso racked his brain, trying to think how to play it.

The passengers and crew trickled in, mostly silent, frightened and completely bewildered. Many were loaded down with duty-free bags; some were festooned with cameras. Several leaned on members of the plane's staff, who—no less bewildered—smiled mechanically. One oldster entered in a wheelchair.

Just to look at them made Arcasso's heart sink. This crowd bore no resemblance to the two men in the Ilyushin: these were U.S. citizens, not disciplined Soviet pilots. It might be possible to keep them quiet for twenty-four hours, but after that . . . Already one or two were demanding their rights and an explanation.

Last came the captain and his copilot, white as sheets, stumbling like sleepwalkers. Arcasso, after a quick aside to the FBI chief to get the drinks going, grabbed the pilots and took them into the kitchen. Now for my act, he thought.

"Congratulations, Captain!" He shook a limp and clammy hand, his strained smile meeting a lackluster eye. A nervous tic twitched at the corner of the captain's mouth. Arcasso grounded him mentally for a good long rest, and the thought of the ominous Ilyushin news made him wonder just how long that rest might be. "I'm Frank Arcasso, Colonel, United States Air Force."

The pilot nodded vaguely. Arcasso felt that if he'd introduced himself as Donald Duck he'd have gotten the same reaction. But he had to snap the man out of it. He needed information badly. "Come on, Captain! What happened?"

The man looked from Arcasso to his copilot, seeking some contact with reality. He wiped his face with the back of his hand. The action drew Arcasso's attention to the beardless face: three months without a shave or a trip to the bathroom . . .

The pilot sighed, utterly drained. "What happened . . ." He repeated the phrase flatly. Intelligence returned unwillingly to his haunted eyes. "All I can tell you is that suddenly the sky goes from dawn to full day, and I'm three thousand miles west of my last position! What happened!" He laughed, an ugly, hysterical sound. "They say this is Denver—Denver as cold as *this* in September?" The voice rose. "This is a nightmare! Soon I'll wake—"

Arcasso gave the pilot a swift, hard, flat-handed smack on one cheek. "Cut that out! You're a senior pilot, not a child!" Strangely, the Jumbo's skipper understood the action. He blinked, making no attempt to rub the dull red patch on his pale face. He spoke more calmly now. "I don't know more than that. Maybe later, not now. You can't imagine the feeling— and then to bring that flying hotel into a strange field . . ." He paused, resuming with more spirit. "Goddammit! I brought that crate in only just below all-up landing weight, the temperature way down— that was the last straw! This could be winter!"

He had to know, sooner or later. "Captain," said Arcasso gently, "I'm going to give it to you straight. This *is* winter. This is December 15."

The pilot stared at him incredulously. His copilot made a strange strangled sound in his throat and passed out. Both men ignored him.

"You stay right there," said Arcasso decisively. "This will all work out, things will be fine." He strode out, wishing he could believe himself. En route he grabbed an FBI man with a tray of glasses. "Two large bourbons—straight—in there, now! And see that those guys stay right there!"

In spite of his crumpled, sloppy suit, the more alert passengers seemed to recognize Arcasso's authority. He fended them off, aided by the local FBI chief.

"Sir, the mike at that desk is working—"

"The doctor here yet?" Arcasso interrupted.

"Just arrived. The hotel's all set—"

"Get the doc in here," said Arcasso, adding grimly, "we could use him." He crossed to the desk and automatically flicked the microphone with a fingernail. "Ladies and gentlemen!" he spoke. "It will be a lot easier for all of us if you'll just settle down and listen." He surveyed the disorderly scene. A crying child added to the pandemonium. He couldn't stand crying children.

"Will somebody keep that kid quiet?" The parents would hate him, but he sensed the others were on his side. To be too apologetic at this moment would be fatal.

"Ladies and gentlemen, my name's Arcasso, Colonel, United States Air Force." Below the neck he was less than convincing, but his face fitted his claim—his gray eyes commanding, his metal claw adding sinister authority. "Right now I speak to you as the representative of the U.S. government. Bear that in mind. I've already heard some demanding their rights. Fine! I go along with that. You *have* your rights"—the claw thumped on the desk—"but along with the rights go obligations."

He let that sink in, scanning the audience, trying to identify the tricky ones. The child screamed again; a sharp slap cut it short.

"What I have to say is Top Secret. I don't like telling you, but I have no option. You won't like hearing it, but you've got no option. Also, I'll tell you the bare minimum. You won't like that either, but this matter involves the security of the nation—which is *you!*"

Arcasso had their attention now; no feet shuffling, no coughing.

"You have accidentally become involved in what I will call an experiment." At one side, the local FBI chief watched him like a hawk. "The experiment has stopped; you are here, and there is no cause for alarm."

A man shouted, "Okay, colonel! That's the commercial—now tell us what the hell's goin' on!" Many nodded, murmuring agreement.

"Right," replied Arcasso. "Here it is. Some of you have heard of a concept called the space-time continuum. If you fully understand that idea, then you're ahead of me, but in everyday language it means that space and time are the same thing.

"I know this sounds like science fiction, but you have to believe that this continuum is a basic requirement in time travel. All of you have heard of that." He paused, grasping his claw in his good hand. "I have to tell you, you are the first time travelers. You left Paris in September. This is December."

For nearly ten seconds there was utter silence. Then a woman screamed, men shouted, children cried. Someone yelled, "He's fainted!"

The doctor and an FBI agent pushed through to the center of the disturbance, lifting a man out, laying him on a bench seat, luckily screened from view. Arcasso remained behind the desk. Let them shout and scream—they were entitled . . .

The FBI chief crossed to him, walking casually, ignoring the racket, his face impassive. "Colonel, the doc says the guy is dead—coronary arrest."

Arcasso nodded, equally phlegmatic. "Get the body out of here—fast—I don't want a fuss." The agent nodded back and headed for the door.

Arcasso turned to his audience. His metal claw slammed down again on the desk. "Okay, that's enough! Settle down—I haven't finished!" He glared at the shocked faces before him, then softened his approach. "You've all had a big shock. You've taken it very well." He lied, " 'Fraid it was too much for one gentleman—he's passed out, he'll have to be hospitalized. Is anyone else feeling ill?"

The FBI chief ushered in two white-coated orderlies carrying a stretcher. Arcasso's prayer was answered. The dead man's face was not covered, and the FBI man effectively blocked the view for most of the audience. The group remained silent as the grim charade was played out. The doors closed.

"No need to worry about him. He'll be well looked after—and at federal expense. Now"—he dismissed the matter—"let's move on. You've accepted the unbelievable part very well." The lie was worth repeating. "You'll find the next item easier to take. Not only have you traveled in time but in space. This is Denver, not New York. You will appreciate we did not plan this—"

"Just one moment! Not so goddam fast!" It was one of the businessmen.

"I'll be obliged if you did not interrupt." Arcasso's tone was hard, menacing. "There'll be time for questions later. As I was saying, this Event was not planned; we are most anxious to have the accounts of your experiences. Four-star accommodations have been arranged and transportation is ready. I suggest you go now and relax in comfort at Uncle Sam's expense. Then you can tell us everything and ask questions." He stopped; it was the best he could do, a blend of prevarication and flattery.

The businessman was tougher than most. "I have to get home—"

"Sir," said Arcasso icily, "we can't delay all these good people with a public discussion of your personal problems."

A FBI agent moved up to the man, taking his arm, talking earnestly, quietly.

"Thank you, ladies and gentlemen. The country can be proud of you." He smiled at the older women; warmed by alcohol, some smiled back. "Don't forget, you have room service for whatever you want"—he wouldn't dream of letting this group loose in a restaurant—"The U.S. government picks up the tab. Anything you want, from a highball to the doctor—just lift your phone. Thank you."

He stepped down, soaked with sweat. Unbelievably,

there was a slight ovation. An older, clear voice called out, "How about you, Colonel?" and got a small laugh.

"You're in the wrong business, Colonel," the FBI chief muttered sardonically. "Don't offer me any gold bricks; I might just buy one."

Behind his stiff smile, Arcasso hated himself—but what else could he do?

Alvin Malin arrived two hours later. Crew and passengers had been established in the hotel. The setup was far from ideal, and things became even stickier when the embargo on phone calls was disclosed. But by that time they had been split up, and were much easier to soothe, cajole, or lean on.

The air Accident Investigation team had flown in and gotten the Jumbo moved to a hangar. There Arcasso briefed his men. He wanted the plane checked out for anything, repeat anything, unusual. He did not mention holes, but warned his team to give special attention to the plane's external surfaces. They were to conduct a minute search of the interior, vacuum floors and seats, and keep the dust for analysis.

When asked what they were looking for, Arcasso said—frankly—he didn't know. His bleak expression stopped any argument.

Malin and four of the agents who had heard Arcasso's address to the passengers and crew took statements from all except the flight deck personnel. Arcasso spoke to them himself.

Around midnight, with *Papa Kilo*'s human freight deep in alcoholic or sedated sleep, Arcasso called a meeting in his hotel room. The doctor gave his opinion that, apart from shock, passengers and crew showed only the expected after-effects of a long flight:

exhaustion, swollen ankles, a little residual airsickness. As for the dead man, his medical record revealed a chronic heart condition. Shock had simply given him the final push.

Malin and his men had a stack of papers, amounting to practically nothing. The plane had vanished between the dawn radio call and the pilot's failure to report two hours later. During that time the passengers and the cabin staff were either fast asleep or dozing. Arcasso had no better luck with the flight deck crew. The engineer said that until the captain had cried out at the suddenly bright sky, he'd seen nothing. Pilot and copilot told the same story: They had been on course, the sun rising slowly behind them; then, in the blink of an eye, they were in broad daylight with land visible far below. By sheer reflex action they had gone to emergency procedure. The ship was well below the programmed flight level. The pilot admitted that for a few seconds he'd lost control—he had no idea where the Jumbo had gone. He'd put the plane into a climb back to operating height and made the distress call.

It was the Ilyushin story all over again: in a word, inexplicable. Finally, the chief of the investigation team phoned. The examination of *Papa Kilo* was not yet completed, but nothing had been found so far.

Malin and Arcasso were left alone in the smoke-filled room. Empty glasses littered the long coffee table, ashtrays overflowed, reports littered the floor. Arcasso sprawled on a couch, dipping now and then into the papers, reading, making notes. Malin was exhausted and sat quietly in a lounge chair, trying to unwind with a cigarette.

With a sudden gesture of disgust, Arcasso threw a report onto the carpet. Malin broke the silence.

"There's not the faintest chance we'll stop this story, Frank. We have to let those people go. All we've gained is a few hours."

"D'you think I don't know that? Why d'you think I pulled Joe's time warp gag?"

Malin rocked gently back and forth, rubbing his hands on his thighs. "A statement has to be released by the Defense Department."

"Not before we get the passengers home," warned Arcasso. "If the TV boys get wind of this . . ."

"Yeah." Malin got up. "The big boss isn't gonna care for this."

"Who is?" Arcasso mashed a cigar butt savagely. "But he's had long enough to argue about Joe's time warp story. D'you have a better idea?"

"We could tell the truth."

Arcasso regarded him thoughtfully. "You don't mean that—you know we can't! Imagine the President getting up and saying 'Sorry, folks, we don't know who or what causes ICARUS—but it ain't us, or the Russians, or any human agency'!"

"The President can stay out of this," Malin retorted, "the Pentagon takes the rap—we might need the Big Man if there's another Event. Christ—that would be a *real* jam!"

"Alvin, we're in the biggest jam in history, right now! Stop playing devil's advocate; you know we have to stick to the story, no matter what." He broke out a fresh cigar. "So the Treasury is out a few million bucks, and we get a little more egg on our face—what's that compared with the effect the truth would have? Christ!—then the shit would really hit the fan!"

Malin shied away from the possibility. Arcasso was right; the immediate future looked grim enough without unleashing further hysteria. "I'm off to the local office; anything you want passed to Washington?"

"No. I have to stay here—fix the oldsters' transportation, talk with the airline, and have a real close look at that plane."

"Okay. I'd better get over to Abdera and fix a little discreet surveillance. Having these poor souls in one place is just about our only lucky break. Abdera Hollow—sounds like a real dump."

"Huh! By tomorrow night it'll be the most famous place on earth!"

Arcasso did not get to look at *Papa Kilo* until later that afternoon. By then his team had found what he had dreaded.

Eleven small holes, each two millimeters in diameter, their distribution random. None in the wings, engines, or freight holds. Otherwise, the search had produced nothing.

Eleven holes, the only clue . . .

But clue to what? He'd have expected eleven holes of that size to have reduced cabin pressure to the point where safety circuits would have been activated and the oxygen masks would have dropped—yet they hadn't. Why? Was the pressure reduction not enough—or had the transition been too fast? Speed. Maybe that had something to do with it. Maybe not . . .

·XI·

Few citizens saw Malin come or go, but those that met him remembered his visit. He began by shaking the sheriff out of his backwoods lethargy—a real live FBI man in *Abdera*?

Malin was much less impressed. He put the fear of

God into the lawman about security and warned him not to trip over any FBI boys. Armed with Mark Freedman's address, he set out for the doctor's office.

As he apologized to Freedman for his unheralded visit, Malin produced his ID card, which modestly described him as a "senior official." Telling the doctor his fantastic story, he began with the part he liked least, CIA Joe's time warp; thereafter he stuck to the facts about the Jumbo. He explained selectively, ending with the assurance that the bureau, acting for a research agency—too secret to be named—was mainly motivated by a desire for the well-being of *Papa Kilo*'s passengers.

After a careful check of the ID card, Freedman had sat back and listened, nodding his head from time to time in sharp, birdlike movements, his eyes roving over his visitor's face, missing nothing.

"Incredible!" said Freedman when Malin had finished, "quite incredible . . . You have a flight list?"

While Freedman scanned the list, Malin studied him, evaluating the sensitive mouth, the high-bridged nose, the dark eyes behind heavy spectacles: a man of intellect, decisive, firm. If his professional abilities matched his attitude and appearance, what was he doing in a hole like Abdera?

Freedman looked up quickly, interrupting Malin's reverie. He tapped the flight list, and Malin noted the strong, slender hands, as sensitive as the face. Freedman slid the paper back across the desk.

"Yes, they're all mine—except this last one. Not local." He spoke with complete certainty.

Malin checked. The last name was that of the dead man. "You're right, doctor. My error." He crossed the name out and returned the list. "What we want is for you to keep an eye on them. If you see anything unusual, we'd like to know. A retainer will be paid, plus expenses."

"You say 'unusual.' That's not very specific."

"Because we can't be specific. We've got no idea what to expect—this has never happened before." The penetrating look he got left Malin with the uncomfortable feeling that Freedman recognized the lie. "You have to judge."

"Surely the medical advisors of the agency you represent have reached some conclusion?"

"For obvious reasons, we can't include anyone in Abdera Hollow," said Malin evasively; a fraction late he saw the trap and countermoved swiftly. "But don't think they could give you any more background than I can. The evidence suggests the subjects went into a state of nonbeing, all their physical and mental functions suspended. None of the men, for instance, needed to shave; no subject complained of thirst or hunger. But the plain fact remains they existed out of time for three months."

"Yes . . ." Freedman sat quite still, his expression revealing nothing. "Okay," he said at last, speaking quickly, "I'll act for you—with one proviso; my patients' interests come first. If, in my opinion, there is a clash of interests, they take precedence."

"The Hippocratic oath, eh?" Malin smiled. "We wouldn't want it any other way." He looked at his watch. "Naturally we will count on your discretion, professionally and otherwise. Here's my card. If you've got anything to say, call one of these numbers. If it's urgent, call the number I've underlined. Ask for me and give your name—that'll get you through the barricades. Failing that, ask for the Special Operations Room—they'll know about you."

He got up and they shook hands. "It's been a pleasure meeting you, doctor. Don't get me wrong, but I hope we don't have to meet again."

If the travelers had hailed from New York City, their return from the dead would have had a considerable impact, even on what is the loneliest city in the world. The Event paralyzed Abdera Hollow.

With all preparations made that they could think of, the FBI lifted the Denver telephone ban at 10 A.M. the next day and chaos began. Within minutes of the first call to Abdera, a stringer rang the local paper in Binghamton. Other calls convinced the editor that something mighty strange was afoot in Abdera, something worth checking out. Two hours later, his excited reporter called and the whole press and TV bandwagon started to roll, avid for the news break of the century. A TV team flew in by helicopter from New York, arriving at Albany County Airport just as the travelers were moving from plane to bus. Every news agency cluttered the lines to Washington. All government PR men had been warned to expect this. They stonewalled: A statement would be "issued shortly" by the Pentagon.

It was difficult to believe that all the commotion centered on a single busload of elderly folk, winding its way up the old road from Interstate 87. They sat amazed at the familiar yet fantastic sight of snow, dramatic evidence that they had indeed lost three months of their lifespan.

Bewildered and apprehensive, they were unaware of the inquisition which awaited them, the accidental fame which would briefly be theirs.

But for the unthinking—the bulk of humanity—the news did surprisingly little, particularly abroad, where many equated the matter with flying saucers. In any case it had occurred in America, where weird things happened all the time. No, the time travelers were less than a nine days' wonder. Men on the moon, UFO's, life on Mars—what would they think of next?

For many U.S. citizens, the Pentagon's announcement of the "accidental entrapment of a civilian plane in a classified experiment in chrono-spatial relationships" put the affair in a vaguely understandable context: The Defense Department was fooling around again. Once it had been the Manhattan Project—which, admittedly, hastened the end of a war a long way back, but went on to produce the most expensive, deadly, and unusable firecracker in history. Then there was Fort Detrick with its equally deadly biological weapons, also rated unusable. And what good came of the space program, nonstick frying pans excepted?

So thought most people over thirty-five, and the older they were the more they thought that way. Twentieth century man, raised on crises and horrors, miracles and marvels, has been practically immunized against anything that fails to touch him personally.

Among the young, whose brains tend to be less ossified, there was intense interest. Campus protests erupted across the country, demanding that "the security wraps be taken off research of such fundamental importance and fantastic implications"—but for once the media were not deaf to presidential pleas, and the young people received minimal coverage.

Scientific and science fiction circles were amazed and totally baffled. Among scientists, the burning question was how it was done—and, that answered, who was doing it. Did no one have the faintest idea where the Research and Development had gone on, or who had been involved in it? Without the solid evidence of the Jumbo, most men of learning would have dismissed the whole affair out of hand.

It was elsewhere, chiefly in the Third World, that political reaction was strongest. Several heads of state, never famous for benevolence to their own people, raised holy hell at this latest example of capitalistic infringement on human rights. The imperialistic hawks, they screamed, admitted the Jumbo incident had been a mistake; a non-American airplane could as easily have been the victim of their irresponsible activities. A powerful lobby demanded and got an emergency meeting of the UN General Assembly.

Hardly anything kills popular interest in a topic as quickly as discussion in the UN. A football score gets more attention than a whole month of the General Assembly's deliberations. The man in the street hardly knew of the Jumbo debate, and if he knew he didn't care.

But there was one curious feature in the so-called debate. The Soviet bloc took no part in lambasting the U.S., and, along with most of the Western world, abstained from voting. The resolution was passed, but the massive abstentions rendered it, even by UN standards, a waste of time.

The Soviet attitude puzzled Washington and the ICARUS Ten. They had told the Soviet Seven in advance of the time warp cover plan, and expected the Russians to make what capital they could in debate. Yet . . .

The reason became obvious a few days later. A second-lead article in *Pravda* casually referred to the ideological aspect of Soviet space-time thought. There followed a great deal of indigestible prose; but for those that sifted through the dross, a few nuggets of gold emerged, notably a reference to "the need for Soviet pioneers in this new field to found their labors on sound Marxist-Leninist principles."

Whatever it conveyed to *Pravda*'s native readers, its significance was not lost on Western intelligence: rather coyly, the USSR had let it be known they too were in the time warp business. To the ICARUS Ten it meant something else. Either the Soviets were giving them discreet backing, or they were taking care not to be upstaged by the U.S. in the possession of this entirely contrived power.

Either way the ICARUS Committee was satisfied. The prime, fearful question remained unanswered, but at least the Jumbo incident, if not closed, was under control. The President, who had some private pull with the Fourth Estate, got the cooperation of the media.

Neither he nor anyone else could stop enterprising free-lance investigators from probing for the secret of the fantastic time warp machine, but the committee lost no sleep over the efforts of these diligent reporters. The real secret was that the machine didn't exist.

A few of the time travelers wrote pieces for the press—"My Lost Three Months" was one of the better titles—but few were published or featured on TV. None of them had anything sensational to say. Government lawyers were in the process of negotiating out-of-court settlements of claims, but small cash advances had been made. That helped to keep everybody happy—and quiet.

The committee remained watchful and apprehensive, hoping against hope that there would be no more Events, comforted by the fact that no other planes had vanished in ICARUS conditions. They were also pleased that no word had come from Mark Freedman. The Soviet silence regarding the Ilyushin's crew cast a small shadow, but with so much else to sweat about the subject was not pursued.

If anyone had asked Frank Arcasso, Alvin Malin, or CIA Joe how he felt about ICARUS, the answers could have been summed up in two words: worried and frightened.

They had no way of knowing how much worse things were about to become.

· XII ·

By February, 1983, Abdera Hollow had sunk back into its old rut, many citizens very tired indeed of the publicity their little town had received from the ill-fated charter flight. Many, too, were jealous of the time travelers, especially when the first handouts arrived, two thousand dollars apiece. Not that the general citizenry could plead poverty. Free-spending reporters had boosted the slack prewinter sports period, but by the end of the year they'd gone. It might be the news story of the decade, but the travelers were not the news. There were limits to the in-depth study of a seventy-year-old woman whose unremarkable life included only this one fantastic moment, about which she was totally ignorant.

The average Abderan took more interest in some of the domestic repercussions of the flight. In his wife's absence, one bereaved husband had speedily taken up with another, younger woman. Marriage was planned. The stormy confrontation between the two women affected most Abderans; they'd known the characters in the drama all their lives. Interest rose when the second woman announced she was pregnant, a state her predecessor had never achieved.

Freedman and his assistant, Jaimie Scott, kept a vigilant eye on their Special List and found that, far from exhibiting unusual signs of decay, they were remarkably healthy. Using a variety of excuses, Freedman was able to examine many of them thoroughly. In pre-Event days most of the elderly folk had had some defect: Rheumatism, arthritis, varicose veins, and heart conditions were common. Freedman found no worsening of their troubles; in fact, in some cases the conditions had marginally improved.

The first really interesting evidence came from a younger member of *Papa Kilo*'s party. Shane de Byl, a pleasant-faced and well-shaped blonde approaching her twenty-first birthday, had now completely recovered from the disastrous love affair which had prompted her to take the tour. She had her two-thousand-dollar government check, and with the expectation of more to come, she believed her big break had arrived.

The daughter of an old Abderan farming family, she had worked locally as a receptionist before the trip. Quite understandably, that post had been filled during her prolonged absence. But with her check safely banked she turned her mind to far more pleasant thoughts. She would have a winter vacation—learn to ski—meet some of those cute young city guys. Better than being chained to a hotel desk all day.

Her venture began well enough. She splurged on her outfit, and, heedless of her aunt's dire warnings, headed for the nearest ski school. Unfortunately, after she'd done deceptively well in the beginners' class, over confidence led her to try an advanced slope. She ended up with a broken leg.

Jaimie Scott set the simple fracture. Generally speaking, doctors regard their female patients' bodies with a detached eye. Often, a body that looks wildly exciting displayed on a dimly lit bed appears very different on an examination couch under cold light. But there can be exceptions.

Doctors are trained to observe: Jaimie Scott, twenty-eight and unattached, could not help noticing her sensational figure, or the fact that she was a genuine blonde. At no time did he get out of line, but he did tend to make more house calls than were strictly necessary. Freedman, who realized what was going on, smiled slyly below his beaky nose: Jaimie was a good boy, and the de Byl girl—he'd helped her into the world—was a reasonable match. Okay, she'd never win a Nobel Prize, but she was a normal, healthy, good-natured young woman—just what Jaimie needed. He watched with amusement as the lad checked back with him on every detail of her treatment. Then the humor suddenly vanished.

They had regular evening sessions discussing current cases. Two weeks after the girl's accident, Scott came into Freedman's office clutching an X ray, a puzzled expression on his face.

"Mark," he said diffidently. "I'd appreciate your opinion."

Scott slipped the negative under the clips and switched on the screen light. It was a photograph of a perfectly ordinary human tibia.

Freedman had no difficulty in guessing whose it was. Really, the boy had a bad case.

But Mark was a doctor, and however trivial a case might be, he gave it all he had. He frowned, concentrating.

"What do you think, Mark?"

"I'd say you've got the wrong . . ." his voice trailed off into silence. He pushed his glasses up on his head, examining the X ray minutely, his nose only inches from the photograph.

"When was it taken?"

"This morning."

"Get some more, all angles." Freedman couldn't take his eyes off the screen; he zoomed in again.

"Already fixed for tomorrow morning."

"Good, good . . ." Freedman nodded vigorously. "Let me see the original shot."

Scott clipped up a second negative. "Taken after I'd set the fracture." He watched anxiously as his senior scrutinized it. "What do you think, Mark?"

The doctor took his time. "I think we should wait for the next batch of pictures. Could be the angle. How old is she?"

"Nearly twenty-one, and very healthy."

"Even so, if that X ray is reliable . . . remarkable! Let me see the negs as soon as you get them. Now—" He moved on to another case.

The next set of pictures only confirmed their opinions. If they had not known what they were looking for—and exactly where to look—they could easily have missed the fracture altogether.

In fourteen days Shane de Byl's leg was as good as new.

That afternoon Freedman called Washington. Malin made no comment, but thanked Freedman and asked to be kept informed. The doctor felt Malin had little interest in the report; the FBI man seemed preoccupied.

Mark Freedman was right. Twelve hours earlier, alarming news from the State Department had electrified the committee, and sent Arcasso streaking half way round the world.

Frank Arcasso felt numb with fatigue despite uncounted cups of metallic-tasting coffee. He'd never

74

been a bomber man, and this ship, a converted Rockwell B-1 with extra fuel-tank space, seemed to him to have been up forever. It was no airliner. They'd refueled three hours into flight, near Honolulu, and five thousand miles out from base, repeating the pattern over Manila. Now, slumped in the copilot's seat, he heard the singsong intonation of the ground controller, Colombo International, Sri Lanka. This special State Department B-1 with its civil registration—the "fire truck"—was used to move diplomats at the highest speed possible. It certainly did that: halfway 'round the world in less than seven hours.

But Arcasso was burdened with a great deal besides fatigue. Repeatedly during the flight, he'd taken out the message that had started this mad dash across the globe. It conveyed no more to him now than it had at first reading. He felt irritable, apprehensive, exhausted.

The brief tropical evening had almost gone when he climbed stiffly out of the plane to be met by a young Defense attaché. He sat silently, oblivious to all the sounds and smells of one of the most exotic islands in the world, as his car raced to the embassy.

Inside the embassy he dropped thankfully into a chair, produced the message, and tossed it across the desk. "This yours?" he growled.

"Yes, Colonel," replied the attaché, an Army captain. "I realize it's vague, but we have a standing order to report anything unusual—"

"I know," cut in Arcasso roughly, "I wrote it. Just gimme the story."

"Well, since I sent the message, I've learned that three nights back—"

"Three goddam nights!" Arcasso exploded. "What—"

The young captain's face flushed with anger. "If you'll let me finish, sir . . . Three nights ago a plane was heard passing low over a small town to the north. The people noticed it—they don't hear many planes up there. They said it crossed from west to east, making a hell of a racket. As I said, that bit came later. Then a call from the police department—they'd gotten a report of a plane wreck in the jungle, believed to be an old U.S. aircraft."

"Yeah," said Arcasso, "that's the thing. What do they mean—old? Old U.S. or old ex-U.S.? There must be stacks of our crates all over. Have you seen it?"

"No, there's been no time. I asked the same questions, but the Colombo police were only repeating what they'd been told."

"So it could be a clapped-out C-47!" To the attaché's surprise, Arcasso smiled. "I may be on a mighty expensive wild goose chase!" The captain could not begin to realize the sense of relief Arcasso felt. "So you haven't seen it yourself?"

"No, sir. It's quite a drive from here, and as soon as I heard you were on the way I decided it best to stay here and get things organized." He hesitated, not anxious to spoil his visitor's sudden good humor. "I don't go crazy for the C-47 idea, sir. There's only one body."

Fear flooded back. Arcasso mentally cursed himself for being so eager to clutch at any straw. He sat back, eyes closed.

"May I fix you a drink, Colonel?"

Arcasso nodded. "Yeah, thanks—anything so long as it's strong." He fumbled for a cigar, forcing himself to think. He had to stop telling himself black was white, if only for the sake of his frayed nerves. Take it easy. . . .

"Where's this body?"

"It reached the city morgue an hour back. You want to see it?" He handed his visitor a large whiskey.

"Thanks. No, let's take the plane first. Where's that?"

The attaché turned to a wall map. "We're here. The town I mentioned is up here. Anuradhapura. Here, just to the east, is Mihintale. The wreck is located a couple of kilometers north of Mihintale."

"How long will it take to get there?"

"Three hours, I guess, to Mihintale." He shrugged. "That last two kilometers could take ten minutes or two hours." He read Arcasso's expression. "Your first time on the island, Colonel?"

"Yeah."

"Believe me, it's a fantastic place. You name it, they've got it. Jungle covers two-thirds of the island. Ten paces off the main road and you're hopelessly lost." He shrugged again. "There are whole cities lost in jungle growth; one up there"—he gestured at the map—"nearly two thousand years old, covered two hundred and fifty square miles. Not that jungle needs that long to cover anything. Six months is enough."

Arcasso hardly heard. "There's no guarantee the low flyer is the one that crashed," he speculated, following his own train of thought.

"No. But like I said, if it fell out of the sky six months back, you could be standing on top of it and not notice. Also, I've checked with the local aviation authorities; they have no knowledge of any plane in that area at the material time."

Frank liked it less and less.

"Okay; no point in theorizing. Sooner we get moving the better."

"With all due respect, Colonel, we'd never find the place in the dark. I suggest we haul out of here at three-thirty, aiming for Mihintale at first light. You could use a little sleep, I imagine, and I'll have time to fix a guide with the local gendarmes."

It made sense. "Okay, but you drive, and let's make it your car."

"You want the low profile?"

"Affirmative, Captain," said Arcasso. "Jesus, yes!"

They drove north out of Colombo along the deserted coast road. Arcasso was still half asleep and suffering from monumental jet lag, hardly noticing anything for the first hour. But slowly he revived, grateful for the cool night wind off the sea. At Puttalam they turned northeast, driving through what seemed like a large tunnel. Strange glittering bugs flashed in the headlights' glare and were gone; once he saw the startled emerald eyes of a leopard. Occasionally something darted across the road. The attaché drove slowly and carefully, pointing out the deep ditches on either side of the narrow, unfenced road. This was the jungle, no place for an accident.

The attaché's timing was perfect. Anuradhapura was only a collection of half-seen shapes when they drove in. By the time the police station had been located and the guide collected, the brief tropical sunrise was over.

Eleven kilometers later they reached Mihintale; their guide directed them onto a narrow, unpaved track, heading north. For ten minutes they bumped and swayed, then stopped. From here on they would walk.

Arcasso found the attaché had known what he was talking about the night before. He had not expected the jungle to be so dark; overhead the treetops formed a continuous roof, excluding all direct sunlight. On the sloping ground—he guessed they were moving round the side of a hill—the thick knee-high scrub was a lot tougher than it looked. Giant creepers, thick as a man's forearm, hung down, their gentle swaying the only perceivable movement; and the harsh, screeching alarm call of unseen parakeets was the only sound in the damp, cool air.

The going was not too bad, for a path had been trampled by the men who had removed the body, but Arcasso sweated as he toiled after the guide. He was learning the hard way that Sri Lanka had plenty of insects, not all of them discouraged by repellent cream.

The guide called out, pointing. Arcasso forgot his discomfort; ahead lay a patch of sky, visible through a hole torn in the jungle roof. Below it lay the cause.

At first Arcasso thought the plane had come down in a small clearing, but he quickly realized the plane had made the space itself. The aircraft lay on its back, the remnants of the undercarriage pointing upwards. He guessed it had hit the treetops with its wheels down; they'd caught, the aircraft somersaulted, spun, and plunged to the jungle floor.

Both wings had been torn off; one hung impaled on a branch, the other was missing. The engine, ripped loose on impact, had carved a path to its resting place twenty meters away; the tail plane was half wrapped around the base of a tree. It was a very bad crash.

Looking at the stripped fuselage, torn and pierced by shattered tree stumps, he thought it resembled a giant slug, shrunken in death. On its crumpled side was a white five-pointed star in a blue roundel.

Arcasso wandered around, picking up pieces of mangled metal, dropping them, hardly aware he did so. The guide stood back respectfully while the attaché took photographs, privately anxious to get the job done before the heat of the day clamped down.

There had been a good many shocks in Frank Arcasso's life, even before ICARUS. Only the thought that he'd met them and somehow gotten by gave him any help now; no matter what, he had to do the routine things.

He inspected the engine, confirming what he already knew. He'd seen one before, in a museum: a Packard-built Rolls-Royce Merlin. He noted the number, his fingers trembling.

Unless he was crazy, or in a nightmare, this was the wreck of an F-51, a Mustang. Offhand, he could not recall when the plane had been phased out of the USAF—the 1950s? Certainly no later.

The wing stuck on the tree provided the greatest shock of all—three broad white stripes were painted from forward to aft. Arcasso's history was rusty, but he was pretty sure those three stripes had been first used as standard identification for Allied aircraft taking part in the invasion of Europe in June, 1944.

And those three stripes, bright and clean, might have been painted yesterday.

Arcasso remembered little of the return journey to Colombo. As they passed through the jungle, the attaché tried to discuss the crash, but was silenced once Arcasso realized he knew next to nothing about aviation.

The attaché prattled on about the ancient culture of Sri Lanka, pointing out a two hundred meter tall dagoba, a relic of a civilization virtually unknown in the West, and went on about a sacred tree under which the Buddha had sat, a tree more than twenty-two hundred years old, and very likely the oldest in the world.

Frank Arcasso let it all roll over him, nursing his apprehensions, yet a fragment of his mind wondered what the contemplative powers of the Buddha would have made of this awful dream.

By the time they reached the outskirts of Colombo, battling with ox carts and crammed buses, he had gotten his mind working, forcing himself to ignore the stunning implications of what he had seen, concentrating on the immediate problem.

The visit to the morgue was an anticlimax. The sad, hideously torn body of a young man conveyed little. But the clothes, the personal possessions, were something else entirely.

The pilot had worn an old-fashioned overall flying suit, a fur-lined zip-up jacket, and an ancient Mae West life preserver. His identity book was the clincher. His face, recognizably that of the corpse, stared up at Arcasso—bright, hopeful eyes, carelessly knotted silk scarf, crew-cut hair. The official stamp, half on the photograph, half on the paper, bore a date: September 9, 1943. Elsewhere, a date of birth: 1923. Arcasso was strangely moved by the face. If they'd met, the youth would have stiffened to attention before a full colonel, yet in years he would have been damn near old enough to be Arcasso's father.

It was crazy, impossible, but a stone cold fact.

Frank managed to take possession of the clothing, papers and dog tags. He thanked the inspector for his cooperation, hinting that the plane had gotten lost on a submarine tracking operation. As a story it had nothing to commend it, but he couldn't dream up a better one, and the chances were the police inspector knew even less about aircraft than the attaché, and was not likely to ever set eyes on the wreck.

He told the attaché the story was false. In fact the plane had been on a spy mission, and the less the attaché knew, the better. He saw the ambassador, produced his letter of authority signed by the President, and requested the body and wreckage be recovered from the local authorities and flown back to the States as soon as possible; the USAF would provide transportation. The ambassador too was left with the impression that he was stuck with a CIA spy operation which had gone sour.

Arcasso collected the attaché's undeveloped film and sent a secret message to "Smith"—which meant the ICARUS secretary, Sarah.

EVENT FOUR POSITIVE STOP COMMENCED 1944 REPEAT 1944 STOP LOCAL SITUATION UNDER CONTROL STOP RETURNING ARCASSO

Exhausted, maddened by insect bites on his neck and ankles, he climbed back into the B-1. He'd said the local situation was under control, and as far as was humanly possible it was. But the security of ICARUS couldn't last. The central question of who or what was responsible for these inexplicable returns from the dead remained unanswered.

The new factor was the sudden expansion in the time scale. If a plane could come back thirty-nine years late, why not one from an even earlier day? Suppose some stick-and-string crate from the twenties or World War I got down safely?

·XIII·

Landing at Washington National, Arcasso went straight to an emergency ICARUS meeting. He had no option—a State Department car met the plane.

In terse sentences he reported his findings and actions. As before, the committee made short work of the immediate practicalities. Arcasso would check out the pilot's USAF records, his AI4 section would examine the wrecked fighter. CIA Joe had the facilities to conduct a postmortem and dispose of the remains. The chairman would arrange for express transportation via the secretary of defense, who was one of the Ten.

And then they were back with the impossible question: Why? Arcasso shied away from that, stating bluntly that whatever the cause, he was convinced the secret could not be kept for long. He added forcefully that they'd better do some heavy thinking on that angle, and soon. "Meanwhile," he concluded, "I need some sleep, even if Jesus Christ is the Prime Mover." No one smiled, least of all Arcasso.

The phone woke him from five hours of uneasy sleep. The President had called a meeting—the first— of the ICARUS Ten for the next day, timed to dovetail with the postmortem report on the body, already airborne in a B-1 fire truck. "It's about time," snarled Arcasso, and tried to get back to sleep.

The rank and prestige of those attending the late night meeting in the White House bespoke the alarming nature of the ICARUS problem. President Robert J. Knowlton waited silently as his guests—Secretary of State Erwin J. Lord, Secretary of Defense Herbert F. Morton, FBI and CIA chiefs Malin and Langbaum, the other members of the ICARUS Committee, and Colonel-General Lebedev of the Soviet Union—made themselves comfortable. Sarah, the secretary, was also in attendance, ready to record the minutes.

The tension was so great that Arcasso, who rated zero in this high-rank collection, felt in no way inferior. They were people bound together by a common, fearful secret, a secret which made rank a triviality.

The President, his famous vote-catching smile conspicuously absent, spoke briefly, introducing Lebedev calmly, unemotionally, as if the presence of a KGB general at a secret presidential conference were an everyday affair. He stated the object of their meeting: to establish, if possible, the cause of the Events. An update would begin the session.

CIA Joe reported on the body of the F-51 pilot. "I hate to be an alarmist," he said, "but I can't avoid it. I can only tell you what the doctors found."

The cause of death had not been established with complete certainty. The postmortem had identified two distinct types of injuries; either could have been fatal. One type was the result of impact, and included a broken neck, a severed jugular, and multiple injuries to chest and arms. But the second set . . .

The body contained metal fragments, widely distributed over chest, abdomen, and legs. The fragments had been identified by ballistics as bits of twenty-millimeter cannon shells, probably German.

As he listened, Arcasso's mind leaped ahead. The back of his neck seemed to crawl and his hair seemed to stand on end. Instinctively he looked at Lebedev, the only other aviator present: His heavy Slavic face had sagged, and sweat glistened on his brow.

CIA Joe went on. The second type—wounds as opposed to injuries—would have caused death by severe hemorrhaging within four or five minutes. But in the case of the impact injuries, death would have been instantaneous. If the pilot had died of wounds, there would have been no loss of blood from the severed jugular—certainly a result of the crash, since a sliver of bamboo had been found in the wound. But owing to the state of the body, the doctors could not state positively that the blood on the neck had come from the severed vein.

Here Joe interrupted the hard facts of the report to make his own comment. Naturally, since the doctors had no idea of the truth, they'd concluded that the pilot, wounded by flak, had lost control and crashed—what more was there to say? But Joe had pressed them. Okay, they couldn't be sure, but weighing all the probabilities, when did they think the man died—in the air, or on hitting the ground?

Although puzzled by what struck them as an irrelevant and academic question, the three doctors reexamined the evidence. Reluctantly, all three agreed that the pilot had died in the crash.

CIA Joe laid the report gently on the desk and looked around the table. "Mr. President, gentlemen: I interrogated the doctors myself; they didn't like giving a firm answer, but answer they did. I am left in no serious doubt that the pilot sustained combat injuries in 1944 which would have killed him within minutes, but that he died in 1983."

Arcasso was not the only one who felt physically sick. The President broke the silence. "Joe, why 1944?"

"Colonel Arcasso has the collateral evidence, sir."

Frank cleared his throat. His mouth was dry and his voice seemed to belong to someone else. Haltingly, he made his report. Pilot and plane had been traced. Both had been logged as missing on operations over Normandy, France, on June 7, 1944.

"Gentlemen, what we've heard is impossible—yet it's happened! I don't know what to say . . ."

The cry for help in the President's voice was not missed by Erwin Lord. The secretary of state was reputed to be the coldest, most logical brain in the goverment, a man whose surname came in for much sardonic word play. "Mr. President," he said, trying to contain the incipient hysteria, "it is said that the solution to a problem lies less in the answers than in the questions posed. Let me ask one. It may appear a flat-footed approach, but I believe we won't get anyplace if we don't take things slowly, one step at a time. My question is this: is ICARUS, in our opinion, of this world—or is it not?" He held up a restraining hand. "Back in my Navy days, it was the custom for the junior officer to answer first—to make sure he was not influenced by his seniors. One more thing. I want a straight yes or no—the supplementaries come later."

To the surprise of some, he directed his cold gaze at Sarah. "You, miss. You've been in this as long as any of us, and are just as entitled to give a view as anyone sitting around this table."

She looked straight at the secretary of state, her voice low, but under control. "ICARUS is not of this world. I think—"

Lord's hand stopped her. "One thing at a time." He glanced sharply at Arcasso.

"I have to agree," said Frank heavily. "Extraterrestrial."

"Colonel-General Lebedev?"

The Russian said bleakly, "I am only an observer."

Defense Secretary Morton threw down his pencil in disgust. "Jesus! This isn't the UN! Don't pussyfoot around—answer as a human being, not a goddam commie!"

Lebedev remained unmoved. "It is not a fair question," he said stolidly.

The President glowered, his gray eyes cold. "A fair question! This isn't a court of law, general!"

"If I may," said Lord softly. "I think I understand our colleague's position. My question was intended to clarify, to clear the way for other questions, based on preceding answers—in fact, the dialectical approach, which he naturally recognized."

Lebedev inclined his head fractionally. The rest of the group eyed the secretary curiously. This was kindergarten stuff, not his normal style.

"For me," Lord continued calmly, "the general's

failure, or unwillingness, to answer is no surprise." He looked directly at the Russian. "And let me say I'm not trying to score cheap political points." He smiled. "If I was, this wouldn't be the audience I'd choose. My lack of surprise is grounded primarily on the belief that the only answer to my first question is that ICARUS is extraterrestrial." He gestured apologetically. "So I've blown my own seniority system of answering. But does anyone believe otherwise?"

"It's crazy!" said Joe angrily. "We *know* we're not responsible, and with the time scale shifted back as far as 1944, neither the Soviet Union nor China were in any state to play technological games—so who else? The British?" He shook his head. "No. And no other combatant nation had any power potential for ICARUS. Much as I dislike saying it, I vote for extraterrestrial. And it scares the hell out of me."

"And you, Mr. President?" Quietly Lord had taken charge of the meeting.

Robert Knowlton's "I concur" was barely audible.

"Anyone disagree? No? So we are agreed that ICARUS is not of this world. This surely means that we accept as a fact that a non-human, extraterrestrial agency, with powers we cannot even begin to grasp, is responsible.

"Let's get back to our Russian colleague's problem, one which is, I think, a great deal worse than ours. Gentlemen, I'm no theologian, but isn't ICARUS beginning to look something like a god? I'm quite certain that if this matter becomes public, an awful lot of people will think so, and maybe act accordingly. There lies General Lebedev's dilemma. He will forgive me for quoting Marx: 'Religion is the opium of the people' . . .

"Atheism is a cornerstone of communism of whatever shade—Marxist/Leninist, Maoist, Trotskyite.

Okay, we in the West may not be very religious, but at least we leave the door open. ICARUS doesn't look like our idea of God, and it would come as a hell of a shock to us, but we'd adjust." He looked directly at the Russian, "But what happens to a creed that for a hundred years has denied the existence of *any* sort of God?"

"No!" Lebedev's fist crashed on the table, his heavy-lidded eyes glaring at the secretary of state. "No! ICARUS is a natural phenomenon which we have not met before—no more than that! Compared with the earth's age, man has only been here a few seconds!" His fierce gaze moved from face to face. "Ice ages changed the world; do you not believe in them because you have never seen one? ICARUS may be a power storm, an event that only happens every thousand years! Until man flew, he had no idea they existed. It is a natural force we do not understand—yet!" He glared. "It is *not* a god!"

Arcasso broke the silence which followed. "How d'you account for the holes in the Ilyushin and the Jumbo, General?"

Lebedev turned his smoldering gaze on the speaker. "They have no significance!" Arcasso did not answer; his expression was enough.

"May I?" The secretary of state glanced inquiringly at the President, who nodded. "General, I did not say ICARUS *was* a god. I said what I think the average person *will* think. Your definition—'a natural force we do not understand'—fits a god as easily as it does a power storm—whatever that may be. We're playing with words; the reality doesn't change. Humanity has worshiped practically every damned thing at one time or another. Okay, call it a power storm. In no time flat ICARUS will become 'the god of the storm.' The return of those two planes is the most incredible event ever—unless," he added, "you happen to be a Christian. No, General. As I said before, we in the West have at least kept the door ajar. You slammed yours shut back in 1917. Now it's been torn off its hinges!"

·XIV·

As time passed, Mark Freedman—while not exactly worried—became faintly uneasy about his Special List patients. The case of the de Byl girl's leg, remarkable as it was, was not conclusive evidence of anything. All the same, few time travelers required his services, though many had been regular patients before the flight. Discreetly, Freedman rechecked some. Old Mrs. Jane's varicose veins looked a lot better. A case of hypertension showed a reduction in blood pressure. And one ancient woman with an arthritic hip was getting around without a stick for the first time in years. She told him it was due to "them government rays," advising him to get some.

Freedman heard nothing from Malin after his report on the girl's leg. Maybe the FBI had lost interest, but he was far too cagey to believe that. Diligently, he wrote up his case histories, watching, listening, saying nothing.

Then, on a late spring morning, a Special did show up: a spry seventy-year-old widow. She had a mind, she said coyly, to marry one of the widowers from the historic trip. They both felt fine, but the old goat, although touching seventy, had some pretty young ideas about, well—bed. Did the doctor think . . . ?

He grabbed the chance to do another physical. Later he described her to Scott as a vintage Rolls-Royce: The suspension might be weaker and the paintwork scratched, but aside from that she appeared to be in fine form.

He gave her a clean bill of health, and suggested that her swain pay a call. His checkup gave the same result. Aside from an insect bite not a darned thing had bothered him since the flight. Freedman had long suspected the man had heart trouble, but the EKG readout and his own observations proved otherwise. A lot of men of forty weren't in as good shape. Freedman gave the union his professional blessing, but warned the man not to overdo the sex.

"If you want to—and can—that's fine," he said. "But no pills, no artificial stimulants."

"Glad to hear you say that, doctor." His patient glanced at the closed door and said in a low, confidential voice, "Guess we've been doin' a little practicin'. Mind you"—he looked conspiratorially at Freedman—"never more than three, mebbe four times a week."

This admission shook Freedman. He'd known the man for twenty years, and in his estimation the patient had never been a sexual flyer. Seven years widowed, he'd shown no signs of deprivation. Now the old devil was back in the game, and still had enough spare energy for a speculative glance at the nurse's tail.

Scott's report told the same story, though Freedman discounted his observation, for all Jaimie's spare time went into observing Shane de Byl. Up and about in record time—but far less keen on skiing—she built no roadblocks in the young doctor's path to her. Passing her by chance in the street, Freedman noted her radiant health and evident happiness, and harbored some uncharitable thoughts about his assistant's conduct off-duty.

* * *

It was after this chance encounter that Freedman evolved a new attitude toward medicine. Until now, he reasoned, the basic aim of his profession had been to maintain or restore a patient's health. What constituted health clearly varied with age. Expressed as a graph, the line would rise from zero at birth, peak near twenty-one, and decline thereafter slowly at first, then heading steeply downward. Freedman was well aware that his mental graph was correct only in the broadest terms. But for him it served its purpose. Any physician knew he could do little about degenerative conditions—a man of ninety complaining of arthritis simply could not be restored to his state at twenty; even if it were possible to eradicate his disease, he still could not move with youthful agility. His aging organs, however healthy, limited him.

Now, as Freedman saw it, a new graph had to be drawn. Given the X factor involved in time travel, the decline was far less steep. Natural degeneration had, he guessed, not only stopped—it had become regeneration. The graph might be a straight line. It might even rise.

Freedman secretly wished for a second "accident." Seventy-odd people were not statistically satisfying. Above all, he burned to know details of the secret time warp device. If the active factor could be isolated . . .

Inwardly he allowed himself to dream. The X factor might lead not to a mere return to health, to an elevation to a new, unknown level of superhealth. Man had gone a long way in that direction with selective breeding of animals—cattle, sheep, and hogs far exceeded their wild forebears in size and health. Was he, quite accidentally, on the verge of doing the same thing for his own species? Freedman did not find that aspect particularly exciting; to produce larger, longer-living humans did not strike him as a meaningful exercise. But to give humanity superhealth for a span of, say, seventy to eighty years—that was another thing altogether. He realized he could not jump to conclusions. The sample was too small, the time scale too narrow; there could be a sudden, steep drop in the graph, a rapid regression.

Even so, the germ of the idea existed. The Wright brothers' first flight had been immensely useful—to know a thing was possible was more than half the battle. Superhealth—raising humanity to a new, amazing level—might just be practical. The active ingredient in the X factor had to be found.

Freedman called Malin and suggested a meeting with the bureau's medical men. To his annoyance, Malin showed up instead.

Although they had met only once before, the doctor's practiced eye took immediate note of the marked change in his visitor. Clearly the man had lost weight, was exhausted and under great stress.

Malin explained, not very successfully, that for security reasons a medical get-together was not possible. He would faithfully report Freedman's views. In due course, he did.

The committee took no notice. The doctor's theory was based, as they well knew, on a totally false premise—and as for the health of a bunch of senior citizens, what was that to men in their situation?

Not unnaturally, Freedman felt somewhat discouraged after Malin's visit, but not enough to lose interest in his Specials. The discouragement lay in Malin's reaction. He was a man, thought Freedman, in need of a long rest. Freedman flirted briefly with the idea of going over Malin's head, but decided to hold his cards, await developments. Events rapidly justified him.

Abdera's butcher was the first to observe the phenomenon. A big-bellied man, devoted to beer and careless of dress, his clumsiness with a meat cleaver made him a frequent visitor to the doctor's office. Shortly after Freedman had devised his theory, the butcher rolled into the office, one thumb roughly bandaged.

Wondering how such a ham-fisted guy had become a butcher, Scott cleaned and stitched up the nasty gash. To keep his patient's mind off the operation, he asked how trade was.

"Not so good, doc," rumbled the man in a deep, beery voice. "Back in the winter it wasn't bad, wasn't bad at all. But now I'm jest fillin' up the deep-freezes. Outa season this town dies." He fell silent, contemplating the dullness of Abdera. " 'Course, thet fuss over them plane folks gave a lift to trade—all them reporters an' TV fellers. Now thet's over and gone." Again he sank into somber silence, but resumed suddenly with greater animation as an intriguing thought came to mind. "Tell you one thing, doc—the durndest thing! Some folks around this town have gone plumb crazy on liver! Jest can't get enough. Lamb's liver is what they want, but I tell 'em, a lamb's only got so much liver, an' I don't have enough to go round." He nodded, saluting his own wisdom. "They settle for any goddam liver. Whaddaya make of thet, doc?"

Scott, now busy taping up the thumb, did not seem concerned. "I've no idea," he said and gave instructions for the future care of the thumb. The butcher, not to be put off, rambled on.

"Yeah, thanks. You know, liver's a fine food, very fine. Folks jest don't eat enough of it. Steaks and more steaks! But *these* folks have cottoned to it in a big way, yes sir!" His voice sank to an even lower pitch. "An' the screwiest thing is who them folks are!" He waited expectantly.

Scott was only too anxious to get rid of him. He stood up. "Oh—who?"

"You an' me, doc, you might say we're in the same line of business," replied the butcher. "I don't shoot off my mouth no more than you do—but I could. You'd be real 'mazed the things I light on. Take a certain widder—week in week out, she gets by on a coupla chops—then, all of a sudden, she's buyin' two steaks, one large, one small, each Friday for the last month! Don't tell me it's for the dawg—she ain't got one."

"What's that to do with your liver addicts?" Scott asked curtly.

"Gee, not a thing, doc! Jest pointin' out I get to see a lotta things." He read Scott's expression correctly. "Yeah, the liver. All them folks from thet plane! Leastways, them or their families—they're the ones that are wild for liver."

Scott froze. Trying to look uninterested, he said offhandedly, "Maybe they got a recipe from radio or TV."

The butcher took his time, regarding his thumb thoughtfully. Slowly he looked up at the doctor, a crafty smile spreading across his swollen drinker's face.

"Mighty strange recipe, doc. Seems them plane folk are the only ones who care for it." His eyes were slits in the folds of fat as his grin deepened. "Take ole Mrs. Groot and thet young niece of hers, de Byl, 'frinstance." His piggy eyes searched Scott's face for some reaction. "Jest the two of 'em, thet's all, but twice this week they've had liver: two pounds on Monday, two pounds Wednesday. Thet's a whole lot of liver fer two females! Mebbe I should get thet recipe!"

Jaimie Scott wasted no time in telling Freedman.

"Yes, very interesting." He looked at Jaimie over the top of his glasses. "But is it the whole story? As far as he's concerned it is, no doubt, but meat's not the only food. We need more information, but we must tread carefully." Until then, Scott had regarded the story as an isolated event, but clearly Mark saw it in a wider context. Jaimie began to see the point. "Okay, Mark, where do we go from here?"

"You tackle Shane unofficially. Don't alarm her, but get all you can from her and her aunt. If you run into any other Special, pump them—discreetly. I'll check with the two on my list for tomorrow. We'll discuss our findings here, tomorrow afternoon."

"Tomorrow afternoon! That's not much time!"

"I don't think there *is* much time." Freedman offered no explanation. "Speculation based on such slim evidence is pointless, but I've got a nasty feeling this is not good news."

When they met the following afternoon, six case histories lay on Freedman's desk: four female, two male. The findings were identical. Apart from liver, each had an abnormal appetite for milk and beef extract.

Freedman ran one hand repeatedly through his thinning silver hair, a sure sign of agitation. "A damned small sample, but it has to be enough. What's your preliminary diagnosis?"

Scott hesitated. "Well, preliminary has to be the word. I'd guess it's a compulsive desire generated by a massive deficiency of vitamin B-12. But I'm at a loss as to what has caused the deficiency."

Freedman nodded. "Yes, that's one way of looking at it. Agreed, the evidence strongly suggests B-12, but I'm not so sure about the deficiency. It may not be an intake to restore imbalance. It may be to stock up for a new requirement."

Scott laughed unconvincingly. "I'm pretty sure neither of the men are pregnant, and neither are Shane or her old aunt. That's another thing," he said apologetically, "I've just remembered Shane said they prefer their liver raw."

Freedman looked at the notes. "I see you estimate each has a daily intake—along with standard foods—of a quart of milk, two to three ounces of beef extract, and a pound of raw liver." Freedman's hand went back to his hair. "That's one hell of a—"

The phone rang. Freedman answered monosyllabically, but something in his manner made Scott watch his face. Briefly their eyes met; Scott saw his colleague's pupils dilate in shock. Twice Freedman asked for a name to be repeated; then the conversation ended abruptly. He replaced the receiver carefully and sat back, staring blankly.

"What's wrong, Mark?"

Scott felt alarmed; Mark was not given to dramatics. "Mark, please tell me."

Freedman spoke, his words coming in unusually short sentences. "Malin—he wants a meeting. Both of us. Washington." He stifled Scott's exclamation of surprise with a single look. "I said no. They're coming here."

"They—who are they?"

Mark pushed his spectacles up until they rested on his head; he rubbed his eyes, pinched the bridge of his nose. "Malin and a Dr. Marinskiya."

Jaimie frowned. "Who's he? Sounds like a Russian."

"She. Tatyana Ivanovna Marinskiya. Malin didn't

elaborate, but she's certainly Russian. The name mean anything to you?"

"A Russian doctor with an FBI agent?" Scott shook his head. "Sounds screwy to me. No, never heard of her—should I have?"

"Yes. She's a big wheel in Soviet cytology, one of the foremost authorities in the world, in fact. She's got a list of papers as long as your arm! The structure of cells, the function of cells, the multiplication of cells— you name it! First the B-12 discovery and now this—I don't like it at all, Jaimie."

"D'you think this may indicate possible tumors?"

"I don't think anything," replied Mark deliberately. "Not tonight. Come on; I've had enough for one day. What we need is a drink, maybe two."

After the unproductive presidential conference, the ICARUS Ten lapsed into tense, apprehensive expectancy. But the committee was not altogether inactive. A secure voice link, operable by line or radio, was set up between each of the Ten and the Special Operations Room. Anywhere, anytime, all of them, including Sarah, could be in instant touch. So far as their duties allowed, none of the Ten moved far from Washington.

The committee concentrated on contingency plans, but now the emphasis was not on "if" but "when" the story broke. After Lebedev's outburst, less concern was felt for the Soviet attitude. The party's line had clearly been decided, and they would stick to it, come what may. To a degree, the committee accepted the idea that ICARUS was a natural, if rare, event. If that could be sold to the world, the U.S. would be in step with the USSR. But none of the Ten believed the story could be made to stick.

None of the Ten believed the story, period. Sarah

had become particularly important to them, for she was the nearest they could get to an average person. Her belief could be the belief of millions, and she thought that ICARUS proved that something far greater than man existed.

Arcasso firmly rejected the natural phenomenon theory. Lebedev's dismissal of the holes in the Ilyushin and the Jumbo cut no ice with him. For nights on end he sat up, filling his den with cigar smoke as he pored over the drawings showing the location of the holes in the two planes.

His wife tried pleading, seduction, and—when that failed—blazing rage. Nothing made a difference. She thought seriously of leaving him. She was an ambitious woman, and even Frank's sudden promotion to brigadier, arranged by the President to give him more weight, gave her little satisfaction. Unlike her husband, she had long dreamed of that single star. But she rapidly discovered that her improved status in the Washington circle of military wives was a poor reward for the increasing tension at home. Frank had taken to spending his twenty-four hours as duty boss in his office, sleeping on a campbed in the operations room. On balance, it was more restful.

One afternoon he was in the ops room when the presidential phone rang. The president of the USSR had been on the hot line. It was in the urgent interest of the United States, he said, for a Soviet doctor to visit the medical team attending the Jumbo passengers. If Knowlton agreed, Tatyana Marinskiya could be in Washington tomorrow, explaining her mission on arrival. Knowlton consented immediately.

Arcasso called an emergency meeting of the committee. Wasting no time on idle surmise, they proposed that Malin should be her escort. If Malin considered it necessary, this doctor in Abdera, Freedman, should be admitted to the ICARUS circle. They didn't care for the idea—but, as Malin pointed out, if a doctor had to be involved, Freedman was the best bet. Naturally Malin had run a check on him. Freedman was very well qualified, and security-wise he was rated sound, although security in the old pre-ICARUS sense was meaningless. The chairman called the President and got his immediate approval.

Malin ran a similar check on Dr. Marinskiya. He was not a medical enthusiast, but he found her academic record impressively long, although cytology meant nothing to him. Lacking time to summon an FBI doctor to explain further, he let it go—trouble would come soon enough without him searching for it. He met her at International Airport the next afternoon.

Doctor Tatyana Ivanovna Marinskiya turned out to be the universal Mother figure. A round-faced, rather dumpy woman, she looked like more of an authority on home-baked cookies than on cells. Dressed in a Robin Hood hat, heavy shoes and a tweed jacket and skirt that certainly had not been made in Paris or London, she was barely feminine enough not to look like a male in drag. On her matronly bosom was a cheap brooch, and her plump hands displayed a number of rings. Malin, who had an eye for jewelry, figured that if he had the gall to give his wife such trinkets, she'd have stuffed them down his throat. He didn't care to imagine his mistress' reaction.

Fortunately for Malin, whose Russian was rusty, she spoke excellent English—with, strangely enough, an English accent. He'd fixed customs and immigration, and within minutes of deplaning, they were on the way to her hotel. For security reasons, there would be no contact with the Soviet embassy.

En route, Malin probed to see just how much she knew. He soon discovered she was completely up to date on all aspects of ICARUS. Malin thought she appeared remarkably calm and cheerful for a person sent here to deal with the mind-boggling mystery of ICARUS. He concluded that she had either swallowed the party line, or was so wrapped up in cytology that she hardly cared. Such people did exist; Malin had a good many specialists on his staff who would gaze fearlessly through the gates of hell to further their knowledge of their field.

Tatyana probed, too. Was Malin a doctor? No? In that case, she said politely, there was little point in involving him in details. In general, her experience with the two Ilyushin pilots would help the medical team attending the Jumbo travelers, and—she added frankly—the American doctors might add to her understanding as well.

Her cheerfulness faded when she learned that the "medical team" consisted of two country doctors, and that the time travelers were not in a sanitorium under observation, but were scattered around, doing whatever they pleased. Malin saw her to her hotel, invited her to dine with him, then left to arrange transportation for the following day.

Next morning they flew to Albany County Airport, where an FBI car met them. During the two-and-a-half-hour journey she said little, smiling politely when he glanced at her, but Malin had no doubt she was quietly observing. During dinner the night before, both had avoided any reference to ICARUS or medicine. But despite their efforts to stick to trivialities, he recognized that behind the motherly apple-pie exterior lay a very keen mind, eager to get to work.

En route, he explained that the doctors she would meet were not yet cleared by ICARUS. If she would be good enough to give him ten minutes to talk with them, Malin would be grateful. She readily agreed. But he read in her watchful eyes something akin to amazement at the way a democracy worked.

Once Malin had briefed Freedman and Scott, he ushered Tatyana into their office, made the introductions, and left. Aside from ICARUS, there were two things Malin couldn't stand: heights and medical talk. He drove around Abdera, getting an idea of the layout. Maybe he'd be called upon to quarantine the joint.

He figured the doctors would be at it for at least two hours; he'd give them a call after a late lunch.

Malin was far too optimistic.

·XVI·

All Malin's telephone call got him was a thinly veiled invitation to get lost. Another two hours passed. With a thousand things piling up in Washington, he felt he would go crazy if he hung around any longer. He returned to Freedman's office and was greeted, if that is the word, with blank stares; he might have been a total stranger. Even the office seemed unfamiliar. The air was blue with the smoke from Freedman's pipe, and pungent with the odor of Russian tobacco. Marinskiya, her jacket off, was drawing diagrams. Scott was reading case notes. Coffee cups, glasses, case histories, books, and a bottle of whiskey cluttered the desk.

Freedman practically threw the FBI man out. Yes, he would report as soon as possible, but right now time did not permit. Malin, surprised by this brusque reception, asked if should return later. Freedman seemed annoyed by his persistence. "Yes, tomorrow," he said. "Or the next day." Pressed by Malin, Freedman said impatiently that Doctor Marinskiya would be staying with him.

Too worried by the implications of Freedman's manner to be annoyed, Malin left for Washington. The doctors had forgotten him before he reached his car.

Freedman liked his Soviet colleague, her simple, direct approach. She had no false modesty about her status, but did not try to pull rank on him.

She had begun by clearing the ground: How much did Freedman know of her specialty? Freedman replied truthfully that he had read with interest one paper of hers, but was hardly up-to-date. Scott, who had graduated from med school much more recently, might know more.

Marinskiya took off her jacket, lit a cigarette, and plunged into a heavily condensed postgraduate course in cytology, amazing both men with her masterly presentation, done straight off the top of her head. She in turn quickly decided that if Freedman was a fair specimen of an American GP, she would have to reevaluate her low opinion of Western medicine.

Questions and answers followed. Marinskiya's bright blue eyes sparkled with enthusiasm, gratified by the Americans' quick understanding. With the whiskey came first names, and Tatyana kicked off her shoes.

But this was no party. Carefully she stuck to the general principles of cytology, making sure there would be no areas of misunderstanding in either language or terminology.

Only when satisfied that both men had grasped the basics did she start on Case ICARUS, Event Two, the Ilyushin-14 pilot and copilot.

From the time they landed, both men had been kept in a KGB sanitorium in Vorkuta. For the first few months their detention had been for security reasons—and, Tatyana added quickly, for psychological examination. Nearly a year had elapsed before any serious interest was taken in their physical condition, apart from standard checks. One of these checkups revealed that a minor complaint of the pilot's (Freedman identified it as athlete's foot) had completely cleared up. Without treatment by powerful antibiotics, that was extremely unusual. Both men were minutely examined. Both were not only fit, they were in excellent condition.

And that, too, said Tatyana candidly, was surprising. Though efficiently run, the sanitorium was a KGB establishment and not famous for luxuries. It was located at Vorkuta, a town well inside the Arctic Circle, bitterly cold in the six-month winter and, as she put it, "unfavorable" for the rest of the year. As a result of the interest the report aroused, KGB approval was obtained and the men were flown three thousand kilometers south to a medical research establishment near Odessa.

Odessa, explained Tatyana patriotically, was in all respects a beautiful place, comparing very favorably with the south of France, the Caribbean, California, or any other resort area. Here the men were re-examined, subjected to extensive tests, and in their off-time allowed to relax, free from close KGB surveillance.

Freedman asked about the men's diet. Tatyana looked at him blankly. What of it? It had been, so far as she knew, a normal, perfectly adequate diet. Freedman nodded, apologizing for the interruption.

The aviators had been in the Odessa establishment less than three weeks when the first sign of trouble was noted. Both complained of feeling tired, although they slept well enough. This was at first attributed to the change in climate, but the condition did not pass; it worsened.

Another week, and neither of the men seemed able to keep his eyes open for more than an hour at a stretch. Fresh examinations revealed nothing, but since both looked as if they might fall asleep standing up, they were hospitalized.

"And here," said Tatyana, her voice husky from talk and too many cigarettes, "I want you to follow most closely. The men were put to bed, extremely lethargic but apparently otherwise fit, on the afternoon of what we afterwards designated Day One.

"By the morning of Day Two, their condition, particularly that of the pilot, had worsened. Even after a good ten hours of sleep, both men fell into a coma soon after being awakened for breakfast. Clinically, the symptoms indicated a terminal diabetic condition. But it was not diabetes. The men were again examined that morning, and a small lesion, less than a centimeter in diameter, was discovered on the left side of the pilot's neck. That was all. It was not regarded as significant, possibly an insect bite—"

Freedman sat up, suddenly alert, but shook his head when Tatyana looked at him inquiringly. "No," he said, "go on."

"By evening the lesion had grown to the size of a pigeon's egg; it was hard to the touch and fibrous around the periphery, resilient at the center. The pilot's coma had deepened; intravenous feeding was ordered. The doctors decided excision was the only answer. Early in the morning of Day Three—the growth by that time the size of a duck's egg—they operated. Surgically it presented no problems, and was completed satisfactorily." Tatyana took a sip of her whiskey, her hand trembling slightly. "Within two hours the man died; cause, cardiac failure."

She paused; Freedman looked grim, Scott pale. "Brace yourselves, my friends, it gets worse. First, no cause for the heart failure could be determined. I am assured that the preoperative check revealed nothing, and the patient's postoperative condition was good. Still he died." She drank again. "Secondly, the tumor had been excised intact; two doctors and three nurses testified to the fact. Placed in a dish, it was put aside for later examination, and was not observed until after the patient's wound had been cleaned, sutured, and dressed. Only then did the surgeon look in the dish. The tumor had ruptured; a serous fluid lay in the bottom of the dish. Under the collapsed skin lay a hollow hemisphere of fibrous tissue about one centimeter thick. No one in the institute had ever seen anything like it. At that point I was summoned from Moscow." Abruptly she stopped. "But I am tired of talking." She produced a paper from her wallet. "A summary of my findings. Read it if you wish; in short, it says I didn't know what I was examining. Excuse me." She got up, padding off silently in her stocking feet to the bathroom.

Freedman skimmed through the paper; both men remained silent. Freedman passed the paper to Scott and went to the phone. He had not warned his wife that they had a guest. He did so, adding he would take Tatyana out for dinner.

Tatyana paid little attention to her meal. She was wrapped up in her subject, talking technically of the cell tissue, drawing diagrams on napkins, using the word *discontinuity* in a context neither Freedman nor Scott understood. But they got the gist of her main argument. The structure of the tumor was entirely new to her, yet the serous fluid appeared upon analysis to be normal. She reserved the most dramatic observation until the end.

Freedman ordered coffee—Would she care for a liqueur? Only water had been taken with the meal. Yes, said Tatyana; vodka. She tossed away three without visible effect. Over the last she ended the story of the Ilyushin pilot.

She cupped her strong hands. "The tumor, like half a small tennis ball—yes? Above the cut top, the collapsed dermal layer." Thumb and forefinger indicated a millimeter's thickness. "Between, the fluid." She stopped, marshaling her thoughts. "A definitive answer is not possible, but I feel"—she placed one hand on her ample breast—"even allowing for evaporation, the fluid present, did not, could not, fill the cavity."

Freedman saw it all too plainly. "You guessed the rupture was due to some other agent, present in the intact tumor, now no longer there."

" 'Guessed' is not correct, Mark," she replied. "I prefer 'evaluated.' "

It was all so conversational, so academic, that Scott was slow to grasp the significance. When he did, however, he thought of Shane, and the color ebbed from his face. "Good God," he whispered huskily, "a parasite!" Tatyana gave him the slightest of nods.

Back in the office Scott brewed coffee. Tatyana shifted gears effortlessly back to whiskey, waiting patiently for the men to settle down. Freedman consulted a book, read briefly, then resumed his seat.

"Now," said Tatyana, "I tell you of the copilot."

For the past two hours the implications of her story had been racing through Mark's mind, but impatient as he was to proceed he admired her methodical approach. One thing at a time.

"First, a question," he said. "It seems to me your conclusion that the cyst was in fact an egg which hatched unobserved is based on two points: the ruptured membrane, and your guess—and frankly, that's all it is—that the serous fluid was insufficient to fill the cavity."

"I come to that." Tatyana was in no way put off by the criticism. "On Day Three, shortly before his colleague died the copilot showed similar extreme symptoms. The lethargy they had in common, but he was slower to pass into deep coma. At this point I arrived; from here the observations are mine, not secondhand. With the experience gained in the first case, we decided against surgery; instead, we watched. Coma developed with the same amazing speed—so did a tumor on his right wrist.

"We kept watch through the night. Nothing happened while I had the duty. I then thought he had little chance of survival beyond the morning. His arm had been secured by bandages so that it lay outside the bedclothes, resting on his stomach, the tumor plainly visible under a spotlight, the room otherwise in darkness."

Scott breathed deeply, his face set, imagining the scene. "At one o'clock in the morning another doctor took over." Anger mounted in her voice. "He denies nodding off, yet he can only say he was suddenly aware that the tumor had ruptured—unobserved." She spat the word out. "Unforgivable! For twelve hours the man's condition remained marginal; yet, strangely, I had the feeling that the standard intensive care given him did little to aid recovery." She smiled at Mark. "A guess, of course. Whatever the reason, by the end of Day Four a slight but general improvement was evident. At the same time the tumor regressed, shriveled. The progress continued at an increasing rate. On Day Seven, an estimated eighty-four hours after the rupture, the tumor lost adhesion and dropped away, leaving a clean wound. Thereafter he recovered quickly."

Mark interrupted. "I don't see the additional evidence—"

"It is this: The arm was secured, a small kidney dish placed under the wrist, resting on the patient's stomach. The bulk of the fluid drained into that, but an irregular row of small stains, none greater than two millimeters in diameter, extended for roughly thirty centimeters across the sheet, away from the man's hand. The inference is obvious."

Shakily Scott asked, "The spots—they were analyzed?"

"Of course. Serous fluid."

Freedman broke the silence. "The actual point of rupture, anything significant?"

Tatyana nodded approvingly. "Some fool cut into the first tumor at that point; by the time I saw it, no useful opinion could be given. In the second case—" She paused. "So far as could be seen—remember, we had decided not to intervene in any way—the opening was circular, perhaps four millimeters in diameter." She shrugged. "Undue significance cannot be attached to size or shape because of natural elasticity of the skin." She shrugged again.

"Getting back to the patient," said Scott, thinking only of Shane, "when you say he recovered, was it to his 'perfect' state, or the way he was before the flight?"

"His pre-flight condition."

"Can you be sure he is not, as you said earlier, perfect? I mean, short of a specific condition, how can you know?"

"Two reasons. His pre-Event health record showed he had a tendency to mild dyspepsia—that returned. Secondly, in his 'perfect' state, his skin was exactly that, resembling a newborn infant. I examined him three days ago; dermatology is not my subject, but he seemed to have a normal quota of skin eruptions for a man of his age."

Freedman tossed his glasses on the desk, pinched the bridge of his nose, and blinked shortsightedly at Tatyana. "But the parasite—" He got no further.

The flat of Tatyana's hand smacked down hard on the desk. "In the case of the pilot the failure is forgivable. In the second case—" She spat the words out with typical Russian fervor. "That imbecile son of a pig, the doctor who fell asleep! A disgrace to Soviet medicine!" She poured herself a generous shot from the near-empty bottle. "Nothing! No trace. In the copilot's case, every square centimeter of the room was checked. I cannot describe the shame I feel admitting this."

Mark quickly intervened. "Yes, but have you inferred anything from the known facts?"

Tatyana accepted his slight reproof, checking her fierce Slavic temperament. "I have inferred," she said slowly, "that the parasite, size and structure unknown, occupied the cyst, which was roughly the size of a table tennis ball, perhaps a little larger. I *guess*"—she stressed the word—"it had legs, possibly wings, and at least an elementary sensory system—how else could either of the parasites have escaped?"

"Presumably you searched the operation theater after the second case?"

"Oh yes. That produced one negative item. The theater staff was positive that the doors had not been opened until well after the discovery that the excised tumor had ruptured. It is possible that it left through the only exit—under the door. The gap had been measured: fifty millimeters."

Silence filled the room. Freedman and Scott were trying to visualize a creature which could occupy the space of a large table tennis ball, capable of passing through a fifty-millimeter slot.

Scott repressed a shudder. He visualized it as a nematode, a human tapeworm, dirty white, glistening with slime.

Freedman had even more nightmarish thoughts. Two parasites were involved; neither had been found. Whatever its structure—he saw it as a fast-moving millipede—he was much more concerned with the creature's brain. Conceived in space, from the moment of birth both creatures had sought escape from the artificial confines of man, and both had made it. Freedman, too, briefly considered tapeworms and at once discarded the idea. Nematodes had none of the physical ability, sensory equipment, or primal urge.

With the careful precision that marked all his movements, Mark took the whiskey bottle, emptied it into his glass, and after a moment's consideration, downed it in one gulp.

"Tomorrow we must consider the implications for our Special List." He spoke calmly. "I think we've had enough for one day."

But despite the whiskey, Freedman couldn't sleep. The discussion, however horrific, had at least dealt with medical practicalities, staggering but observed facts. Now, alone in the darkness, he felt that most awful fear—the fear of something unknown, incomprehensible—tearing at his insides. Somewhere up there lay the cause: some body, some thing. . . .

Essentially a simple, cheerful girl, Shane de Byl was bright enough to know she had no great brain. Okay, she could live with that. She knew she had a fine body, and the instincts to enjoy it and to use it for its proper function, children. But not just yet.

By 1983, those women who sought it had long won the battle for equality. But Shane was cast in an older, more elemental mold, and she saw her purpose in life as the enjoyment of her youth, later her husband and children, and in due course her grandchildren. Not that she had consciously worked it out. But had she been pressed, that would have been her answer.

Secretly she delighted in her body, watching its magical progression from puberty, from skinny flatness to ample, gentle curves. Every morning, flanked by a mirror on one side, an open window on the other, she had her private session of self-admiration, turning this way and that, craning her neck to see herself from all angles, conscious of the fresh air that added to her awareness by its chill touch.

She enjoyed too the approaches of men as natural tributes to an attractive girl, but lately she had repulsed all advances.

Jaimie was the man she wanted and intended to marry, even if he did not know it yet. Jaimie filled her thoughts, and the others could go jump in the nearest available lake. Shane was a nice, old-fashioned girl.

So when Jaimie asked her, as a favor, to allow herself to be examined by a specialist—purely in the interests of science—she was happy to oblige. She had no interest in knowing why, nor did she mind old Freedman being present. He had brought her into the world, and mentally she had already assigned him the task of helping her with her first child.

But she felt a faint twinge of disappointment when the specialist turned out to be a woman. She felt defensive before another female—especially this one, with her funny accent and cold, sharp manner. She might be a big wheel someplace, Shane decided, but she was still woman enough to feel jealous of Shane's splendid breasts, when hers showed all too clearly the weight of her years.

The examination was certainly thorough. Shane felt there was not a single inch the specialist did not examine with chilling dispassion; she was glad Jaimie was not present.

And then a whole stack of questions, that made no sense to her. Did she feel well? What a stupid question! Her broken leg seemed to fascinate the woman.

Old Freedman said little during the examination or the questioning, but he asked the question that got the specialist away from her leg. Had she recently suffered from any ailments, no matter how slight? Strange, really—she'd tried hard to remember, for Doc Freedman in his funny old voice seemed very anxious to know, his dark eyes watching her intently. For his sake, she thought hard, finally remembering a spot on her arm that had itched.

She indicated the area, and wished she hadn't. Doc and the woman examined the whole arm as if they were looking for gold. Finding nothing, they questioned her again about the location, and the more she thought about it, the less sure she was where it had been. The specialist, ignoring Shane as a person while her strong fingers kneaded the muscles of her arm, said to Freedman that she didn't think X ray would reveal anything. That alarmed Shane: but Freedman, who did not regard her as a dummy, calmed her fears.

When she left, bruises were beginning to appear on her arm. Stupid old cow! Carrying on about a bite she'd forgotten, something that happened way back, after that crazy flight.

Two more Specials came in for checkups that morning. Freedman introduced Tatyana Marinskiya as "a colleague from Europe." She said nothing, sticking to a nod and a smile, but she listened carefully. Freedman slipped in questions about insect bites without raising his patients' suspicions. The first recalled nothing. The second, a seventy-year-old widow, said yes, she'd had a bite about the time she got back. She'd been a regular martyr to insects all her life, she explained at length. The smallest bite would blow up . . .

Nodding understandingly, Freedman stemmed the flood of reminiscence. Had that particular bite given her a bad time?

Funny he should ask, said the widow. No, it hadn't. She'd rubbed it with some ointment, and that was the last she'd thought of it until now.

Treating Tatyana to a lunch of hamburgers and coffee at Mom's Diner, Mark casually named the unknown parasite. It had to be called something, he said, and *Xeno* struck him as apt, being Greek for "Stranger." It sure as hell was that.

When they returned to the office, they found Scott eating lunch with one hand while writing his case notes with the other. He had one item: a Special had recalled a bite on her breast. She was sure of the timing; she'd figured it was a flea bite collected in a particularly seedy hotel she'd stayed in on the tour. Scott had examined the area—the breastbone, where the tissue over the sternum has little thickness—and found no sign of anything.

Tatyana remained silent. Leaning back in her chair, she lit one of her black Russian cigarettes, eased her shoes off under the desk, and asked Mark his views on Xeno.

First of all, said Freedman, the Soviet experience demonstrated that Xeno found the human body an acceptable host. Their scant knowledge of the creature made speculation on how or why a waste of time. He would concentrate on the practicalities of dealing with the intruder. With only two cases to study, it was impossible to form hard and fast opinions, but he felt the indications were that after a dormant period, the embryo established an exceedingly close relationship with its host—witness the sudden death of the pilot on surgical separation. Tentatively, he felt that surgical intervention at the earliest moment might still be the answer, but speed of an unprecedented order would be necessary; minutes could count.

Scott was horrified by Mark's calm, dispassionate appraisal, but Tatyana listened with deep attention. She was an eminent authority in cytology, but had no specialized knowledge of parasites—certainly nothing to compare to Freedman's expertise. In the ten years before he settled in Abdera, he had deliberately sought a varied medical experience around the world. In Africa he had become familiar with bilharzia, caused by the parasite *schistosoma*, whose life cycle was hardly less fantastic than that of Xeno.

Freedman turned to the *Papa Kilo* victims. The evidence was scant, but he had no serious doubt that some, possibly all, had been implanted. He based his case on the insect bites and the inordinate craving for foods high in vitamin B-12. True, neither of the Russians appeared to have this desire; perhaps, he said tactfully, their "social environment" made it difficult for such cravings to be known or satisfied.

As to the time scale, in the Ilyushin case some four-teen months had elapsed before the acute stage began. If the dormant stage was always that long, then, at least in Abdera, they had time to think and prepare. Currently, he ruled out exploratory surgery, for the exact locations of the bites or implants were uncertain, and to go digging during the dormant stage for something that was evidently very small, without knowing what to look for, would certainly be a waste of time. No, they must wait, and be prepared to attack the par-asites at various stages of active growth with the knife, radio therapy, or chemotherapy. The recovery of a fully grown Xeno was of vital importance to greater understanding. "Obviously, no two or three doctors can tackle this threat," he said. "Potentially we have seventy-odd patients, all likely to require sophisticated treatment around the same time. I shall put this to Malin immediately."

Tatyana nodded vigorously. "The problem cannot be met in this clandestine way. I too will take the same line with my government and Mr. Malin. Total coop-eration! Immediate hospitalization of all patients!"

"Yes . . ." Mark regarded her thoughtfully. "But here in the States it's not that easy. Interference with a citizen's rights—well, interference he or she objects to—is political dynamite."

She glared as if it was his fault. "They must be *made* to obey! In the Soviet Union . . ."

As evening closed in, Tatyana Marinskiya left for Al-bany on the first leg of her journey home. Both sides would keep in close touch; she would like to return the moment anything developed. The good-byes said, she moved to enter the car, then paused, turning to Scott, holding his arm in a viselike grip. "Don't worry, Jaimie," she said solemnly. "She is a good, strong girl. I know the type—strong!" Then she embraced him in true Russian style. Freedman watched, smiling, and was embraced in his turn.

Freedman sensed she yearned to talk about the deeper implications of ICARUS. Perhaps time did not allow it—or was there some other reason?

Within minutes of her departure Freedman was talking with Malin, giving him the essential facts. Xeno was an unknown parasite. The Jumbo crew and passengers were almost certainly affected. A meeting at the earliest moment was essential. Drastic action must be taken. A written report would be ready the next day.

Scott listened, anxious to hear Malin's reaction, but Freedman hung up, shaking his head. "Too soon, Jaimie. Malin's practically speechless. I don't blame him. Give him time," he smiled thinly. "Like until tomorrow." He clapped his assistant on the shoulder. "Come on, my boy! Help me to get the report written. It's a nasty situation, but don't despair. Already we know a great deal more than the Russians did, and with luck we've got five or six months to get organized."

Freedman wrote swiftly, revised and wrote again, tossing the sheets to Scott, who hunted and pecked out the final copy on a typewriter.

At 7:00 P.M. they broke for a hasty supper. Before leaving for Mom's, Scott excused himself; he had a call to make.

Freedman smiled to himself; he could guess who was being called.

Two minutes later Scott burst into Freedman's office, his face chalk white.

"Mark! I called Shane—got her aunt—" He swallowed. "Shane's gone to bed—says she feels very tired!"

An innocent-sounding sentence, but an invisible, icy hand clutched at Freedman's heart.

· XVIII ·

Malin's personal secretary had known for a long time that he was mixed up in something very sensitive—and judging by the increasing strain he showed, something pretty important. Her first guess had been marital problems; she knew all about his mistress, and suspected Mrs. Malin was also well informed. But she'd tossed that theory away months ago. Whatever it was, it had to be a lot more serious than sex.

Even so, she was not prepared for the sight of Malin as he passed unsteadily through her office, saying nothing, looking as if he'd just seen a ghost. Dr. Freedman had brought this on, no doubt. To her he was only a name, but Malin had given strict orders that Freedman should be connected with him anytime, anyplace, no matter what.

And Freedman had called. After that, she knew nothing. Her boss hadn't made any calls through her, but he had two private phones.

Should she call Mrs. Malin, warn her that her husband looked sick? No, that would be indiscreet—and indiscretion was a secretary's one unforgivable error. She'd do nothing.

* * *

Malin felt as ghastly as he looked. Freedman's terse report far exceeded his worst fears. For several minutes he had sat, hand still on the phone, forcing his brain to battle with this new crisis.

Parasites! God almighty—where had they come from? What were they? Well, so much for Lebedev's power storm theory. Freedman had conveyed the urgency he felt. To convene the committee would waste time.

He got the President on the ICARUS line, taking a slightly perverse pleasure in being the first to give him the bad news. Shaken, the President agreed to a meeting of the Ten; he'd be free at nine that evening; would this doctor be there?

No, said Malin, thinking quickly, but the Soviet specialist was arriving from Abdera. If she had hard news, he'd bring her.

At eight thirty he met her plane. Within minutes they were talking urgently in the security of his car as they raced toward the White House. She had hard news all right.

Eight of the Ten were present. Formalities had been dispensed with totally—no handshakes, no chitchat, just grim silence until the President strode in and took the chair. Without preamble, he called on Malin to update them. Malin repeated Freedman's verbal report, then introduced the Soviet doctor. She had details.

Tatyana felt tired and worried. During her journey she'd taken her first long look at the wider implications of ICARUS. As a good Soviet citizen and party member, she had until this time concentrated on her duty, the narrow medical aspect and nothing else. The rest did not concern her; other, higher comrades in party and government dealt with that. But some of the undisciplined freedom, the diversity of thought, she'd observed in the States had gotten through. For the first time in her life she was asking herself questions, and she did not like the answers.

Her account was cold and factual and made her audience suitably uncomfortable. The only hope she offered—their expressions showed they snatched at it—was the possible breathing space of six months before the full weight of the Xenos fell upon them.

The President thanked her. Did anyone have a question?

"Yes," said Arcasso. "The small holes in the Ilyushin and Jumbo *Papa Kilo*—could they be connected to these bites?"

Tatyana shrugged helplessly. "I have no idea. Parasites, insects"—she waved a plump hand irritably—"I know little. Ask your Dr. Freedman; he has wide medical experience and is very well read in insect biology." She changed the subject. "What is of vital importance is to prepare for what must come. I'd be happy to assist, but three doctors are hopelessly inadequate. There must be more, plus laboratory and surgical facilities—a hospital, in fact—including cobalt ray machines." She saw the anguish on several faces. "Yes, the secret of ICARUS is endangered, but will it be any better if you do nothing?"

"Doctor," said the President, "our country has never sat on its hands in a crisis, and we won't start now. But we have to consider the good of the whole nation, indeed, the world. The news is horrifying. Imagine the reaction of a world totally unprepared for these dreadful revelations! ICARUS material *must* be restricted to a minimum number of people, as I'm sure your government will agree."

"Very probably," said Tatyana, "but it doesn't alter my views. Also, do not overlook that it's *your* government, not mine, that faces this immediate problem."

"Mr. President," said CIA Joe, "the Army must have a suitable hospital we could use. I agree with our Russian colleague; like it or not, the ICARUS Staff has to be greatly expanded. I don't think that's too serious. What *does* worry me—security-wise—is how the hell we get all these Abdera folk in there without comment."

The discussion went on for quite a while, ending with the drafting of a presidential directive to the Chief of Staff, Armed Forces. A suitable Army hospital was to be found, cleared of existing patients and restaffed with appropriate service personnel, all of whom would be inducted into the ICARUS group. Doctors Freedman and Scott would be asked to cooperate with the hospital, the former acting as an advisor on additional equipment and as a member of the hospital's medical committee. Action was to be taken immediately; the hospital was to be fully operational in three months time.

On the side, the FBI would keep track of all who had been in *Papa Kilo* on its fateful flight. The FBI and CIA would be jointly responsible for producing whatever scheme could get them all into the hospital with a minimum of publicity.

As a first step, Malin would at once consult with Doctor Freedman regarding future planning and obtain his views, as the man on the spot, on how best to maintain secrecy in Abdera.

The meeting ended. All were satisfied with the progress made, quite certain that in three months time, well ahead of the predicted crisis, the organization to meet it would be ready. Once more, the larger implications were, by unspoken agreement, shelved.

Pouring herself a stiff whiskey—Malin had provided a bedside bottle—Tatyana Marinskiya felt satisfied, too. These Americans certainly moved when they had to. When their capitalistic society finally crumbled, and they took the path of socialism to communism, might they not become the most powerful socialist state?

She washed away that unpatriotic thought with a second slug of whiskey, dropped gratefully into bed, and slept almost at once.

But in Abdera Hollow, deep in the Catskill country of Rip Van Winkle, perhaps a dozen people slept even more soundly.

And in a small suburban house on the outskirts of Lafayette, Louisiana, two children were deep in the same sick sleep, oblivious to the wrangling of their parents downstairs. Not for the first time, they argued about spending their government handout. Hell, they'd collected two thousand bucks apiece—eight thousand for the family—and had the prospect of more.

High over Central America, bound for Atlanta, Georgia, a young stewardess confided to a colleague that she could hardly keep her eyes open.

• XIX •

Mark did not completely allay Jaimie's fears, but he succeeded in quieting them. To jump to hasty conclusions was unprofessional and no way to help Shane. Wasn't it possible, for instance, that the aunt was too shy to say that Shane had the curse, felt lousy, and had hit the sack?

That slowed Jamie up. He confessed he had no idea of Shane's menstrual cycle, but recalled she'd been out of sorts maybe a month back.

They finished the report around midnight and, carefully nursing his fragile hope, Jaimie went home to his two-room apartment. Mark said he'd lock up and go home, too. He lied. Alone, he lit his pipe, read notes, and brooded about Xeno.

At 2:00 A.M. he drove to his modest house, left his car in the driveway, and let himself in quietly. His wife, long since accustomed to his irregular hours, had not waited up.

For a time he pattered around his den, pretending to prepare for bed. But his mind was far too active for sleep. He poured a small whiskey, drowned it with soda, lit another pipe, and lay down on the sofa with a book. All along he'd known he'd wind up with this particular volume. The subject was insects. It was better to grapple with the immediate problem, anyway; the more frightening implications must wait.

It has been said that if all the world's animals, man included, were put into one pan of a cosmic set of scales, and all the world's insects into the other, the insects would outweigh the animals. Perhaps an unconscious realization of the staggering scope and variety of the insect horde lay at the root of humanity's dislike and fear of insects.

Freedman found their world absorbing. A lot of his spare time went into study of all forms of wild life, but animals and birds were practically human compared to insects, his deepest interest.

This fascination for biology had been a major factor in his decision to settle in Abdera Hollow. Globetrotting had ended in marriage, and there he had faced a choice: carve out a reputation and earn big money in the city, or forget all that and do the things he liked. His wife was amenable either way, so Abdera Hollow won.

Now his hobby assumed new importance. Xeno had to be an insect, regardless of its orgin. It was also a parasite, using a totally different species as a womb and a food supply for its young. From that leaped a new and frightening line of speculation that he firmly thrust aside, for it had no bearing on the immediate problem.

In principal, Xeno was nothing new. A number of insects parasitized cattle, horses, man, other insects—the list of hosts was endless. The method of attack varied with the victim's size. A predator whose host was of comparable size usually paralyzed its victim with a sting and implanted its eggs, leaving the host to be eaten alive by its young when they emerged. Larger creatures like man or cattle were implanted secretly and painlessly, but in every case that Mark could recall, the basic method was the same: they implanted their hosts by means of an egg-layer, or ovipositor. It might be long and thin or short and stout, but it always had incredible penetrating power.

And if the ichneumon fly could bore into trees, seek and find its hidden, helpless prey, might not Xeno have penetrated the plane? If that were true, the Xeno's ovipositor would be measured in meters, and Xeno itself could be a great deal bigger than man.

Freedman rejected that theory. There was always some correlation between the fully grown specimen and the egg at the point of hatching. Again he thought how vital it was to recover a newborn Xeno.

In any case, an insect's size was limited by the relative inefficiency of its respiratory system. All insects had breathing tubes—spiracles—of one sort or another; and these simply could not extract enough oxygen to support a creature the size of a cat, let alone a man. None of them had lungs, thank god.

But did Xeno bridge that gap? If so, then in theory it could be bigger than a man. It could be any size, until some other limiting factor stepped in. Imagine a wasp the size of a man. The sheer mass of the abdomen—the lungs would certainly develop there—would be so great that the damned thing would break at its slender thorax the first time it tried to pull a high-g turn.

He'd tell Malin he didn't believe implantation had been done from outside the plane. He'd tell him . . .

The book slipped unnoticed from his hand and Freedman slept. With his open mouth, his beak-like nose, and the light reflected in his glasses, he looked very much like one of his imagined insects.

The insistent trilling of the phone woke him. Rubbing a stiff neck, he got up and crossed the room to answer.

"Freedman." Yawning, he glanced at the clock; not yet seven in the morning. "Sure . . . I'll be tied up at the county hospital until after lunch. Be back here at four. . . . Right."

Further sleep was out of the question. He picked up the book, stared speculatively at the photograph of the ichneumon fly, resisted the impulse to continue reading, and shuffled off to placate his wife with a cup of coffee.

Across town, less than half a mile away, Jaimie Scott was also up and about. Mark had calmed him down somewhat; but he had spent a restless night, his professional mind filled with a mixture of foreboding and deep concern for Shane. Freedman was well satisfied with Jaimie's development as a doctor; but aside from that, Jaimie was young, naive—and hopelessly in love for the first time in his life.

While shaving, showering, and dressing, he tried repeatedly to think of a good excuse to call Shane without exciting her fears or her aunt's suspicions. Invention failed him. For a while he stood by the window, drinking the cup of coffee that passed for breakfast, gazing out at what promised to be a beautiful June morning. Already the climbing sun was burning away the mist that lay in the hollow.

Abdera Hollow would never win a prize for outstanding beauty, but the view from Scott's second-floor window was by no means bad. He lived in a house perched on the rim of the hollow. Abdera had a certain charm, especially now, when the trees were in full foliage, half submerging the red roofs and white walls in a green sea, hiding the imperfections—the vacant lots, the occasional derelict building. The natives might find the town low on excitement, but for a city-dweller's vacation—his short vacation—Abdera could be highly restful.

But Jaimie had no eyes for the scenery. He stared at the ridge of a roof on the far side of Main Street—Shane's roof, which sheltered all his hopes for joy and fears of the unknown.

With Mark away on his biweekly visit to the county hospital, Jaimie had plenty to occupy him during the morning. If Shane was okay, he knew she'd be off for an interview for a hotel job; no point in phoning before noon.

Twenty kilometers away at the hospital, Freedman was equally busy. Like his junior partner, he too had his fears, but his older, more disciplined mind held them under better control. Each patient he visited got his full attention, but as he moved from room to room he speculated briefly on the purpose of Malin's coming visit. Malin had said nothing, but the urgency in his voice had been unmistakable.

Unlike Jaimie, he noted with pleasure the brilliance of the day. The small, modern hospital was flooded with sunlight, giving a lift to all inside. Even that battle-ax of a head nurse smiled and said hello.

Freedman would remember that morning. Even he, cautious and alert, had no inkling of the change that was coming, of the terror that would soon descend upon his community.

It began as he drove slowly back to Abdera. Well ahead of schedule, he pulled off the road at a favorite lakeside spot; he would allow himself a ten-minute break, watching the waterfowl. He found a mallard particularly handsome. The drake's brilliant bottle-green head pleased him; soon that vivid color would be lost in the summer molt.

Mark was scarcely three paces from the car when the phone buzzed. "Goddam!" Still watching the duck, he answered.

The pleasure of the day, his preoccupation with the duck, abruptly vanished. Scott was calling from Shane's house. He'd phoned, not liked the answer he got, and gone over to see her. As casually as he could, aware the aunt could be listening, he said, "I'd be glad if you dropped by on your way back." Freedman agreed and drove off quickly, suddenly pressed for time. Two men wanted him urgently, Malin and Scott. Neither had explained why.

So, in a bedroom incongruously bright with sunlight, Freedman saw his first Xeno victim. She lay sleeping, outwardly a normal, healthy young woman. But, as Scott explained, with the exception of a short half hour of dreamy consciousness, she had slept solidly for twenty hours, and on her arm a slight swelling had appeared. She stirred as Mark examined her, but showed no signs of coming to. He straightened up, glancing at his watch. In thirty minutes Malin would arrive.

"What's wrong with Shane, doctor?" asked the aunt anxiously. Freedman shook his head. "It's too early to say. A thorough examination and tests will have to be made. I'll arrange an ambulance."

"You mean she's got to go into the hospital?" said the woman in growing alarm. "It's not serious, is it? I mean, she's going to be okay?" She cast around for a comforting answer. "Maybe it's this weather; this heat takes it outa you." She laughed unconvincingly. "I've only been up myself for a couple of hours, but it feels like the day's been going on forever—and Shane's a growing girl." She yawned, emphasizing her point.

Mark's face remained impassive. "We'll know more later," he said. "I'll tell the hospital to call you when the ambulance is coming." He shut his case. "Don't worry—just let her sleep."

The aunt looked at her niece doubtfully. "Well, I guess a good sleep never done anybody no harm." Her practical female mind asserted itself. "Maybe the hospital's the best place. I can't go runnin' up and down stairs, not at my age." They left her packing an overnight bag for Shane.

Once clear of the house, Scott turned to Freedman. "Mark, this is it! What can we *do*?"

Freedman turned on him fiercely. "We don't panic!"

"But the time scale! Tatyana figured we had months—"

Again Mark cut him short. "Never mind what she said. Tatyana was wrong!" He got in his car. "Get back to the office—and don't drive fast."

Freedman called the hospital and arranged for the ambulance, then spoke to the head of surgery, an old friend. "Slim? This is Mark. Look, I can't say much right now, but I suspect you're going to get a lot of business from me in the very near future. . . . No, I can't explain—just take my word. Stop all non-urgent admissions, and if you can discharge any patients, do it. . . . No. . . . No. . . . I can't tell, there could be twenty admissions from me in the next two or three days. . . . No, not full emergency procedure, not yet. I'll call you later. I've just arranged the admission of the first one—"

By the time he had finished, two patients had already left the office, annoyed by the brusque attention Scott had given them. He was desperate to talk with Freedman. He almost ran down the corridor to his senior's office, arriving at the same time as Malin.

Freedman surveyed his two visitors: both looked haggard and eager to talk. With a sharp glance at Jaimie, he gave priority to Malin.

Malin plunged into the presidential directive to set up an ICARUS hospital. When he got to the target date, Freedman stopped him.

"Won't do, Malin—not now." Quickly he told him of Shane de Byl.

"But Marinskiya said—"

"Yes," Scott interrupted. "Why this time difference? And why Shane?"

Mark's hand, half raised from the desk, silenced them. "The Soviets had only two cases—insufficient evidence." He spoke quickly, urgency forcing him into verbal shorthand. "The difference in climate and sunlight may be significant. Vorkuta is above the Arctic Circle; intense cold, six months of semidarkness." He concentrated on Jaimie. "Shane is the youngest and therefore perhaps the best host." He shrugged. "All that is beside the point. Xeno is here now, never mind why." He turned to Malin. "Forget your Army hospital; the action is going to be here, in Nash County Hospital." Again his raised hand stopped Malin. "Security's your problem. Other doctors—and surgeons—*must* be involved."

"No!" Scott said decisively. "Not Shane—not surgery!"

"No, not Shane," agreed Mark quietly. "She's our first case, the first chance to discover what we're up against. That's vital."

Scott hated him at that moment and his expression showed it.

"And you know it." Freedman was unmoved as he returned Scott's stare. "Get over to the hospital, Jaimie. Full intensive care facilities at immediate standby. Keep as complete a record as you can of her condition, but no medication or X rays. Set up a camera; shots every half hour—more if you think it's necessary. I'll be over as soon as I can. I don't think it's likely, but if the cyst ruptures before I arrive—*get that specimen!*"

Scott left without a word.

Malin had been doing some fast thinking. "You think this girl's first because she's the youngest?"

Freedman nodded. "Very possibly."

"How old is she?"

"Twenty-one—why?"

"Well," said Malin slowly, "I'm thinking of the

other folks on the plane. Certainly there were two or three kids and a couple of stewardesses of about your girl's age."

Freedman tossed his glasses on the desk in a gesture of hopelessness. "It's no good—you'll never keep this quiet! Everyone that was in that plane is in danger, especially the young. The situation here is bad enough, but the others must be held under observation and the doctors told what little we know."

"That does it," said Malin. "Nash County becomes the ICARUS hospital center. It's not a perfect answer—there isn't one—but it's the best we can do for the patients and security. It's a tricky proposition, setting up a federal operation that fast, but that's a headache for the President. I'm putting you in charge of this thing, Mark."

"Me?" Freedman looked up sharply. "I'm in this by accident. I'll do all I can, but I'm only a GP!"

"True," agreed Malin, not prepared to argue, "but you know a hell of a lot more than anybody else, and there's no time." He looked directly at Freedman. "Mark, I'm not asking. I'm *telling* you you have the job."

Mark felt neither pleased nor sorry. His mind was struggling with the problems of his patients. Shane's aunt, for example, could well be on the threshold of the acute phase. She was alone now, and if she passed out, how would he or anyone else know?

"Can I use your phone?" Malin asked.

"Go ahead," said Mark absently.

Within two minutes Malin had the New York FBI office buzzing like an overturned beehive. He wanted a mobile field HQ unit in Abdera that night; New York had better not be late.

Then he called Washington. "Frank? Alvin. This is an open line. That scheme is a dead duck. Forget the three-month deadline—it's *now*. I'm lining up a local non-Army facility and I want you to clear it with the big man. Tell him . . ." Malin was dimly aware of another phone ringing, of Freedman talking. But he went on rapidly, suggesting the selective releases of ICARUS letters. ". . . And all those other folk we met back in Denver, especially those under twenty-five—the committee had better think of some way to get them here. . . . yes, all of them. . . . I'm staying here. By midnight I'll have a proper communication link. You'll get all the dope then." He hung up.

Freedman was staring at him. "If it's any comfort," he said, getting up, "you haven't jumped the gun. There are two more cases—and one's the second youngest on my list!"

Having driven like a lunatic to the hospital, Jaimie had plenty of time to prepare for Shane's arrival. His nervous state raised a good deal of curiosity, and caused a hostile confrontation between him and administration. The battle-ax at the desk retreated before his determination to get what he wanted, but she told him that she would report his disgraceful conduct to Freedman, the control committee, and anyone else who'd listen. Jaimie could not have cared less.

Once Shane was safely in the first-floor room assigned to her, he slowed down. She lay still, her breathing barely noticeable, yet she looked so healthy, so beautiful. Jaimie pulled himself together and, assisted by a nurse, took an EKG reading. He also checked Shane's temperature, pulse rate, and respiration. All were subnormal, but not enough to worry him. He concentrated on the cyst, his hands trembling. This lump, already more than two centimeters in diameter, brought on by something hideous, something completely alien to her world, was nonetheless a part of Shane.

He sent the nurse for the photographer, glad to have a few moments alone. In an attempt to blot out the fear and anguish he was feeling, he dictated his findings into his recorder.

Freedman arrived and found no fault with Jaimie's preparations. Shane lay on her side, her strapped right arm clearly visible, the bed flanked by all the daunting paraphernalia of modern medicine. To one side stood a camera, mounted on a tripod clamped in position. The overhead light had been dimmed, the curtains drawn; a single spotlight illuminated the target area on the girl's arm and the shallow dish beneath it.

Satisfied, Freedman hurried off to the emergency meeting of the hospital control board, picking up Malin in the reception area en route.

During the ten-minute drive to the hospital, Malin had made up his mind. A decision had to be made without referring back to Washington, and he was the one to make it.

After an introduction by Freedman, he informed the board that the passengers and crew of the *Papa Kilo* flight had contracted an unidentified sickness during the course of their flight. How many would be affected could not be known, but the bulk of the passengers hailed from Abdera, and—subject to presidential approval—he was putting the hospital under federal control. Dr. Freedman, who had the twin advantages of knowing most of the patients professionally and knowing more about this sickness that anyone else, would assume operational control of the hospital on behalf of the United States Government.

The doctors and senior nurses absorbed this in shocked silence. One or two looked at Malin as if he'd suddenly grown an extra head. Freedman's speech was terse. This was an emergency. The drastic action was justified. The patients would be his personal responsibility. Any questions?

Staggered by the speed of the takeover, no one spoke.

"Okay," Freedman continued, "we have one hundred and ten beds. Sheila," he addressed the head nurse, "how many vacancies do we have right now?"

"As of half an hour ago, thirty-nine."

"Make it thirty-seven—there are two more on the way. There may be a dozen or more before morning." Freedman looked at Dr. Lewis, the head of surgery and the hospital's senior physician. "Slim?"

Slim understood the unspoken question. "There's no time to stand around. I fully support this action, and Mark's in control"—he went on, half joking—"so long as he doesn't see himself with a knife in my operating rooms! I've already stopped all nonurgent admissions and ten patients will be discharged tomorrow. That gives us forty-seven beds. What is the potential figure, Mark?"

Freedman looked at Malin.

"As a rough guess, I'd say *Papa Kilo* had between eighty and ninety on board."

Malin got up. "By midnight there'll be an FBI guard on this place—not to get in your hair but to keep intruders off your backs. Thank you."

As Malin left, Freedman was launching into a description of the Xeno cycle.

By 11:00 P.M. five calls for help had reached Freedman via his answering service. Four times an ambulance made the run to Abdera, lights flashing, but sirens silent on his orders. Within the hospital everyone worked feverishly, all differences and rivalries forgotten. Patients were moved to clear wards and groups of rooms. Slim and Mark examined the first two cases after Shane. One of them was her aunt. The cyst, located on her neck, presented no problems for the surgeon. Freedman made the decision: Operate.

The frenetic activity in Nash County Hospital was reflected clear across the States. Washington hastily approved Malin's action and the President phoned the governor. Four Army doctors, two of them parasitologists, were dispatched to the hospital at once, and the FBI got down to locating and bringing in the eighteen non-Abderan passengers and the crew of *Papa Kilo*.

Ten of the passengers and one crew member were found within an hour. Ten were induced by a mixture of threats and hints of even larger federal compensation to make the trip to Abdera—by service transportation. The stewardess could not be moved. She already lay in an Atlanta hospital, a sore puzzle to the doctors.

The missing seven worried Washington. Five were in one family. Neighbors in Lafayette, Louisiana, said they'd gone on a short vacation in their camper, destination unknown. That was bad enough. But what made the ICARUS group really sweat were the other two, the pilot and copilot. The pilot—on his first operational flight since *Papa Kilo*—was driving a Jumbo over the Atlantic, bound for Europe, and the FBI located the copilot on a stopover in Bombay.

Freedman knew nothing of these latest developments and would have paid small attention if he had. His slight figure was seen everywhere in the hospital, arranging, ordering, helping—and, above all, steadying others with his calmness.

At midnight he took over from Scott, ordering him

back to Abdera. To save time, an ambulance would be stationed at their office. Scott would guard the telephone throughout the night. At first light he was to start checking all Specials.

Jaimie did not want to leave Shane; but the silent, tense hours he'd passed in her room had given him time to adjust. Secretly he felt relieved that Mark was taking over, doubting his own ability to remain calm and objective in dealing with Shane's inevitable crisis. He had no such doubts about Mark.

Alone, Freedman settled down to his vigil, half his mind busy with other problems, reviewing decisions already made, evaluating new ones. Slim had the first of his two surgical cases on the table. Seven other admissions were being treated like Shane; three had to be put in one room, under the supervision of a senior nurse. This was all the overstretched staff could provide. In an adjoining room the hospital's only other camera was rigged over the cyst on the collarbone of a sixty-nine year old widow.

Mark doubted if any further cases would be found before morning. Most Specials would be in bed anyway, with no one to tell the difference between sleep and coma. A message from Malin told of forthcoming reinforcement by U.S. Government personnel and material, but tonight's battle had to be fought with what they had.

Freedman turned off the overhead light to see the EKG scan more clearly, relying on it to alert him of any change in his patient's condition. He sat on a high stool, watching her arm under the cold, bright spotlight, the silence broken only by the audio blips of the EKG machine. Now and then he gently felt the lump with a gloved hand, estimating the size of this alien life that grew almost visibly, draining the resources of its victim for its own unknown purpose. As a human being Mark fought against horror; as a doctor, wonder and fascination held him.

Around two A.M. the head nurse dropped by with coffee. Angrily he waved her away. She put the cup on the cart beside him and left only too gladly. She was not a fanciful woman, but the darkened room, with Freedman bowed over his work like a vulture over its prey, chilled her.

Freedman ignored the coffee. He dictated notes rapidly in a low voice, and, with the cyst growing at an ever-increasing rate, took photographs every ten minutes. All the while he listened to the steady blipping of the machine. With infinite care he laid his hand lightly on the cyst's domed top, which had now changed color from healthy pink to dirty yellow. Gently his sensitive fingers explored the periphery, recognizing the growing hardness, just as Tatyana had described.

And then—

It took all his training, all his personal discipline not to snatch his hand away. Beneath his probing fingertips, something moved: a slow, writhing movement.

Carefully he withdrew his hand, his heart pounding. He paused, wiped his brow with his arm, picked up the recorder, and spoke, grasping the camera cable in his other hand. He waited, excited and apprehensive. Soon he would know.

Freedman could not be certain of the exact moment of rupture. Perhaps his gaze lingered a fraction too long on the EKG scan, but when he looked again the cyst had changed.

The stretched skin still gleamed in the cold light. But in the very center of the swelling, a brighter reflection, a pinhead of fluid, lay on the skin—and as he watched, it grew.

Instantly he pressed the camera switch, filling the room for a microsecond with blinding electronic light, the silence broken only by the click and whirr of shutter and film-shift. He switched on the microphone, spoke softly, and left the recorder running: from here on he would need a free hand.

The pool of fluid increased in size, losing its sharp convexity. Now the size of a match head, a trace of blood discolored its edge. Freedman took another shot, tightening his eyes against the flash. The fluid had now formed an irregular patch as big as a bean. Light danced on its trembling surface. He guessed the surface tension would soon fail—or was the movement due to something else?

The process speeded up. For some reason, the patch broke. A thin trickle of blood-streaked fluid coursed slowly down the girl's arm, revealing a cavity.

Unconsciously, Freedman held his breath. Serous fluid welled out of the cavity in small, irregular pulses. Breathlessly he described the change, his mouth dry with excitement and barely contained fear.

The domed top of the cyst lost shape: faint wrinkles

appeared in the satiny skin, its color changing from putrescent yellow to dirty, lifeless white.

And through the yellow fluid, hesitantly, a head—triangular, alien . . .

Again the lightning flash. The head pulled back momentarily, then reappeared.

No bigger than an ear of corn, with two small black eyes, set well apart, it stared with frightening sentience at a strange world. Once more the camera flash, but this time the head did not recoil.

Freedman reached for a pair of forceps. With his attention focused on the alien, his hand fumbled. The forceps slipped, clattering on the table-top.

The head tilted sharply, aware of the noise.

Great God! The thing could *hear*.

He had the forceps now, and their cold, familiar shape gave comfort. Not yet; wait. . . .

The head moved forward in a smooth, serpentine action. Behind the head, a short neck of equal width, and behind that the first suggestion of a wider, thicker body, straining to free itself from the surrounding flesh.

Taking another shot, Freedman felt a new rush of fear. The alien not only saw and heard, it had the ability to learn, to understand that the bright blink of light posed no threat, for its struggle to emerge did not stop.

Two clawlike black pincers appeared, grasping the edge of the cavity to gain purchase. The head bent downwards and the back was suddenly visible, arched. With one swift, flipping action the rest of the body and tail emerged, whipping upwards, falling with a faint, nauseating splat on the girl's arm.

It took all of Freedman's self-control to press the shutter release. Xeno resembled no larva he had ever seen or heard of. Instinctively he pulled back, his face twisted in a shocked grimace. The closest approximation to Xeno he could make among earthly species was a fully mature scorpion. But there were differences.

Scorpions are arthropods, not true insects, but like insects they have six legs. Xeno had twelve. Freedman watched in growing horror as he saw what he thought were short legs uncurl in an unearthly manner, and as they did so, straighten, jointing themselves like sections of a fishing rod. The process complete, the legs shook off traces of the nurturing serous fluid, pair by pair, with a fastidiously obscene action, testing themselves—as if they had no relation to the motionless, muddy-white body they supported.

The body was unlike that of a scorpion: smooth, unsegmented, it ended in a long tail, a smooth whiplike structure that flexed from side to side.

And then, in a movement that should have warned him, the tail arched upwards and forwards over the back.

It had to be *now*.

With a swift, stabbing motion Freedman struck, grasping the parasite around the body. Through the steel to his fingers, from fingers to brain, came the sensation of a softness that repulsed him. Then, with stupifying speed, he felt a swift resistance, a hardening, a fantastic transformation from butter to rock.

He lifted it clear of the girl's arm. It remained rigid, tail arched, legs splayed. Holding it under the brilliant light, he forced himself to lean forward, to observe, to learn.

But scientific observation vanished as the insect gave a sudden and incredibly strong wriggle. He tightened his grip, nauseated by the powerful, writhing motion; the strength, the boneless, snakelike movement was unnatural, frightening in its own right. Suddenly it was still, stiff, the expressionless eyes, not black but a very dark brown with a hint of gold, staring\directly at him.

It took all of Freedman's willpower to control his revulsion, his fear, to go on observing. He was aware of two things. Through the forceps he felt a regular, rapid pulsation. Synchronous with it, two minute apertures in the masklike face opened and closed.

The revelation almost made him lose his grip on the forceps. It would have been better for him if he had.

Xeno *breathed*! No insect could—not like this.

Staggered, he failed to observe the slight movement, the adjustment of the tail as the creature centered it down its line of sight. He saw the tail pulsate and half guessed the reason. But he was far too late. Something splashed on the left lens of his glasses. He felt a tiny warm spot on one side of his nose—warmth that grew in milliseconds to intense heat, blinding pain. Then darkness fell.

The telephone jolted Scott from an uneasy sleep, his head resting on arms at his desk. He fumbled for the receiver. What he heard cleared his sleep-drugged mind instantly.

Forgetting his jacket, he stumbled out into the cold predawn blackness. The ambulance driver, leaning against his car, tossed away a cigarette.

"Where to, doc?"

Scott stared at him, glassy-eyed. "Where? . . . No, no! Take over in there, the phone." He dug out his keys, dropped them. He swore, fighting hysteria as he searched frantically.

The driver found them. "You okay, doc?"

The cold, wet gravel bit into his knees. He scrambled up unsteadily. "Yeah. Hospital—guard the phone."

The driver watched him go. Scott's car lurched, stalled, started again, and sprayed gravel as it shot down the driveway without headlights. The man headed for the brightly lit doorway. This was certainly one helluva night.

Scott's wild appearance passed unnoticed in the chaos at the hospital. Nurses screamed orders, white-coated figures ran in every direction. The air was electric with panic. He ran, too—straight to Shane's room.

Freedman lay on a stretcher, Slim bent over him. Light filled the room. Shane lay as he had left her, but a swift glance at the EKG machine reassured him.

The surgeon looked up, his face shiny with sweat. He was still in his green O.R. clothes, mask around his neck. Scott took in the fallen stool, the scattered instruments and dishes.

"For Christ's sake—what's happened?"

"How the hell do I know!" snarled the surgeon.

"Mark—is he dead?"

"No."

Jaimie dropped beside the still figure. Mark's face, without his glasses, looked strangely unfamiliar, defenseless.

"There," said Slim, moving closer. "Don't touch!" he added sharply.

Slightly to one side and above the bridge of Mark's nose, at the beginning of his left eyebrow, was a small red spot, the surrounding hairs frizzled, burned.

"What makes you think—" Jaimie stopped, mesmerized by the spot.

Slim mopped his face with his mask. "A guess. I was on my way to see Mark; I heard a horrible scream from Carter's room—he was on the same camera watch. I ran in—" he shuddered. "Carter was on the floor—dead! Right eye practically burned out!" His mouth trembled. "Jesus! Just one scream, and he was dead in seconds!"

"But what—"

"Christ! How should I know!" Slim checked himself. "Something—don't ask me what—must have spurted out." He shrugged helplessly. "It has to be that. Mark was lucky—his glasses saved him." He nodded in the direction of the table. The familiar spectacles lay in a dish, the left lens discolored. "Analysis may give us some idea."

Scott looked from Mark to Shane and back to the surgeon. "Guess we'd better move Mark."

"Yeah?" Slim laughed disbelievingly. "Where to? All rooms are full! The nurse watching three of your people collapsed an hour back—exhaustion, hysteria—she got the last spare room." He rubbed his face wearily. "Leave him—unless you've a better idea."

He picked up a pair of forceps, lifted the spectacles carefully into a jar, and capped it. "They're *your* patients now."

"Yeah," said Scott helplessly. Two very tired, frightened men searched each other's eyes.

"You have any idea what the hell's going on? I mean, what's hit us?"

Jaimie could only shake his head.

·XXII·

For nearly an hour he worked. Shane had improved since he last saw her at midnight. At least he was sure she was no worse; the crisis had to be over.

To look at the cyst, now blackening round its periphery, almost made him sick, but it matched the description Tatyana had given of the copilot's, and the Russian had recovered.

He transferred the EKG machine to Mark. The readings were better than he'd dared to hope for. He was struck by the similarity of their conditions, although he could see no reason for it.

With both patients comfortable, he turned reluctantly to the camera and recorder, dreading what he would find. Forty exposures had been made. Only then did he realize that he should complete the record. When—if—Mark recovered, he'd be angry if Scott had failed him. He rang for the photographer and, while waiting, concentrated on the recorder.

Someone had switched it off. He rewound it, listening to a lot of blank tape until a high-pitched gabble told him he had reached Mark's last entry.

But he did not want to hear it right then. Trying hard to sound unconcerned, he read in the time, a brief, disjointed account of events, and the condition of both his patients.

The photographer peered around the door, scared and jumpy after his experience with the second camera and the dead doctor. Scott explained that he wanted a final, professional shot of the collapsed cyst, another of Mark's injury, and then some very fast action in processing the film.

Alone once more, he rewound the tape back to midnight, then quickly forward to the first signs of the cyst's activity.

The next twenty minutes were the worst in Jaimie's young life. He listened, picturing the scene, as Mark's voice lost its customary calm objectivity when the rupture of the cyst began. He heard Mark's quick indrawn breath as the Xeno appeared, the tremor in his voice as he described its astonishing breathing system. Listening, Scott could not take his eyes off the cyst, as if the whole awful scene were being reenacted before him.

Then the clink of steel on glass, the scrape of the stool on the floor. The last description, Mark speaking rapidly, as if he sensed that time was short. A sudden cry, itself cut short; a crash—then silence.

Malin found Scott hunched on the stool, head buried in hands. The sight infuriated the FBI man; he shook the young doctor's shoulder roughly.

"C'mon—snap out of it! Is Freedman going to make it?"

Slowly Jaimie came back, the nightmare still lingering in his eyes.

"Malin . . ." He spoke in a dull, flat voice. "Yes, I guess he'll survive."

Malin flared up. "Well, you should sure as Christ be doing something, not just sitting here!"

"Wait a minute, Mr. FBI Man. Let me tell you something." Jaimie stiffened with anger. "We don't know what is responsible for his state—or Shane's. Both are improving under their own power. Neither I nor anybody else is going to try anything fancy, understood?" He continued less aggressively. "Meanwhile, we're not sitting around. Tests are being run right now, the film's being developed. As for me sitting on my ass, you just listen to what I've heard on Mark's recording."

"Save it," said Malin hastily, "we have a meeting." His anger had receded. "Can you leave them?"

Scott got off his stool and contemplated the recumbent figures, the two most important people in his life. "Yes," he said heavily, "there's little else I can do right now." As he walked to the conference room Scott noticed the time: five thirty. He wasn't sure whether that was A.M. or P.M.

Slim was there, still in his operating clothes, along

144

with another doctor, the head nurse—looking ten years older—and two senior nurses, one pouring coffee. All appeared uncertain, tense, leaderless.

Malin took charge. Although he too had been up all night, he had not been involved in this first battle with Xeno. His audience listened quietly to the news: Four Army doctors would join them by mid-morning, and a dozen nurses were flying in. Additional equipment was on the way. It made little impression on these, the walking wounded, who were more concerned with their one dead doctor, a senior nurse whose mad screaming had only been stilled by a hypodermic needle, and Freedman, whose fate hung in the balance.

Slim spoke. Three non-Abderan passengers of *Papa Kilo* had been brought in, bringing the ICARUS admission total to thirty-four. One patient had died, cause not yet known. At least twenty-two cysts had ruptured, and two had been removed in an embryonic state.

Scott asked if any parasites had been obtained. Slim exploded. There had been precious little time, he said bitterly—moving patients around, clearing wards, getting the newcomers settled. And anyway, he continued angrily, how could they expect results from his hard-pressed staff when the five cases under close observation resulted in the death of one doctor, Freedman's collapse, and a nurse going crazy?

"Okay," said Malin. "Let's cool it, shall we? No one's blaming anyone. We have to work out where to go from here. I'll be frank. My problem is to restrict the knowledge of ICARUS to a minimum number of people; so far as I can, I've done it. This hospital is covered by my boys, and in another four hours no one will cough within a mile of here without my knowing about it. But the real problem is yours—to handle all ICARUS cases. If you need more staff and equipment than we're providing, say so. What you do is your business. It's a major setback that Dr. Freedman is out of action, but we all know he attached great importance to getting hold of one of—one of these things. I think that priority still stands. Any comments?"

"Sure," said Slim impatiently, "we need a specimen more than ever, but let's just take a look at what we know. We've had twenty-two ruptures and gotten nowhere. In the process we have one dead and two out of action. I think the substance on Mark's glasses will give us a lead, and the lab's on it right now." He paused. "Whatever, the thing's damned dangerous and mighty fast on its feet."

Malin suppressed a shudder. "We don't even know what it looks like—"

"I do," said Scott. In a harsh, strained voice he gave Mark's description.

Malin looked as if he would faint. Slim broke the appalled silence. "Jesus Christ! You say he said six *pairs* of legs—not six legs?"

"Mark said it two ways: six pairs and, a little later, twelve legs." He added, "He held the thing in a pair of forceps before it struck."

Slim brooded on that for a moment, then he held out his arm, imitating the action. It was too much for Malin; he made some excuse about other problems and left. No one noticed. "It's reasonable to assume Mark held it at arm's length," said Slim, contemplating his extended arm. "Make it close to a meter from his face." He tried to sound casual. "Two shots known to have been fired; one victim hit square in the eye and the other saved by his glasses. That's pretty sharp spitting."

"It comes to this. We've got the two embryos safely dead in alcohol, but we need a full term specimen."

"I'll get it." Scott hardly recognized his own voice.

"Okay," said Slim, "but we don't want any more trouble. Full protective clothing." His stare stiffened the head nurse. "Break out a decontamination suit—the whole bit, including respirator." He eyed Jaimie. "Make that two outfits."

Even as they talked, cysts were rupturing. A hysterical nurse had thought she saw something jump off a bed, moving incredibly fast. She thought it went under a door.

Only two cases remained, one fast approaching the crisis point, giving Scott little time to indulge his personal fear. Suited-up, booted, and gloved, he shuffled into the room. There would be no EKG, no camera—and no Slim. At the last moment, an urgent message from the lab had called him away. He'd clapped Scott on the shoulder: "Sorry, Jaimie; it's all yours."

He stood uncertainly at the foot of the bed. A nurse closed the door behind him, increasing his sense of alienation. He stared at the patient, an elderly man with a fast-growing cyst on his wrist; the patient would simply have to take his chances—recovery of the specimen was crucial. Ever practical, Slim had ruled out fooling with a kidney dish; Scott carried a chrome-steel bucket with a close-fitting lid. Inside, a liter of formalin sloshed around.

Sweat steamed up his respirator lenses, but Scott had neither the time nor the inclination to do much about it. A finger behind the cheek-piece improved his vision quickly. He peered down, breathing heavily, a nightmare figure in his own right, feeling scared and alone. To him the patient was part of the thing he sought, not a human being.

But he had little time for thought. Events moved with terrifying speed. The spot of fluid was already there, growing, pulsing, then welling out. For the first time he saw the alien head, triangular, deadly. He screamed within himself, clinging desperately to Mark's clear description, hearing again his calm voice. He forced himself to hold on, to wait.

Momentarily the head froze as the tiny eyes, black and shining, took in the surroundings, eying Scott malevolently. Suddenly—although he expected it, the action still made him jump—the awful arching of the back as it slid out, the sinuous flip, the disgusting splat—and the alien lay fully exposed on the man's arm.

Scott struck without hesitation, but his grasp of the forceps was less than perfect. For one heart-stopping second he thought he had failed; he gripped with all his strength and lifted.

That was the most horrible moment. The creature seemed weightless; it might have been made of polystyrene. But God, what strength.

Like Freedman before him, he felt the reaction to his steel grip, the body hardening, wriggling with unbelievable energy. Scott fought his rising panic. Shaken by the Xeno's writhing, he turned his wrist so that he had a safe view from the side, out of range of the creature's deadly venom. It struggled desperately to face him, to turn its whole body. The tail curved forward above the dirty-white, glistening back.

Moving his hand toward the bucket lid, he must have relaxed fractionally, his mad urge to be rid of the creature making his mind run ahead of events. The Xeno made one great effort, straining its head one way, its tail the other. He had a photographic image of the creature, head and tail in alignment. Something splashed on his mask: He cried out, his grip failed.

Fortunately, his hand was above the bucket. The

creature dropped, clawing at the rim; its undeveloped legs failed to find a grip on the smooth steel.

Scott slammed down the lid, nearly spilling the bucket, and pressed with all his strength. For several seconds he gave way to panic, half sobbing, half laughing. When he had recovered his composure he found he was on his knees, both gloved hands holding the lid down. The bucket was shaking, and he had no idea if the motion was due to him or his captive.

The trees beyond the hopsital lawns were black silhouettes, sharply etched against the pink dawn sky. Slim Lewis, pausing in the main entrance, could just make out the unfamiliar shape of an army-type command vehicle parked in the driveway. He took a deep breath of the cold, clean air, which penetrated his cotton operating greens and sent a chill through his body. He shivered, but made no move to go back inside. Never had he been so grateful to see a new day. He felt light-headed with fatigue, although it was by no means the first time he had worked through a night. But there had never been a night like this last one. He hoped against hope that there never would be again.

His tired brain made no attempt to grapple with the wider implications of what had happened, concentrating instead on what lay immediately before him. That was enough; more than enough.

Five bodies, including the hapless doctor's, lay in the mortuary, and the eighty-odd patients, he thought grimly, don't look much different. To avoid panic and to keep them quiet, they were all under heavy sedation. Most of the staff, meanwhile, had been powered by pep pills for some time.

Still, not all the news was bad. Freedman showed signs of a remarkably fast recovery; respiration, pulse, color, all had improved. Right now young Scott—who'd done a fine job getting the specimen—was back with Freedman and this girl he was so keen on, keeping them company while he drained his second large medicinal brandy.

The specimen. He and Jaimie had raised the lid just long enough to satisfy themselves that the thing was dead. It was certainly that, floating upside down, legs spread, horrific even in death. They had searched the hospital, every room, every cupboard, but had found nothing. Where the hell had these awful things gone? Still, that was another problem, and not his.

What other good news? Well, any minute now, the fresh doctors and nurses they desperately needed were due to arrive.

He looked down the driveway. Judging by the flashlights and the crunch of boots on gravel, the whole place was crawling with FBI men.

Crawling . . .

He shivered again; this time the action had nothing to do with his thin clothing.

• XXIII •

"And how about the rest?" said the President.

"All non-Abderans are accounted for, sir. The pilot's in the hospital in Frankfurt; the copilot likewise in India. A stewardess is hospitalized in Georgia. All the rest, except the Louisiana family, are in the ICARUS hospital."

"And the family?"

"Not so good, sir. A highway patrol report just in before I left said a camper had been found off the road east of Baton Rouge. Two adults in a coma and three kids, two of them dead. It has to be them." Arcasso hesitated. "Anyway, I'm working on that assumption and have ordered their transportation, alive or dead, to the ICARUS hospital."

The third figure in the Oval Office spoke. "Any news break?"

"The local FBI is handling it, Mr. Secretary," began Arcasso, "down there it's just another accident—"

Erwin Lord shook his head. "I mean the bigger boys."

The President interrupted. "Don't underrate the locals. So far we've kept the press off the scent, but if the story breaks anywhere, there'll be no holding press or TV. And I'm afraid it's breaking."

Lord retained his Abe Lincoln pose, arms relaxed on the sides of his chair. He raised one eyebrow. "There are times when I envy our—*my*—Soviet colleague."

The President frowned. At times his S of S was an affected bastard. The irony was that it was completely unnecessary. Lord could run rings around him as a brain, but he lacked the intangibles a top man needed: magnetism, charisma.

"But this," Lord continued smoothly, "is not one of them. We must now fall back on our second line—the time travelers have contracted some strange sickness 'out there.'" He smiled cynically. "Admit that it is dangerous to them, but not to us. That will give the big thrill and no pain."

"Obviously," said the President edgily.

Arcasso stood up. It was nearly two P.M.; he'd been out of the operations room for almost an hour. "If you'll excuse me, Mr. President—"

"Okay, Frank." Knowlton nodded. "Keep me informed. I've canceled all today's appointments."

* * *

Freedman felt he was at the bottom of a deep tank of water, and knew he must swim up to the dimly lit surface. He struggled, but however desperately he did so, he made little headway. Yet there was progress, for the light above grew stronger. The dancing surface ceased to be water, splintering into an infinity of brilliant, blinding fragments. Unaccountably, the light was suddenly replaced by the distorted, anxious face of Jaimie. His mouth was moving but saying nothing. Suddenly a roaring sound filled his head and, just as suddenly, faded sharply. Now he could hear Jaimie. Why in God's name was he shouting?

Scott held the twitching arms of his senior. "It's okay, Mark. Just relax; you're doing fine."

Freedman shivered. He'd never realized what an ugly mess Jaimie's face was: enlarged pores, blackheads. And his eyes: They weren't full of innocence, they were blank. The thickest ox in creation would be ashamed to own an expression like that. And what had he been shaving with—a lawn mower?"

Scott's face moved in and out of focus. Mark sat up, and the world spun crazily. He was aware of a hand on his back; his acute tactile sense identified four—no, five pressure points.

"You're okay," murmured Scott. "Take it easy, Mark."

"For God's sake stop shouting!" yelled Freedman.

Scott bent over his colleague, trying to catch the faint muttering. As he lowered Mark gently onto the bed, Freedman glared at him, his mouth trembling. Scott got the idea. "You want to sit up? All right. Stay right there."

Freedman's hands rested on his knees, his body leaning forward. Scott took a chance, released his hold, and hurriedly got an armchair alongside. He grabbed the swaying figure, lifting him from bed to chair.

For a while Freedman sat leaning forward, hands on knees, head down, waiting for the world to stop spinning. Slowly the tumult subsided, and he sat up straight.

"Where the hell are my glasses?"

Freedman's voice was stronger but still only barely intelligible. "Sure, Mark; I'll get 'em."

Thank God the young fool had stopped shouting. Freedman leaned back, closing his eyes. There was something he should remember; something vitally important.

His head was pounding.

Scott returned and leaned over him, noting the improvement in his color. Freedman's eyes opened slowly; the pupils were less contracted and reacted much better to the light.

"How are you feeling, Mark?"

Freedman took the glasses and put them on clumsily. "Better," he said tersely. "Still feel strange, but it's coming back to me slowly. How's Shane?"

"Still not conscious yet, but progressing."

Mark nodded. "Order a glass of warm milk," he said quietly. "We've got to talk." He remained silent while Scott phoned, relieved that his mind and vision were swiftly returning to normal.

"Okay, Jaimie. Sit down. It's still tough for me to look up. What happened after I failed?" He emphasized the last word bitterly.

"Come on, Mark!" protested Scott. "You can't blame—"

"Forget it!" Mark retorted sharply. "I failed. Don't waste time. Tell me what's been going on."

The head nurse arrived with the milk in the middle of Jaimie's recital; one cold stare from Mark kept her silent. Modestly, Jaimie soft-pedaled his capture of the specimen, passing quickly to the current state of affairs in the hospital.

"You've done well, Jaimie," said Freedman, "better than I—"

This Scott would not let pass. "Mark, for God's sake, be fair to yourself. I was scared as hell. It was your description that stopped me from falling apart. Without you—" He stopped, looking away.

Both men were embarrassed. Mark had known for a long time that Jaimie had a strong streak of hero worship for him as a professional.

"You mean—just this once you actually listened to something I said?" A wry grin spread across his face.

Scott managed a strained smile. "Just this once."

"Okay," said Freedman, "is the lab report in? And the Xeno—what has happened there?"

"Nothing yet from the lab. As for the specimen, Slim says we need a crack biologist to tackle it. That specimen has cost us plenty, and he for one was not prepared to louse it up. As I said, we've got some high-priced professionals on the way."

Mark nodded in agreement, he had no time to speak. From the bed came a low-pitched moan. Jaimie was there instantly.

"What's goin' on?" Shane's voice was weak. "God—I'm thirsty."

Mark proffered his milk. "Give her this."

Jaimie took it, cradling Shane's head as if it were a Ming vase. She drank and looked vaguely about her. But before she could get the questions straight in her mind, sleep reclaimed her. Scott returned, satisfied that she was asleep and not in coma.

Mark appreciated the change. He said softly, "Get me out of here. Get a wheelchair and call Slim—"

"You should get some sleep as well," said Scott.

"The speed with which you've revived is amazing, but you're still not ready—"

"I know all that," retorted Freedman irritably. "Go get that chair!"

Freedman held his meeting in the conference room. His first action was to send a new doctor with a guide to check out and collect all the time travelers left in Abdera. He then listened to a report on the patients. With two exceptions, they appeared to be recovering well, the speed varying with the age of the individual.

The lab technician gave his preliminary report. He began with a startling statement: The substance on Freedman's glasses and Scott's respirator was harmless.

At that Slim Lewis, a waxen-faced, brooding figure, exploded. Then how come one man had died, and Dr. Freedman here had been flattened for fourteen hours? *Harmless?*

Freedman took it calmly, quietly telling the technician to proceed.

"I said it *is* harmless; I didn't say it *was*. The substance has a very short active phase. I believe that in air it oxidized, breaking down quickly into inert components. I worked back from that assumption." He looked appealingly at Freedman, who gave him an encouraging nod. "I'm no toxicologist, but for my money this is an exotoxin, a protein. It looks like an alkaloid of some sort. I'd guess its an alkylhalide, pretty close to dimethylaniline. And there's something else; there's a vesicant present, a blistering agent. In the simplest terms, I think that when this stuff hits the target, the vesicant burns the skin, letting in the protein. From then on it acts like snake venom." Looking at one of the new arrivals, he added, "This officer here agrees."

"Colonel Featherstone; specialty, biological warfare," the man said laconically. "I go along with that. A very efficient system; what shakes me is the speed at which this stuff breaks down."

"Everything about Xeno is fast," Mark observed. "At this point I'm interested in a possible antidote. You have any views, Colonel?"

"No, sir. It appears that that doctor who was attacked died before he hit the floor. The nervous system is blasted out of existence. An antidote may be technically possible, but if this toxin does act within two seconds of impact, what time is there for antidotes?"

Scott broke in. "Mark, I saw you after you'd been hit. Your eyebrow looked singed. It could be that the hairs took the main force of the burning agent. By the time the droplet hit your skin, the vesicant had lost some of its strength, took longer to open you up—and in that time the venom was already oxidizing, losing power."

"It's a theory," agreed Mark. "But what counts is knowledge—and what do we know? First, we can rule out any practical antidote, so the only defense is protective clothing. Secondly, to date these creatures have only attacked when provoked. As far as the human hosts of these parasites are concerned, it's obvious we are powerless, except in the very early stages, when surgical intervention may be effective.

"It may be best to let them go full term. In the case of this group it may be too late for action. I've got a feeling that all the victims who are still in Abdera will have reached or passed the crisis point already. The emergence time-frame of the Xenos in those admitted here is incredibly short."

"You talk as if there may be more," said the colonel.

Freedman shrugged and spoke to the technician. "Martin, I'd like to take a look at the specimen." As the man left, Freedman glanced around the room. "Do we have a biologist who is prepared to handle the dissection?"

The colonel nodded. "Captain Koslowski of Walter Reed. Right now he's working on the embryos."

Martin returned with a large specimen jar, placing it on the table before Freedman, who leaned forward. "Yes," he said softly, remembering. The rest crowded around. Only Scott held back: He'd already seen quite enough.

The creature hung tail down, the tip of the head just breaking the surface, the legs stiff and spread out, giving the illusion of claws.

"Christ Almighty!" The colonel spoke in a hushed whisper. "You mean to tell me that came out of a human?"

If Freedman felt any horror he did not show it. "Eight to ten centimeters from tip to tail, I'd say. You can hardly see them, but I observed two apertures below the eyes—see those two faint marks? I wondered if I'd dreamed that bit. Now I see I didn't. I wish I had."

"Rudimentary mandibles probably," the colonel interjected. "I'd say the thing's weapon system is the main interest; that's really off the track."

"Not at all," replied Freedman. "It ejects instead of injecting, otherwise it's similar to the scorpion—and ejection is a weapon known in nature. There's a fish that shoots down its prey from underwater. No—concentrate on the apertures. They're not rudimentary mandibles or sensors; the photographs will show that—Jaimie, where are the prints? I'm convinced they're nostrils."

Featherstone regarded him carefully. "You don't mean spiracles, doctor?"

"No. Name one insect with spiracles in the head."

The Army man looked alarmed. "You realize what you're saying?"

"Damn right I do! Don't forget, I've seen one of these things alive and close up! Those apertures open and shut rhythmically." He pointed at the jar. "Look at the buoyancy of the body—that's significant. You can bet there'll be some sort of lung."

"If you're right"—the colonel frowned as he spoke— "Then these things could *grow*! Giant ants are strictly science fiction—all insects are limited in size by the inefficiency of their oxygen gathering. But *this*!"

"Exactly," said Freedman. "And thirty to forty of these things are loose. They're very quick, adaptable, and have a high degree of intelligence—how else could they all have escaped?" He turned his tired gaze to the window. "They're out there, gentlemen—they're fast, mean, and deadly. This crisis isn't over. On the contrary, it's just beginning!"

· XXIV ·

The first days after the coming of Xeno were an enormous strain on all concerned. But as the days became weeks and nothing was found and nothing happened, it seemed the danger existed only in Freedman's mind.

Most of the patients recovered, although two more died in the hospital and five were discovered, that first morning, dead in their beds at home. All of them were old.

As Secretary Lord predicted, the world at large accepted the story that the time travelers suffered from a special noninfectious disease, painless and generally harmless unless the victim was old and had a serious heart condition. The cause, it was suggested, was prolonged exposure to "cosmic radiation," a result of the plane's accidental entrapment in the "chrono-spatial" experiment. Air transportation suffered for a time, but otherwise the world went on much as before. Folks forgot; UFO's, a missing plane, little green men—what else is new?

The survivors recovered rapidly, reverting to their preflight state of health.

Shane de Byl recovered faster than most: In three days the cyst shriveled and fell away. Within a month she showed no more than a very shallow depression, the scar not much worse than a bad vaccination mark. With no great effort she put the whole affair firmly behind her and got down to the serious business of trapping the lovelorn but shy Jaimie.

The Treasury came up with another "interim" sweetener of two thousand dollars for each *Papa Kilo* victim, and Shane was quick to use that as a lever. Maybe, she said to Jaimie, she should use the money to get out of Abdera and set herself up in, say, New York City? This and similar ruses got Jaimie moving in the right direction: By week six of the Xenos' time on earth she had maneuvered him into proposing. She made him sweat for twenty-four hours, then accepted. She announced that they would marry in the spring.

Week six, mid-August, the summer almost spent. Already the leaves were turning color, but Freedman refused to even consider a vacation, saying he was too wrapped up in the Xeno crisis to get away. He packed his protesting family off, glad to see them go.

Three weeks earlier the last of the FBI had pulled out. The extra hospital staff had also left, having been sworn to secrecy by Malin. None had been told the full story of ICARUS, and few had seen the Xeno specimen. It had been an inexplicable nightmare for these people, best forgotten as quickly as possible—especially with the FBI leaning on them. In general the tension eased, but not for Freedman.

Malin called on him to convey the thanks of the bureau. Just as Mark began to think how nice it was of a busy guy like Malin to take the trouble, Malin added that Tatyana Marinskiya wanted to talk with him—how would it be if she dropped by? A date was fixed for the following week.

In his current mood, Mark didn't care if she came or not—she or anyone else. His sole interest was the aliens, which he felt certain still lived. He was determined to know their origin.

The dissection of the specimen had proved him right in one respect. There were two lungs, strangely joined at their posterior end. And there were other equally puzzling features about the respiratory system. The biologist and Freedman agreed: Xeno could not be classified as a true insect. Nor was it a true arthropod. Yet it had some features of both, and special characteristics of its own.

The weapon system, for example: The poison-sac and the fine discharge tube in the tail had a complicated network of powerful muscles, which evidently contracted sharply and in fixed sequence, propelling the poison on its way.

But the nastiest surprise was the eyes. They were unquestionably related to the higher earthly mammals, including man, with nothing in common with the compound lenses of the average insect. Freedman had been justified in thinking the eyes intelligent; the picture they would present to the Xeno's brain was assessed as slightly superior to that of a dog. The implications of the discovery were not lost on the examiners: The brain, large by insect standards but tiny by mammalian, had to be good enough to process and evaluate the picture.

All this had been spelled out to the ICARUS Committee, and Freedman had added that roughly seventy-five of these creatures had probably escaped. Admittedly, no trace of them had been found, but there was still every reason to be on guard. The biologist opined that this weird creature might well have considerable difficulty in adapting to conditions on Earth. In all probability, a relatively complex creature like this could not survive for long.

The committee clutched at his idea: He had to be right. Nothing had been seen of the creatures—they could have been eaten by birds or cats or any predatory animal. It was the ostrich syndrome all over again. But as the weeks passed the committee and the biologist felt a growing confidence in the theory. They were military men and politicians, lacking background knowledge or the time to acquire it, and few wanted to dig deeply. Erwin Lord was an exception. He didn't believe that if they ignored this particular problem it would go away. Arcasso was another.

But of all the ICARUS group, Freedman was best qualified to evaluate the Xeno. In background, experience, and general knowledge, he was in a unique position. Most importantly, he had the mental toughness to face it.

As soon as he was strong enough, he made the first of many searches of the hospital area, disregarding Scott's plea to wear protective clothing on the grounds that it would cause comment. The search he'd ordered on the first day had been unproductive, but he had a shrewd suspicion that after seeing Xeno's photograph—and knowing its lethal power—the FBI men weren't trying all that hard.

His own searches were a very different matter. Using a long stick and wearing wraparound dental glasses, he poked around the areas of high probability—under stones and fallen branches, in hollow trees—but he found nothing. But he hardly expected to. Forty creatures were estimated to have escaped in the vicinity of the hospital; the chances of finding one in the surrounding countryside were astronomically remote. But his failure to find even the slightest evidence did not weaken his conviction. They were out there, somewhere—alive.

Freedman glimpsed the car as it headed into his parking lot. Tatyana. The car had FBI written all over it; he could spot one a block away. He stayed behind his desk; she'd be in soon enough, and these days he conserved his energy. It would be a very long time before he fully recovered from his brush with Xeno—if ever.

Tatyana was escorted by a large middle-aged man with iron-gray hair, steady eyes, a face made sinister by a puckered scar on one cheek, and a certain air of curiosity. Freedman figured he was FBI, even if he'd never seen one so badly dressed.

Tatyana enveloped Mark in her arms and a cloud of cheap scent. The greeting over, she held him at arm's length and surveyed his face.

"Mark Freedman, comrade! You have been through much! You are still not strong." She peered intently at the small pit in his forehead, half hidden by an eyebrow. "So lucky—so lucky!" she murmured, shaking her head slowly. "You must rest. Sit down." Her powerful arms steered him into his chair. Only then did she remember her companion. She pointed dramatically at him, in a manner worthy of the Kirov Ballet. "Mark, my friend—this is Brigadier Arcasso"—she rolled the name—"United States Air Force and a member of the ICARUS committee."

"My God, you did that well," said Arcasso, smiling at Tatyana. "I wish I could bring you with me everywhere." He walked to Freedman, holding out his hand. "Glad to know you, doctor. Please call me Frank." The awkward way he produced his ID card alerted Mark to his artificial arm, the hand buried deep in a sagging pocket. "Alvin Malin has told me a lot about you. He's tied up, so I came along as Tatyana's escort." He grinned again. "Or maybe it's the other way around."

Freedman smiled back. He liked this big man, his easy style; from the way Tatyana was beaming, he saw that she felt the same way.

While his secretary fixed coffee, they stuck to trivia; but for all the good humor, tension lay close to the surface. The coffee served and the secretary gone, Tatyana got down to business.

She'd seen his photographs, read Scott's report, Mark's description of the birth of the Xeno, and the biologist's report on the creature's anatomy. She had come from Moscow, she said, to clear up some points and to solicit Mark's views as the most experienced Xeno man in the world.

Freedman dug out a file from his safe—a present from Malin—and handed around some enlargements of Xeno. Arcasso was not put off, as Malin had been, by the horrific pictures. He listened intently while the doctors discussed anatomy; but when they moved to survival probability, he joined in. Did Xeno's makeup give any idea of its likely range of temperature toleration? "After all, doc, it looks like a scorpion's half-brother, and they don't go crazy over snow and ice." He looked at Tatyana for support.

"Possible," she said, kicking off her shoes. The action reminded Mark; he produced whiskey and three glasses.

"And you've had one damn cold night up here."

Freedman glanced at him sharply. "You monitor our weather?"

"Yes, sir. The USAF Weather Center runs me a daily report."

"Well, I agree with Tatyana that it's possible, but although I can't point to any hard evidence, I wouldn't bank on Xeno folding."

"Me neither."

The gloomy confidence in Arcasso's voice surprised Mark. "What's your reading?"

"It's these goddam holes. If the eggs got in that way, then I guess the parent had to be outside the plane. And, baby, at *Papa Kilo*'s altitude it's cold outside!"

"No." Freedman shook his head. "Guesswork. The plane must have gone out of space and time into unknowable conditions. Okay, so that's guesswork, too, but I prefer it to yours. Particularly as I don't go along with the implantation from outside idea."

"But goddammit, doc—the holes have got to mean *something!*"

"Agreed, but how do they fit in? Okay, assume the parent bored the holes with its ovipositor—that's standard procedure, except it drilled through metal, not wood. It inserts its ovipositor, seeks and finds all the passengers—just the way the ichneumon fly hunts grubs hidden in a tree—and implants them. If that's the case, we're stuck with two questions. Although the aircraft was sealed, the Xeno knew suitable hosts existed inside. I find that a tough proposition to believe. And secondly, the scale's completely out of whack."

"What scale, Mark?"

He looked at Tatyana. "Xeno's horrible and terribly dangerous, but its features are not all that abnormal. In general, it conforms to the laws of nature as we know them. It doesn't have X-ray eyes, or a laser beam as a weapon, and there's nothing outlandish about its general proportions—admittedly, twelve legs strikes one as pretty strange, but I'm not so sure there isn't a looper caterpillar with twelve, and there's the centipede. To me, in very general terms, it looks highly practical—do you follow?"

Arcasso nodded.

"Proportions." Freedman emphasized the word. "Take the Xeno egg. It must be very small, almost microscopic. In nature there is a very rough ratio between mother and egg. A robin's egg is smaller than a chicken's, whose egg is smaller than that of a goose— and that hardly compares with an ostrich's."

"What has this got to do with Xeno?" asked Tatyana, faintly impatient.

"If the parent implanted the Jumbo passengers from outside," Freedman said, "all you have to do is measure the distance between the nearest hole and the furthest passenger and you have a rough estimate of the ovipositor's length." He looked at Arcasso. "None of those holes was aft of the midship section, right?"

"Affirmative," said Arcasso.

"I've made that measurement," Freedman continued. "Assuming the body to be twice as long as the ovipositor—a fair average for earthly insects—I wind up with the parent Xeno just a smidgen smaller than the aircraft."

"But that is not possible!" Tatyana glared at him. "You cannot believe that!"

"No, I don't. Two reasons, both proportional. The ovipositor would have to be fantastically thin and fine compared with the body, and the idea of such a vast creature producing pinhead-sized eggs is too much for me."

Arcasso helped himself to the whiskey with some urgency. "Okay, so you toss away the outside theory. You reckon the bastards bored their way in?"

"It makes more sense," conceded Mark, "but it creates new problems. Assume they went in and out the holes; it's strange that not one got trapped. And another, bigger problem: the Xeno we captured has no boring equipment; the mouth's adapted for sucking, but it sure as hell couldn't suck or blow a hole in an airplane! So my guess is that the parent Xeno was smaller and has at least two capabilities ours doesn't have."

"Hold it there for a moment." Frank marshaled his thoughts. "You say the parents could have been smaller—small enough, maybe, to get in or out of the holes?"

"Yes, I think so."

"How about this, then? Suppose they didn't get *in* that way, only *out*?"

Both Mark and Tatyana waited for him to go on.

"Okay, so I'm stuck with a big problem—how did they get in in the first place? Someone once said that if you could solve the space-time dimension you could turn a tennis ball inside-out without cutting it. Well now, whoever or whatever could pull this trick with our aircraft wouldn't have much trouble with the tennis ball! Suppose the plane was opened up, accidentally letting in the Xenos? They lay their eggs and go someplace else—except those trapped when the ICARUS figure activated the cosmic regurgitator and put the plane together again. I guess eleven Xenos were trapped in the Jumbo, and smartly blasted their way out. How about that?"

Tatyana toyed nervously with a ring and waited for Mark to speak.

Freedman pushed his glasses up on his head and

pinched his nose. "That's a very ingenious answer, Frank. I don't know a damned thing about the fourth dimension, but the rest fits better than most ideas."

"Glad I came along, doctor. I've spent whole nights trying to come up with something better." He lit another cigar, then remembered. "Aw, doc—I'm sorry! I interrupted you. You were saying the parent had capabilities ours hasn't?"

"Yes," said Freedman. "Ours has no blasting equipment, and even more significant, no sex organs." He added cautiously, "No identified sex organs, that is."

Arcasso looked at the statement from several angles before replying. "Well, that has to be a comfort—doesn't it? But isn't that new to earth? I mean you can have a neutered man or cat, but *someone* has to cut his balls off." He remembered Tatyana. "Sorry, ma'am."

She placed a hand on his, shaking it gently, looking at him with amusement. "Frank—I've heard about balls."

Mark regarded them thoughtfully. "Sex is the missing link here," he said ambiguously, pushing the bottle towards Tatyana, who was looking somewhat longer at Frank Arcasso than was strictly necessary. "Nature has tried everything, but at some stage, sex has to be in there in some form. And that's what I'm really afraid of—with no sex capability in our specimen, plus that lack of blasting equipment, I fear we're only looking at one stage of Xeno's development. If it follows the insect pattern of egg, larva, pupa, and adult, then what we have is the larval form. Sex seldom appears until the final, adult stage."

Arcasso stared again at the enlarged photograph. "Jesus! You think that's the second stage. What'll the adult look like?"

Mark gave an exaggerated shrug.

"Jesus!" repeated Arcasso, turning to Tatyana. "What d' you think?"

"My view is worthless. If Mark says so, that is enough for me." She downed her drink in one gulp and banged the glass down, her manner suddenly different. Lighting another black cigarette, she eyed both men with an openly calculating expression. "Mark, here we are all friends. Officially"—she tapped the Order of Lenin on her breast—"I came for this talk, but . . ." She shook her head as she refilled her glass.

Freedman could tell she was struggling with something.

"Of course, I'm pleased to see you, Tatyana," he said, "but I had been wondering why you came." He tapped the file before him. "You could have worked all this out."

She gave him a swift glance. "Yes." She tapped her glass. "Don't think it is this—but it helps." She paused again, smiling faintly. "Mark, Frank, six months ago I was a good Communist, a dedicated party member, certain of where we were going, confident of the soundness of Marxist-Leninist principles." She drained her glass and stared at it pensively.

Arcasso shifted uneasily in his chair.

"Don't hurry me, Frank. I'm on a lonely and dangerous road"—her voice increased in intensity—"a road the party teaches me does not exist! I cannot talk about it with anyone—even now there are only seven of us in ICARUS, all staunch party members. I am not in on the discussions. I only report and answer questions. But I can see in my comrades' faces that they, too, have those same questions which cannot be asked."

Freedman and Arcasso exchanged glances, both trying to understand her problem.

"Until your photographs arrived, we ignored the

wider implications of ICARUS. Until that moment no real evidence of extraterrestrial life existed. Now it does.

"No longer can we talk about 'power storms.' " She spat the term out contemptuously. "Incredibly, the planes were lost in time and space. That was bad enough—but now, Xeno!" Her haunted eyes stared at Freedman. "Never mind what Xeno is to us—what is it to whatever exists out *there*?"

Freedman broke the strained silence, speaking softly. "Who knows—who *can* know? In our human arrogance we immediately think this thing comes straight from God—"

"But God does not exist!" cried Tatyana desperately. "For us he *cannot* exist!"

"Let me finish," Freedman cut in sharply. "To me, it's plain that somewhere in time and space another world—call it what you like—exists. Clearly, Xeno is not God, for it is a parasite and must live on something else. It does not follow that Xeno's host is God— in fact the argument is unsatisfying. By definition, God must be perfect, and by human standard cannot possibly be infested with vermin." His voice sank. "But there may be one or a hundred stages before one reaches that perfection."

"Mark," said Arcasso, not looking at Tatyana, "I've given a lot of time to this. We're working with mighty little evidence—"

Freedman nodded. "Sure—but even a reasonably intelligent person could work out the existence of aircraft from an airline ticket."

"Right." Frank smiled at Tatyana, trying to ease her tension. "So you figure—and I've gotten that far myself—that there's something up there?"

Mark shrugged helplessly. "Could be Xeno's host is a cosmic version of John the Baptist, or Francis of Assisi. Xeno may live off a saint—or maybe the saint's dog."

Tatyana burst out. "But this is madness! This is the late twentieth century! God does not exist!"

"Call it what you like. It, Them, God, or whatever," said Frank stolidly, "but something out there supports Xeno. And that something has powers we can only guess at. From where I stand, that something looks very much like God. It may not be the sort of God we're used to contemplating, but it's *there*! If you deny that something's existence, then you, lady, and your comrades, have got problems!"

·XXV·

By Western standards the conference room bordered on the archaic. Deep, claret-colored brocade lined the walls, enlivened by ornate gilded mirrors, spotty with age. Doors, windows, and baseboards were white, the carpet gold and cream; the curtains matched the brocade. The two pictures were on opposing walls: Karl Marx stared at Lenin, who was too busy orating to look back.

From across the center table, covered with a deep red chenille cloth, Tatyana looked at the two most powerful men in her vast country: the president and the premier—also general secretary of the Communist Party. Although her expression remained impassive, her heart beat that much faster. The president, formal and polite, smiled and offered her a cigarette.

She nodded her thanks, taking in the two men, both clad in dark blue suits and white shirts. On the president's left lapel were three small medals; the premier had two. Tatyana drew comfort from her own Order of Lenin. It had been awarded to her for her work and was proof of her loyalty as a good party member and patriot.

She launched into her report, hesitantly at first, but gaining confidence as she progressed. The men sat quite still, listening intently, showing no emotion. When her factual account ended, they asked the predictable questions regarding the nature of the insect. Both men were interested, but not, it seemed, to the degree she had expected. She replied in the same matter-of-fact manner, waiting for the bigger, more important questions.

As she answered, she felt the pressure growing within her; she fought a mad impulse to break out of the confines their manner imposed. But no—these were top party members, heirs to the portraits on the wall.

Finally the inevitable question. "Comrade Marinskaya," asked the Russian premier, "what are your own thoughts on the origins of Xeno?"

"Comrade President," she began, her heart pounding, "that is difficult for me to answer. Rightly, our ICARUS security is very tight; there are only seven or eight who know the secret. I am your only medical member—and I became involved because this was thought to be a problem in my field, cytology. It is not. My qualifications for ICARUS/Xeno are not good."

The general secretary frowned. She was not answering the question.

She read his mind. "I must explain," she said, glancing at him, "for you to understand. I have been your medical representative with the Americans. Forced by events, they have seven or eight specialists; also this Dr. Freedman, who has a considerable knowledge of natural history, especially of insects and arthropods."

She was speaking faster, the words tumbling out, desperate to finish before they interrupted.

"No doubt they could answer your question. I cannot. Theirs is a much wider approach which transcends my biomedical background, which goes back to more philosophical, elemental questions."

"Comrade Doctor," said the president sternly, "are you sure you want to continue this line?"

She hesitated, then, "Yes! For the good of us all—yes!" Both men frowned at her. Undaunted, she turned her attention to her document wallet. "I will show you." She produced two full-plate color enlargements, passing them across the table. She tapped the photograph before the general secretary, noting his tremor of disgust.

"Xeno." She spoke coldly, reciting facts. "Born of a man, aged sixty-eight. The dissection of this specimen revealed a brain greatly superior to any earthly insect. Exact comparison is not possible, but it may be as intelligent as the brain of a dog."

Thinking she had veered from her earlier approach, the president sounded less frosty. "Well, that is not much. And the Americans think some of these creatures have survived?"

"Yes. Freedman has no doubts at all, thinking it will survive because of its intelligence, speed, and adaptability. He feels it may even have adapted in some ways since it arrived. That is incredible, but adaptation has to be a matter of degree; even Xeno cannot become something totally different in one generation in a new environment."

"You have already said that!" the premier said sharply.

She nodded, a tremulous gesture of defiance. "Yes. It is part of the vital, elemental question. Even allowing for some adaptation, one is forced to the conclusion that in its other world it parasitized a life form not unlike ours."

"Pure supposition!" the president snapped.

"The Americans don't think so, Comrade President. This is a complex creature, with complex needs. Clearly those needs are met by man, therefore Xeno's normal host must have similar characteristics—and that is only a beginning." She spoke slowly. "The Americans believe that out of our space and time there are Beings vastly superior to us—how else could they break through barriers we did not even know existed? They have the ability to pluck aircraft from our skies—and enough consideration to return them. The Americans think Xeno is an accident—that it is a tiny parasite on the body of one of these Beings, even as we have parasites on and in us. The physical size of the Beings the Americans infer from the effect Xeno has on us. For humans it can be a life-or-death situation. If the accidental theory is correct, then—Xeno is no more troublesome to these Beings than—" she hesitated, then pressed on boldly—"than the seventy or eighty different sorts of life in your mouth, Comrade President, right now!"

"I am amazed," the general secretary spoke with deliberation, "that you, Comrade Doctor, should repeat these fairy tales! You sound like an old peasant woman! You seriously say the Americans *believe* in a race of superhuman giants?"

Tatyana nodded, not trusting her voice.

"Total, absolute rubbish!"

"Comrade President," she said doggedly, "that is the American view."

"And you, Tatyana Ivanovna." The general secretary gave her one more chance. "Do you subscribe to this belief?" His tone was reasonable, his voice soft, but the warning was plain.

Ever since leaving Freedman she had dreaded this moment, unsure how she would face it. She felt as if she were two separate persons, one sitting back horrified at what the other said.

"Comrades! All my life I have worked for Mother Russia and the party!" She placed one hand on her Order of Lenin. "I am no dissident. I know the future is ours. But I also know it is no service to our cause to blindly follow an incorrect path." She could not turn back now. "Because it was thought Lysenko's theories were in accordance with party doctrine, he was believed: The damage that did to Soviet science took years to repair! Truth is absolute; it cannot be bent to meet doctrine. To do so is to be a traitor to party and state."

"In other words," said the general secretary icily, "you agree with the Americans."

"What else can we believe? General Lebedev's power storm cannot be true." She appealed again to the president. "What can I believe?"

"This is pure speculation, creating a new world from a single insect!" The president paused. Tatyana did not have the nerve to contradict him, but her expression left him in little doubt of her true feelings.

"The Americans"—contempt showed in his voice—"are inventing another world, peopled by superhuman giants! A cosmic Disneyland. Really, Tatyana Ivanovna, how can a woman of science like yourself believe this fantasy? What do these superhumans want with our aircraft—do they play with them or what? And why do they return them? For a race as intelligent as your American friends would have us believe, it seems to me to be a pointless pastime." He smiled thinly, but getting no response from Tatyana, his tone hardened. "Admittedly, these Events are inexplicable so far, but the American answer is not intellectually satisfying to me, or," he added pointedly, "to any good Communist."

After the meeting, she wandered aimlessly, her mind in chaos. Outside the Kremlin, instead of heading northeast, across Red Square for the metro and her flat in Sokolniki, she walked south, past the barbaric splendors of St. Basil's Cathedral, finding herself at last beside the Moscow River, staring blindly at the turbid, muddy water.

Whatever the leaders might say, the American theory struck her as both plausible and practical. Their total rejection of the U.S. hypothesis staggered her—particularly as no alternative solution was offered. Worse still, her intuition told her that the president had been less than honest. He had denied the idea not because he didn't believe it, but because he was afraid to believe it. Lysenko's genetics had fitted party dogma. Hard, practical results had proved him wrong, but the party had stuck by its favorite, long after the scientific world had rejected him. Not that the party loved Lysenko. But the invalidation of his theories inevitably hurt the party.

Across the river in Gorky Park the leaves were falling, a chill warning of the approach of the dreaded Russian winter. She turned away, feeling suddenly ill.

In North America Fall had come, too. The riot of color in the Northeastern States gave way to bare branches, whose decaying leaves had carpeted the ground.

But this year was different. Beneath the warm protective covering of the leaves lay the Xenos, making the magical change from larva to pupa.

No human found one, but birds and small animals noted them. They were slightly iridescent and irregular in shape, yet no more bizarre than the pupae of a moth. Still, some inner sense caused all earthly life to instinctively withdraw.

So, in the gathering strength of a North American winter, the aliens lay unmolested, imperceptibly changing, growing.

In the somewhat milder climate of Louisiana, a few more grew in peace; another lay quiescent beneath a dogwood tree in Georgia. And across the world others were in limbo, in Odessa in the Soviet Ukraine, in India, and in Frankfurt, Germany. But if the Xenos remained hidden, ICARUS did not. What both the Russians and Americans had feared happened, and in circumstances totally beyond their control.

London's Heathrow Airport, one of the busiest in the world, had a feature not found in all airports. Many British children and quite a few adults were addicted to plane-spotting, and the airport authority had thoughtfully provided an observation deck where, for a small fee, the enthusiasts could indulge their sport.

The essential equipment for plane-spotting was a pair of binoculars, a notebook, and pencil. Less vital, but still desirable, was a VHF transistor radio. The devotees would watch and listen to the arrival and departure of planes throughout daylight hours, noting the type of each aircraft, its airline, and its side number. To those not addicted, the pastime seemed pointless. But the enthusiast, often wet and cold, would return home delighted to have spotted a real exotic—a private flying harem with an Arabian registration, or an ancient DC-3 wearing the colors of some minor African state.

Around 11:00 A.M. on a fine mid-September day, the deck was crowded. One deck higher a television camera crew waited for a VIP arrival. The crew boss had his own transistor, and the cameras practiced on incoming aircraft.

Behind the blank tinted windows of the control tower an endless game of three-dimensional chess is played. Information pours in nonstop, from West Drayton—Air Traffic Control for Southern England—from aircraft, and from the airport's own radar.

At 11:00 A.M. the complex organization ticked over quietly, a Rolls-Royce of air control, with West Drayton watching all planes, no matter how small, from the ground up to forty thousand meters, and out to three-fifty kilometers. Cover was complete, down to anything that moved on the ground, even trucks in the remote service areas.

A GCA—Ground Control Approach—operator relaxed to light a cigarette. His visual display unit told him nothing was scheduled to land on his runway, 28 Left, until 11:04—a long wait in Heathrow's scale of operations. All the same, he watched his radar.

Suddenly he sat bolt-upright, staring in incredulous horror. Well within his radar's range, perhaps a thousand meters from the runway's threshold, a green-glowing blob materialized out of nowhere, slowly approaching, left of the runway centerline.

He reacted automatically, one hand pressing the alarm button alerting every position in the control room, the other thumbing his transmitter switch.

"Aircraft on approach–come right!" Urgently he repeated his message. "Come right!"

Whoever the stranger was, the safest action was to bring him in. The operator sweated; the bloke was so damn low.

"Maintain present height!"

He'd brought thousands of planes in; his sixth sense screamed that the plane was in trouble. To order him to climb at that speed could be fatal.

Only seconds had elapsed, but the senior controller, Roger Ford, was peering at the scope over his shoulder. "Christ!"

He too saw the Jumbo taxiing round for takeoff on Runway 28 Right. He knew that nothing he could do in the next ten seconds could alter events. He jumped back to his desk, calling another assistant. "Hold all traffic for 28 Left!" He pressed an emergency call button. "Fire and ambulance—threshold of Runway 28 Left—go!"

The shock waves generated by the green blob spread fast. Orders were issued diverting the incoming line of planes. The ambulance call triggered other alerts: the operating theater, the airport police, the local hospital, and that least publicized part of any airport, the morgue.

The plane did not answer. To the GCA operator the seconds crawled; he could only watch the slow, remorseless approach of the two planes.

Roger Ford struggled to keep his binoculars steady. In twenty years of experience he'd never had an emergency like this. He held the plane, so close to the Jumbo, and so low. Unconsciously, his body bent as he willed the stranger to come left. *Come left!*

At the very last moment the stranger's port wing lifted, almost scraping over the Jumbo's high tail plane. For a second Ford could see the shadow of the intruder darken the after end of the Jumbo—which, unaware of its narrow escape, trundled on. Ford had no time to relax; but at least one disaster had been avoided. Now he had a better view—and he almost dropped his binoculars.

Never had he seen an aircraft like it, or one in such

a condition. It had four ancient propeller engines, one feathered; part of the port wing and the tail plane were missing, and there appeared to be a large jagged hole in the fuselage. As he watched, a red flare arched upwards from the plane.

The spindly undercarriage—no nose wheel—hit the runway hard. The aircraft bounced sickeningly, coming down again on one wheel, tail well up. The other wheel touched and the tail dropped. As it careened crazily down the runway, Ford saw the starboard undercarriage slowly buckling. The machine slued round, off the concrete and onto the grass, the starboard wing brushing the surface. Tensed up, pulling for the pilot, Ford could not help shutting his eyes. When he looked again the machine had come to rest, one wing and the remnants of the tail in the air, like a singed moth.

Ambulances and fire trucks closed in. Foam was jetted onto the engine cowlings. He sighed with relief, but his strongest emotion was admiration: whoever he was, the pilot was a real aviator. What the hell it was all about he'd soon find out; right now his prime consideration was the airport. Streaking past that pile of junk might not do the cash customers' morale much good. But at least Runway 28 Left was clear. Firemen had ladders up, hacking at the canopy. With luck the crew had made it, thanks to an outstanding pilot.

But lower down, on the observation deck, the expert eyes of a score of school children knew what they saw, even if they were astonished by the sight. Some guessed they were watching a movie in the making.

For the real buffs, one glance had been enough. The plane was a B-17, and the sharper-eyed had spotted the insignia of the 8th U.S. Air Force.

Above them, the waiting TV cameras had followed

the whole incident, zoom lenses giving vivid close-up shots.

Beyond all hope of concealment, *Eager Virgin*, lead plane of 497 Bombardment Group, USAF, had returned—thirty-nine years late.

The news reached Washington at 6:45 A.M. local. Again Arcasso was the Duty ICARUS officer. By 7:00 A.M. he had awakened the committee and President Knowlton with the bad news, and was on the phone to the U.S. embassy in London, yelling for the ambassador. Five hours ahead (in London it was midday) all radio and TV channels carried the flash. The whole system of selective release of presidential letters failed even to start, a victim of its own security. Had they known, the British authorities would have done their best to clamp down on ICARUS. As it was, the President saw the TV film via satellite over breakfast.

A flying saucer would have caused less comment. UFO's had been in and out of the news for fifty years; many photographs and some film existed, much of it undoubtedly bogus. But this was very different.

The crew included a sergeant gunner who had married an English girl in 1943; they had had a son, born a week before the father had been lost over the Ruhr. The child had followed his father, joining the Royal Air Force.

The film of the father, twenty-four when he disappeared, meeting his son, a squadron leader of forty, was a scoop of incredible strength.

The bewildered, youthful sergeant, still in flak jacket and baseball cap, was faced with a shocked and tearful wife of sixty, each clearly recognizing the other. But the most poignant moment was when the confused father, confronted by this senior version of himself, called him "sir."

An interview with little green men would have been nothing in comparison; most viewers would have thought them a gag. But anyone with eyes in his head, watching the faces of father, wife, and son reunited after thirty years, could see that this was real and human.

ICARUS's cover was hopelessly blown. After a hurried hot-line consultation, the presidents of the United States and the Soviet Union issued a joint statement admitting the return of three planes, emphasizing that the truth had been concealed for the best of reasons, but offering no explanation—and no mention of Xeno.

The immediate world reaction was one of total shock. The Western news media, recognizing not just the story of the century but maybe of all time gave it all they had. But for all their effort, the U.S. government refused access to the B-17 crew. Their isolation was necessary for their own good—"space sickness" remained a possibility. Many newsmen scented something, but soon learned—off the record—that Fort Knox was a piggy bank compared to the B-17. Unauthorized intruders would be shot on sight.

The press pounced on the story worldwide, dredging up all available details on *Papa Kilo*, running stories on the new and incredible time travel device the U.S. Army had. But the stories, however fantastic they might be, were less than the whole truth, for one secret remained intact—the press had no idea of Xeno's existence.

At first, the Soviet government released nothing for internal consumption, but news of this caliber could not be long concealed. Like a slow-rising tide, it seeped through a thousand crevices into the Communist fortress. The statement in *Pravda* referring to the "space-time continuum" came far too late. The Kremlin release made it sound like a matter of no great importance, even a trifle boring, an attitude quickly abandoned when an Armenian physicist came up with a theory that suggested the planes had gotten mixed up with "black holes." Without inquiring too deeply how he knew about the planes, the Kremlin jumped at his theory. It looked good, explaining ICARUS in purely mechanistic terms. He received a sudden promotion, a fast transfer to Moscow University, and orders to develop his thesis. The only snag was his total ignorance of Xeno.

In the States, speculation ran wild, and took in everything from black holes to the Second Coming. But there again, Xeno was not known.

Freedman thought it unwise to withhold this vital item, but on that point the Soviets had been adamant—no reference to Xeno. The secretary of state could hardly believe the Kremlin could be so shortsighted; but, placating soul that he was, he was only too happy to go along with them. If nothing more was heard of the aliens, so much the better—but if Doctor Freedman was right . . .

Secretary Lord apart, the rest of the committee quietly prayed that they'd heard the last of the Abderan Xenos, and they took good care of the crew of *Eager Virgin*. Isolated in a wing of an Air Force hospital when not being tested, interrogated, or lectured, they had nothing to beef about. The food and accommodations were excellent, and the nurses were obliging enough to meet other urgent needs. In a reeducation seminar, the crew agreed that the Pill was one giant advance since 1944.

With the exception of the sergeant gunner, none of the men were married or seriously attached at the time of the plane's disappearance. Their reunions with surviving relatives only added to their sense of alienation. The bombardier, his reactions still razor-sharp after thirty combat missions, confronted his younger brother, a pear-shaped family man weighed down with forty extra years, a man whose most traumatic experience had been witnessing an auto accident. They stared awkwardly at each other, separated by more than the years, trying to find something to say. They parted with many promises, all insincere, to "keep in touch," each relieved that the ordeal was over. For the airman, the crew members were his brothers, the guys you relied on—not that sad, dumpy man.

Their isolation forced the tightly knit crew of *Eager Virgin* back to each other. All belonging to the exclusive club of fighting men, a club in which there are no honorary members, they clung together, none anxious to face a world in which they would be freaks and that struck them as equally weird. Men with *hairdos*? And *handbags*? Jee-sus Christ!

As for ICARUS, that was just one more puzzle. To be plucked out of the flak-torn sky over the Ruhr and tossed straight into this crazy world, forty years AWOL—hell, that was more than enough to be dealing with. Many of their feelings were totally inexplicable to the shrinks. One moment to be scared blind of FW-190's over Essen, their only thought to stay in the combat box—and the next instant to be back in the States, transported to unimaginable comfort, good chow, dames, and unrationed liquor—and these crazy quacks going on about *insect bites*!

Eager Virgin itself revealed nothing new. No significant holes were found, and this was hardly surprising; flak and cannon shells had made plenty.

* * *

For many complex reasons, tension grew in the Soviet ICARUS group. Only the president and the party's general secretary had heard Tatyana Marinskiya's report, and they did not see fit to pass it to the rest. But the others soon had wind of her visit. A good private intelligence network, highly desirable to top people anywhere, was vital in the Soviet Union. Their exclusion from her Kremlin visit, and her denials, only made them think harder. The KGB chief took action; he knew she had been in Abdera Hollow and had talked with Malin, Arcasso, and the local doctor. He took it from there.

Any respectable intelligence service has its sleepers, agents on ice, people with a completely clean record who could be activated when necessary. And no outfit had a bigger collection of sleepers than the KGB. Within twenty-four hours, an innocuous phone call in New York—punctuated with a well-remembered codeword—led to a meeting in Central Park. Possibly influenced by a concern for his parents, who still resided in the Soviet Union, the sleeper obediently left for Abdera the next day, his task to discover the recent goings-on, especially those that involved the doctor. His journey was wasted. By the time he reached Abdera, the world's top journalists had stripped the locals of news—all but those who knew anything about Xeno. They had gone. Malin had moved fast.

Mark tried to talk with Jaimie about the situation, but his young associate lived and breathed little but his forthcoming marriage. He was happy to go along with the Washington view that all the Xenos had died in the alien and unfriendly environment of earth. Subconsciously, the younger man refused to allow the frail shell of his happiness to be touched in any way. Freedman understood; he'd passed the same way once, but now he had an old man's more cynical view of love. The difference between the two men was as simple as this: Jaimie couldn't wait for spring; Mark dreaded it.

But weeks passed and nothing happened. This strengthened the Washington viewpoint but in no way weakened Freedman's. He continued his lonely searches of woods and fields whenever he could spare the time—convinced that spring would bring something more than flowers.

·XXVI·

With all the fixings Shane had set her young heart on, she and Jaimie were married in the first week of April, 1984. If Mark had been ungenerous enough to ask his junior, on the wedding morning, what the word ICARUS meant, he felt sure he'd have gotten a blank, uncomprehending stare. As Mark confided to his wife, Jaimie had as bad a case as he had seen in years, and the girl was no better.

A small house was waiting for them, freshly painted, up on the rim of the Hollow. Shane firmly believed that money was for spending, and the latest treasury grant had refitted the kitchen with everything Madison Avenue could con a girl into buying, from a floor-to-ceiling freezer the size of two telephone booths to a Cuisinart food processor. The fact that she could scarcely boil water hardly fazed her, and Jaimie, if so directed, was ready to live happily ever after on pre-prepared, prepackaged and predigested TV dinners.

Uncomfortable in his hired tux, Mark watched the young couple leave for their Hawaiian honeymoon, smiling a bit ruefully, knowing that life could not possibly live up to their shining expectations—and, deeper in his mind, thinking of the shadow of Xeno which hung over them all.

Beside him—literally, the unbidden wedding guest—was Tatyana. While surprised at her sudden reappearance, he was happy to see her frank, open smile. And Tatyana proved no lead balloon, infusing the rather stiff celebration with a touch of Russian earthiness. Even Shane warmed to her, although she was taken slightly aback when, at the reception, the Russian woman planted her strong, capable hands on the bride's hips and stared hard into her eyes.

"Ah, yes! Jaimie is lucky! You have a good pelvic girdle; you will bear him many sons." Her mood changed and she laughed, a loud, joyous sound. "But not too soon! Make him work hard for them!" She shook Shane's arms. "Remember—a marriage is made in bed! Forget yourself—please him!" She faced Jaimie. "And you, tovarich, forget yourself. Take her, be good to her in bed—and please *her*!" She embraced them both, "It is as simple as that!"

Mark looked away, trying not to laugh. For all their imagined sophistication, her sincere, practical approach had them both blushing.

The honeymoon lasted two weeks. The couple returned, bright-eyed and eager to set up house, still delighted with everything, especially each other. At Jaimie's invitation, Mark and his wife came over for drinks soon after their return. Everything was so new, Mark could almost hear the crunched-up plastic furniture wrappers expanding in the closet. One arm around his wife, Jaimie said he'd be back in the office first thing in the morning. Freedman didn't want to rush him, but secretly he was glad. Any moment now he'd need help.

It had been a cold spring, but on the day the young

couple returned, the weather changed dramatically, bringing a day jewel-bright and warm. Mrs. Freedman remarked upon it, saying she hoped it was a good omen for Shane and Jaimie. Shane accepted that happily, quite sure the world rotated entirely for their benefit. Mark nodded agreement with his wife, doing his best to mask his anxiety. This was the time he dreaded most, the awakening of nature.

Two days passed; the weather held and the miracle of spring began. Jaimie settled back into the routine, treading carefully with Mark, aware that his senior's temper these days had a very short fuse. Jaimie knew Mark was worried, as he was, about Xeno, but he had no real idea of the extent of that worry. With Jaimie taking his share of the work load, Mark went off on solitary searches, returning ill-tempered, silent. He wanted to talk, but his training stopped him; his fears were based on guesswork, not facts. He could be wrong: Every single Xeno might long since have vanished into a predator's stomach. Perhaps there was no cause for alarm. On the other hand . . .

Jake Steward, retired carpenter, a poor angler and part-time lush, was out early. He seldom cared about catching anything, contenting himself with the solitude and fresh air.

So there he stood beside the reed-lined lake, his large belly warmed by his first slug of the day, at peace with the world, watching his bobbing float with mindless contentment.

A sharp burst of unfamiliar sound broke his reverie. What the hell was it? He peered around, seeing nothing. He settled down again, resuming his peaceful reverie.

Something flashed past, jerking him back to reality.

Despite all his years of fishing, he knew remarkably little about wildlife. A bird? Had to be. Again he ignored it, and with practiced ease pulled out his hip flask.

Even as he drank, he spotted something out of the corner of one eye, glistening in the growing sun. It was moving very fast and was lost in an instant behind him.

And as he dismissed the image from his booze-clouded mind, a blinding, searing flash dismissed him from life. The near-empty flask splashed into the still waters of the lake a split second before he fell face down among the reeds, the Xeno hideously busy upon his neck.

The farmer who found him assumed old Jake, whom he'd known for years, had had a heart attack. He climbed back on his tractor, reflecting on the frailty of life and comforting himself with the thought that there were worse ways to go. He headed for a phone; he'd let the cops break it to Jake's old woman.

The police called the county police surgeon, Freedman. He drove out to the location, suspecting nothing. The state trooper pulled back the sheet. A single glance at the pallid face and Mark was alert, looking for the unusual. He found it. On the back of the victim's neck, a blister, smaller than a match-head.

He stared at the mark, tingling with shock. With the aid of the trooper, he turned the body on its back. His intuition had been right: On the neck, two sets of faint red pressure marks, and centered between them a neat puncture, located exactly on the man's carotid artery.

"What d'you think, doc?" The trooper's eyes were just as sharp as Freedman's, but medically untrained.

He'd seen the hole, but it was, he guessed, too small to be lethal, and there was no blood. Maybe it was a boil the guy had beheaded shaving. "His color's a bit strange, but it's heart failure, ain't it?"

"Could be." Mark stared at the dead man's face, his mind racing. "Get the body over to the hospital. I'd like to have a closer look."

The trooper immediately turned professional. "Somethin' screwy about it, doctor? Mebbe his old woman stuck a poison dart in him," he grinned, "hoping to pick up on the insurance."

"No. Nothing like that." He wished it was that simple.

Within an hour he and Slim Lewis were conducting a postmortem, with Tatyana an absorbed, silent witness. Lab tests on the blister and a blood sample would take more time than Freedman could afford, but he thought he had enough to go on; Slim agreed.

Old Jake had either been killed or stunned by venom. Xeno had then somehow located the main artery in the neck, held itself in position by pincerlike claws—these caused the red marks—and sucked out some of the man's blood. If Jake had been alive when Xeno fastened onto his neck, then he had been killed by an embolism, an air bubble, created by the sudden extraction of blood.

Freedman drove slowly back to his office, Tatyana beside him, nervously puffing one of her strong black cigarettes, filling the car with acrid smoke. His mind was still reeling with the impact of these new, awful facts. She broke the silence.

"This is not good, Mark," she said heavily.

"You have a way with understatement," he said edgily.

"Please?" She looked puzzled.

"Forget it."

She began again. "There can be no doubt that this is the work of Xeno—"

"None!" he snapped. "You saw the singed neck hairs surrounding the blister." He touched his own eyebrow, remembering. "For me, that settled all doubts."

Tatyana lowered her window, tossing away her cigarette butt, staring without interest at the view.

"And shut that window!"

As she did so, the significance of his terse order dawned upon her. "You think—"

"I don't know what to think, but I'm not taking any chances! I never doubted they'd survive. There are maybe forty or fifty of them out there. God knows what form they've taken, but I'm damned sure they'll be fast."

"Fast . . . and deadly." Tatyana whispered the words, shivering. Her Slavic temperament asserted itself. "No—no! It is impossible! No God would do this—"

"Really, Tatyana!" Mark scoffed, "I expected more than that from you! Such arrogance! Just because we're in touch with an extraterrestrial entity with superhuman powers, people immediately assume it has to be the Ultimate—call it what you will." His tone softened. "For all we know, we may have attracted the passing attention of a beggar outside the pearly gates— a guy unable to get in!"

Tatyana looked at him doubtfully, not fully understanding his quick speech. "Mark, you must not joke with me."

For a second his haunted eyes regarded her. "I'm not joking, my dear. And let me tell you something else: The biblical God sent seven plagues upon Egypt, so don't bank on benevolence from on high."

They remained silent for the rest of the journey.

* * *

Malin's reactions were wholly predictable. "Are you sure?" he asked repeatedly, rousing Freedman to a frenzy of rage.

"Of course I'm sure!" he yelled into the phone. "Xeno is back—and it's a goddamned vampire!"

In Nash County, the death of Jake the fisherman caused little comment. Those who knew him expressed surprise that his heart had packed it in before his rye-soaked liver, but that was all. Freedman certified coronary arrest as the cause of death, and was technically correct in so doing. He had no need of Malin's urgent pleas to keep quiet about the rest. Maybe he was wrong; maybe there was only one Xeno left. He was as human as the next man: Lacking any idea how to combat the threat, he could only hope it didn't exist.

But before Jake kept his last appointment at the crematorium, Freedman's worst fears were confirmed by a small piece in the local newspaper.

At the bottom of an inside page, under "Baton Rouge Vampire," was a piece recounting the discovery of two victims, well outside city limits, each with a neck puncture.

Freedman read the item twice, then reached for his phone. Malin confirmed that the local doctors had not noted any areas of blistered skin. Mark felt sure the blisters were there but that, lacking his experience, the doctors had missed the deadly signs.

"We have to face it," he said. "We can't kid ourselves that only one or two have survived."

"But what can we *do*?" replied Malin irritably. "The committee's gone nuts thinking. We've considered everything—napalm on the local woods, total evacuation—you name it."

"You're wasting your time. Until we know what we

are up against, planning can't even begin. Right now we don't even know if Xeno walks or flies." He added grimly, "All we know for sure is what it lives on—let's hope it doesn't need a meal too often!"

The Louisiana news made up Tatyana's mind. She remained a patriot. Russia could have the same problem; it was her duty to return to inform her countrymen what she had learned.

Mark returned her parting embrace with equal affection, an unusual act for him. As a professional she had his respect; and he admired her warmth, her expansive, generous nature as a woman.

"Come back soon," he added as optimistically as he could. "Let's hope for better days."

Her eyes glistened. "No, Mark. I do not think we will meet again."

· XXVII ·

May was no great month commercially in Abdera Hollow. But it was still a very good time to be there, especially for those folks who liked simply relaxing in the open air.

Thursday, May 3, 1984, was just such a day. On Main Street, the stores opened in the early morning. The rest of Abdera yawned, stretched, and got down to another day.

Up on the ridge the Scotts breakfasted. Jaimie enthused over his wife's culinary masterpiece, an uncracked boiled egg. She was pleased, and they clasped hands over the table and kissed. Both dimly recognized her cooking had a long way to go, but that egg represented a distinct advance.

Usually Jaimie walked down to the office, leaving the car for Shane. Invariably they met for lunch in Mom's diner, a relief for both of them; he would then drive her home, or wherever she wanted to go. But this particular morning, he decided to ride to work; he'd pick her up at noon.

Very probably the decision saved his life.

Mark Freedman got up a lot earlier. He ate a light breakfast and was out of the house by six thirty, walking in the woods. He saw nothing, and everything appeared the same as it did on any other spring morning—until he was on his way back. He could not decide exactly when it dawned on him, for it happened gradually. But there came a moment when he stopped, listening.

Down in Abdera, a tractor started up, a car horn blared, a dog barked. High above, a plane rumbled past, and in the distance, birds chattered and sang. In the *distance.*

For several minutes he remained still, listening with the growing certainty that he was dreadfully alone. Not a single bird sang; there was no sound at all, no movement. He guessed there wasn't a bird within a hundred yards of him. His presence might have driven some away, but certainly not all. Anyway, if they'd fled at his approach, he'd have heard the alarm calls, and they wouldn't have gone far; there are few birds that don't know the exact limits of their territory. The distant racket emphasized the pool of silence in which he stood.

Freedman bit his lip, cursing himself for being such a crazy fool; he swore that if he got out of this alive he'd never do such a stupid thing again. He walked slowly, sweating with fear, scanning the trees. In three minutes, he was back in bird-occupied territory. He stopped, mopping his face, his hand trembling. Exactly what it meant he could not yet know, but he felt certain he had been very close to a Xeno. He'd never noticed this pool of silence during the winter; that could be for several reasons, none having anything to do with Xeno. On the other hand, maybe Xeno had not worried the birds then because it was inactive, whereas now . . . He shut his front door with considerable relief.

He realized just how lucky he'd been an hour later.

It began up on the ridge, not very far from where he had walked. A woman hanging out her washing was the first victim. A nosy neighbor—Abdera had more than its share—was studying the wash with great interest, for a good line of laundry tells an awful lot to a practiced eye. She saw it all.

The attack sent her into screaming hysterics, which brought another neighbor running, and she called the sheriff. He was a slow-moving, slow-witted man, a throwback to the spitoon-marksmen of an earlier age, full of wisdom, hard on the tough guys, yet a soft touch at heart. In fact, handling the town drunk was his forte. He lived in a fantasy world based on a diet of westerns and far too much TV. He had a flair for the dramatic, arriving with siren wailing, his car a galaxy of flashing lights. He listened to the woman's incoherent babbling, paused to inspect the stretched-out figure, and—for once—did the right thing. He called Freedman.

Mark arrived quickly, guessing the cause. By then the woman had been moved into her house. His cold authority drove the chattering group of neighbors out, ordering them to go home and stay there. The woman was alive. A word from him sent the sheriff scurrying to call an ambulance while he examined her.

He had no doubt the nosy neighbor had saved her. On her neck was a minute blister; on her throat, the marks and a very small puncture. He made her comfortable, then turned to the neighbor. There was nothing more he could do for the victim; survival depended upon her natural defenses. Maybe the woman's hair, like his own eyebrow, had absorbed some of the venom's strength.

The eyewitness, calmed by Freedman's presence and a stiff slug of rye, told what she had seen.

She happened, she said, to see young Mrs. Kennedy hanging out the wash. Out of the corner of her eye she'd spotted something—exactly what she couldn't say—on the roof of a nearby house. She had seen it only when it moved. It was about the size of a small bird, she guessed, and it swooped down, very fast, in a straight line for the victim's back.

There she paused, overcome by the memory. It took another shot of rye to get her going again.

"It was so fast—I can't tell you! It made a funny kinda noise." She amended that, "Leastways, I think it did."

"How big d'you think it was?"

"Gee, doctor, it's hard to tell." She tried. "I'd say it was about the size of a thrush, but"—she went on warmly—"it sure as hell wasn't no thrush! It went like—like an arrow, yet it seemed to pull up short—I'd swear to that—yeah, it pulled up short"—one hand described a loop—"went over like that. It was then she fell straight down, like she'd been hit with a rock. I was so amazed! I couldn't believe my eyes! One moment—"

"Okay, okay," said Mark soothingly, "take it easy. Now, this bird"—he used the word deliberately—"just think back for a moment. What did it look like? You've got a pretty sharp pair of eyes," he said encouragingly. "Can you describe it for me?"

"Well, doctor, I don't rightly know," said the woman helplessly. "I can't say why, but it was like no bird I've ever seen. It was after it did this sorta circle"—again the hand described a vertical loop—"that was—"

Mark cut her short. The rest he could guess, and he felt sure she'd relapse into hysterics telling it. "One thing at a time. Think back; it was on the ridge of this roof. Take it slowly, from there."

Obediently, she tried. "It took off. There was this funny noise. Yes!" she cried triumphantly, "that's it! I know why I didn't think it was a bird! It had short wings—but they didn't flap, they were kinda stiff. It coulda been a tiny airplane!"

"You're doing fine," said Freedman. "Now think hard about that noise. You said it was 'funny.' Try to tell me what it sounded like."

The woman looked at the sheriff, breathing heavily through his open mouth, then at Freedman, pale but collected. "I guess it was a kinda rude noise, but funny," she said hesitantly.

Freedman could think of only one rude noise. "You mean it sounded like someone breaking wind?"

"Yes." Eager to retain the doctor's good opinion of her powers of observation, she took the plunge. "But not what I'd call normal. Sorta high-pitched."

"Yes, I understand." His mind, far ahead of any computer, was intensely busy, picking out many disparate factors, oblivious to the sheriff's grin.

"Okay," he said at last, "what happened after this thing made the loop?"

"It seemed to fly off to one side, then came in again. It seemed like it hung on her neck. It was brown, light brown." The memory was too much for her, and she broke into tears. Freedman took her shoulders in his hands.

"Come on. There isn't much more—is there?"

She lifted her tear-stained face to him. "No. It seemed to hang on her," she said again. "I opened the window and screamed—I musta been outa my mind! This thing took off like a bat. I didn't see it after that."

He left her under sedation. What happened to the sheriff he neither knew nor cared. He collected his patient and drove slowly back to the hospital, thinking.

For his money the nosy neighbor was a good observer, which was a lucky break. She said Xeno ended its strike with a loop. Why should it do that? Such a complex action had to be a carry-over from its other world. If the theory that Xeno was no more than a flea of the gods stood up, then why did it do this? Maybe the venom acted as a local anesthetic. A pattern was emerging: two attacks, both from the back. Not only was Xeno wary of humans, it also knew the front from the back. The neighbor's scream, which had in all probability saved Mrs. Kennedy's life, gave a clear indication that, like its larval form, the adult Xeno could hear.

What else? Well, it flew; but if the report was correct, and he did not doubt that it was, the method of propulsion was like nothing on earth. No; that wasn't quite right. Squids used jet propulsion, but certainly no bird.

Rigid wings and that high-pitched noise; yes, it had to be a jet. That strange junction at the base of the lungs noted in the larval form, took on a new significance, as did Jaimie's comment on, and his own experience with, the creature's feather weight. The picture was getting clearer, but not clear enough. There was so much more he needed to discover. Before engaging an enemy, know him. Wild swipes in the dark got you nowhere.

Turning onto Main, his wish was granted.

A young construction worker, stripped to the waist, stood at the bottom of a ladder. Across the street, from the shadow of the roof's overhang, a brown shape, faintly iridescent in the sun, shot down, traveling at incredible speed.

Freedman braked hard. The Xeno flattened out, streaking straight and level for the youth's back. Three meters short it pulled up in a loop. The youth fell like a tree; the Xeno made a sharp banking turn, its wings distinct, raked back, swallow-shaped and gleaming. The wings folded over the fallen figure as Xeno dropped onto the youth's neck, paused, then shuffled obscenely sideways like a crab, centering itself. Suddenly it was still.

There were few people in the street; those who saw were petrified.

Freedman never knew how much his inaction was due to that same freezing horror, or to his dispassionate desire to understand. He watched, mind and body in slow motion. Eons of time elapsed before he could shift into drive; more passed before his hand hit the horn. The car jolted forward, blaring sound; he stopped short of the body, struck by a new wave of horror. The Xeno did not move. Instantly he realized this had to be the same one that had attacked Mrs. Kennedy: It had learned that mere noise was not harmful.

To his credit, Freedman did not hesitate; flinging the door open, he half fell out of the car, yet with no clear idea of what he should do. The Xeno knew. For the first time a man faced it; it took off. Freedman caught a fleeting glimpse of the creature, saw the body swell explosively to twice its size. It seemed to leap into the air, flashing away. For the first time he heard that unmistakable sound, so accurately described by the woman. The Xeno darted back to a rooftop, a brown, glistening shape.

Freedman stood trembling, facing it. At that distance he could not see detail, but it appeared to change shape; he guessed it was ingesting air. For one heart-stopping moment he thought it would come for him. Then it was gone, flashing low over the housetops, heading for the trees, the sound faint and fading in sharp intermittent bursts.

Freedman's legs felt like jelly. Slowly he bent over the youth. He had been a lot less lucky than Mrs. Kennedy.

Once he had a grip on himself, Freedman wasted little time. Ignoring the crowd that gathered, he forced his way back to the car. There was nothing he could do. The boy was dead; his duty lay with the living. Waving aside questions, he drove off. In his office he called his wife, telling her to stay indoors and make sure all doors and screens were shut, then shouted the same order to his bewildered staff. He called Malin, but he had scarcely uttered a sentence when Malin shouted him down. A man had been struck dead outside Central Park Zoo: Hundreds had seen the attacking Xeno. Another body had been found in Branch Brook Park in New Jersey. New York City was not in a panic—not yet, that took time. But there were some pretty scared people along Fifth Avenue, and there'd be a helluva lot more, once the news hit radio and TV.

Freedman listened in shocked silence. Until this moment, he'd thought of Xeno as a local problem. Malin gave him no chance to think before going on to another chilling item. There could be no serious doubt that only one Xeno had hatched in the whole of Georgia. But already there had been two attacks within twenty-four hours, and both victims were dead due to loss of blood or embolisms. Freedman hung up, pushed his glasses up to his forehead, and covered his face with his hands. The Georgia item was nasty, really nasty. If the thing fed daily . . .

His thoughts on the sinister implications of that news were interrupted by Jaimie bursting in. He had been on house calls and was still ignorant of the latest developments. Freedman spelled it out coldly. As Mark ended, Jaimie reached for the phone. Another phone rang and Freedman took the call: a third victim, a male, on the outskirts of town; dead. As he dropped the phone, Jaimie too put down his receiver. His face was white: Shane did not answer.

"Okay," said Freedman bleakly, "so she doesn't answer. You want to go chasing off back home? Suppose she's out—and she may very well be—what then? You think cruising around Abdera is the fastest way to find her? You stay right here, phone around—and don't forget there are two patients waiting for *you*, and you know as well as I do that neither of them is suffering from athlete's foot!" His tone softened. "Go on, Jaimie. I know it's tough, but if we're going to lick Xeno, we'll do it with brains, not panic. Get the secretary to phone neighbors, stores—it'll be a lot faster than tearing around town."

Alone, Freedman reached for the phone. It rang as he touched it: the local radio station. They'd heard he'd seen something crazy on Main: What was it? What was going on? There had been a flock of calls, folks were scared. Calls to the sheriff had failed to elicit any satisfactory answers.

The newsman paused. "Doc—there's a flash coming in now from New York City—" he paused again —"it sounds mightly like what I've heard you ran into on

Main Street. A guy's dead, killed—it says here—by a bat or something. What the hell was it?"

"Why ask me?" retorted Freedman.

"Aw, c'mon, doc," said the newsman urgently, "I know you—we did a piece together on wildlife around here a year back. If anyone has an idea, you do! What was it? Is there a tie-up with the time travelers—and what should folks do? Give me *something,* doc!"

"Okay, you want my advice. Don't panic, and don't create panic. People should stay indoors, and if they have to go out, drive, don't walk." In his mind he saw the youth falling. "And if possible, don't go out alone. That's it. Don't bother me, I'm busy." He slammed the phone down. Immediately it rang again: the sheriff, incoherent, babbling with fear. Mark shouted for him to get a grip on himself, repeated his advice, and left the phone off its cradle.

He sat back, wiping his brow. In as many minutes, two people had wanted his advice. If he felt helpless, what about ordinary folk who knew nothing? Three—no, four cases reported around Abdera; how about the hospital area? There'd surely be more up there. And if Xeno fed daily . . .

Without warning the door burst open: Shane. He restrained himself from chewing her out when he saw her face. He jumped up and steered her to a chair. She looked very bad, forehead beaded in sweat yet cold to his touch, her golden hair disheveled, shoes scuffed, and a large hole in one stocking.

"Mark!" she gasped, gripping his hand fiercely, "Mark—it was awful!"

"Okay," he said soothingly. Clearly the girl was frightened out of her wits. "It's okay now. Just relax." His compelling gaze kept her on the right side of hysteria. "Relax—you're safe." Slowly he got through to her. "Does Jaimie know—" He didn't bother to finish such a futile question. If Jaimie knew she had arrived he'd have been fussing over her like a mother hen.

"My hair," she said, pushing it back from her face, and Mark knew she was over the immediate shock. "No. Jaimie wouldn't know what—" She shuddered again. "He'd go crazy. You—" Her grip tightened on his hand.

Freedman felt he had the weight of the world on his shoulders; once more he was cast as the father figure. "Okay, tell me." Although still very scared, she was uninjured aside from some scratches.

"Jaimie had the car this morning. I started off, walking down to town. We were meeting for lunch—" She broke off. "Oh, God!"

"Yes. Go on." Mark knew all about her cooking and Jaimie's defensive ploy. "It's all right now. Take your time."

"I—I wanted to do a little shopping. I'd gotten as far as the end of the road—you know, where you turn down the hill—" Her face squeezed up in terror as she relived the moment. "Suddenly there was this funny noise. It seemed like it was right behind me!"

Freedman's growing impatience vanished; he sat very still. "Yes?"

"Something shot past me, terribly fast. At first I thought it was a bird—boy, was it moving! I think it flew around me, kinda circling, two or three times." She shuddered. "I stopped, real scared. I'd never seen a bird like that in my life."

Freedman nodded, his face impassive. "What happened then?"

Her beautiful eyes were wide with shock. "Suddenly, this thing was on my *arm*!" She grabbed her opposing forearm with one hand. "There! For a second I was too scared and shocked to move. It disgusted me—it felt cold, so *cold*! And its eyes . . . kinda human, but not human—you know what I mean. It only stayed a second or two I suppose, but it seemed like a whole lifetime to me! I think it moved; I guess I yelled, tried to shake it off. Then the craziest thing—it sorta swelled up, then it was gone—so fast!" She gestured sharply. "Just like that—gone!"

Freedman let out a long-held breath. "And that was all?"

She laughed nervously. "You want more?"

"No." Whole new avenues of thought opened up, thoughts that needed time. But at this moment he had to get as much out of her as possible. Once Jaimie arrived, she'd cry all over him, he'd be protective, and that would be the end of questions for that day. And by tomorrow she'd have forgotten details. He reached across the desk, taking her hand in his; the gesture appeared impulsive, but was entirely calculated. "Shane; you've had a very unpleasant experience." He spoke softly, staring into her eyes. "That thing's pretty nasty." He tightened his grip on her hand. "It's already killed two or three people." She'd find that out soon enough. "What it is, we don't know yet. To help us track it down, we have to learn all we can about it. You've seen more of it than anybody else. I want you to think hard, then tell me what it looked like."

She stared at him blankly, trying to absorb all he said.

"Gee, Mark—I was so scared! Like I said, it was cold—and a funny sorta shiny brown which seemed to change color, like shot satin or mother-of-pearl."

"Iridescent?"

"I guess so. But that was no bird. It was smooth, no feathers—and flying, it went like an arrow. And those eyes! They were real strange. I can't explain. Creepy."

Freedman struggled to keep calm.

"Okay, Shane. Let's concentrate on those eyes. See if you can remember what they were like."

"I know it sounds stupid"—her nervous laugh irritated him—"but they looked kinda human."

"You mean they had expression?"

"No—not really. They were just cold. They seemed to look right through me."

"Well, why did you think they looked human?" Mark sought the simplest words. "For instance, was there a colored center, surrounded by white?"

She tried. "Gee, Mark, I'm sorry. I don't know."

"Think back," he urged. "There was this thing, sitting on your arm—I know, you don't want to think about it, it's horrible, but you must try, Shane."

She did her best, gripping his hand, her eyes shut, grimacing in disgust. "I want to help . . ." She opened her eyes. "I'm pretty sure there was no white part—and I've got a sneaky feeling the eyes were sort of golden. There's one thing I do remember. It weighed practically nothing."

"That's good, Shane," said Mark encouragingly. "Anything else? *Anything*." He didn't want to put ideas in her head. She desperately wanted to help, to live up to her new status as a doctor's wife; if he gave a lead, she'd follow. "You mentioned legs; what can you recall about them?"

Shane came up with nothing.

"Okay. You said it seemed to swell up before it flew away. Try to go back to that moment; did all of it swell—or just part?"

"I—I think, but I can't say for sure, I think only the body swelled. It happened so fast! The mouth—I think—opened, the body blew up like a balloon—and then it took off." She started crying. "Gee, Mark, you must think I'm terribly stupid!"

"You've told me quite a lot, my dear." As a human,

he sympathized with her; as a scientist he could have screamed. "You've been very—"

Jaimie burst in. "Mark—*Shane!*"

Mark switched off as the couple practically smothered each other, thinking of the little he'd learned.

Jaimie was full of questions; he clamped Shane tightly in his arms. Mark butted in. "She's okay, Jaimie. A nasty shock, that's all, so slow down." He looked meaningfully at his junior, then at his wife. "Shane, you'd better go fix your face." The moment she had gone, fear banished by vanity, he dropped the father act, speaking urgently. "Now you listen, Jaimie: Don't lead her with questions. Play it down; that way you may get more out of her." He didn't sound hopeful. "Don't push—and don't suggest answers—got it?

"Okay," Mark continued, "now get over to the diner. Make it fast—and keep in front of her. No, don't argue. I've got a hunch Xeno prefers attacking single humans."

"Godalmighty," said Jaimie fervently, still trailing mentally. "She was lucky! You think it had already fed? Jesus! It's horrible." He tried to recover his professional calm, but his voice remained high-pitched, strained. "Why d'you think it left her alone?"

Freedman shrugged. "I'm working on it."

"Yeah. I thought Main looked pretty deserted." He tried to laugh. "I don't think there'll be many more patients today. Hey—how about Maisie?" She was his receptionist.

"Oh, God!" Freedman had forgotten her. "You'd better take her over as well."

"And you?"

"Bring me back something, anything," replied Mark carelessly. "No, I'm not just thinking of my own skin, although as of right now, its true I'm too valuable to risk. But I want time to think."

"From what Maisie said, you took a mighty big chance this morning."

"Maybe."

He watched the trio run, hunched forward as if against rain, and heaved a sigh of relief as they disappeared into the diner. He looked at the empty, sunlit street, the black shadows under the roof eaves now so sinister. How could he let them go out? he wondered. But what else could he do? what could anyone do? Perhaps helmets could be improvised, something to protect the back of the neck. The main thing was to destroy the Xenos, and that couldn't be done without knowledge.

The second phone was ringing. Let it.

What had he learned from the girl? Confirmation that Xeno used jet propulsion. Partial confirmation that Xeno had an exceedingly good optical system, far ahead of any insect. *Golden* eyes? Maybe. Were they similar to a bird's—a bird of prey? Pure guesswork: Shane had added very little, but he was stone-cold certain she had not been attacked. Why?

Could it be that a person who had harbored a parasite contained some trace element that made them unattractive as a food source? If so, how the hell did Xeno know?

He hurried back to his office and the time travelers' files. The phone was still ringing; he dropped the receiver on his desk and ignored it.

With Shane's experience in mind, he quickly read the post-emergence records, but they suggested nothing to him. He slumped back in his chair. How *did* Xeno know? Could it be smell? Just because humans were badly equipped with that sensor, they tended to underrate it: Most animals were way in front, and a good many insects. A male moth could pick up the scent of the pheromones of a female of the same species one or two kilometers distant, so there was nothing way-out in Xeno detecting the inedible at, say, a hundred meters.

Okay: Even assuming that—and it was going out on a limb to do so, for there was no supporting evidence—why did Xeno bother with Shane at all? Why land on her—just to confirm the fact? Or could it be that like him, it sought intelligence of its enemy?

The unattractive thought was blown out of his mind as Jaimie came in, white-faced and breathing heavily. Somewhere behind him a woman was crying. They were back, safe, but lunch had been a disaster. Mom, scared blind, couldn't concentrate on her cooking. Worse, the radio had been on.

In the area covering Abdera and the county hospital, ten or twelve people had died, and at least two more further afield, in Westchester County. On the Governor's orders, the director of civil defense was assuming control of upstate New York.

"Civil defense!" Jaimie tried to laugh. "That'll sure scare Xeno!" He gave Mark a rather squashed hamburger.

"Thanks. We have to start somewhere, Jaimie, and the first thing's to stop panic." He looked out of the window. A car went slowly past; Mark recognized a neighbor and watched as he turned the car into his driveway. But the driver didn't leave it there and walk the few meters to his front door; he drove the car across the grass and spring flowers, then scuttled like a scared rabbit from car to porch.

The reign of terror had begun.

The smallest stone dropped in a pool creates ripples, Xeno was a large, ugly rock, and the waves spread clear around the world. Press and TV were quick to relate the bizarre events in New York State with the time travelers, their guesswork rapidly confirmed by the happenings in Louisiana; and the whole thing was sewn up when a reporter, working back from the attacks in Georgia, discovered that one of *Papa Kilo*'s stewardesses had been hospitalized in the area. After that there was no holding off the Fourth Estate, whatever the White House said. Within hours the news from the States blew the lid off the situation in Frankfurt, Germany, where the police were puzzled by two unexplained deaths.

What had been the closest secret in Washington and Moscow alarmed and frightened people all over the world—except in the Soviet bloc. Moscow's firm hand kept the wraps on Xeno.

The uproar in the States forced the President to make a statement on TV. He came clean, saying the creatures had been "picked up" by the time travelers, admitting the news had been withheld to avoid "unnecessary panic." Only in the latter part of his statement was he less than honest, saying that the exact number of these creatures was known, and expressing his certain conviction they would be hunted down and destroyed. As for any fresh arrivals, the know-how existed to deal with them. He ended with a few well-chosen platitudes pleading for calm.

Frank Arcasso watched the broadcast at home, glowering at the screen, sprawled on a couch, cigar jammed in his mouth. The big man had been careful not to use the word *Xeno*: Few people in 1984 had any command of classical languages, but there were enough to know the word meant "stranger," and that could sound too sinister. Much more important, he'd made no mention of the larger implications.

In general, Frank went along with the President, although he thought he was a bit too optimistic about the ease with which Xeno would be wiped out. Sure they would get it, but it could take a great deal more work than the statement implied. But how about the bigger, more vital question—from what sort of world did Xeno come? On that, not a single word. Frank knew that in making any announcement without Russian approval the President was breaking their agreement; under the circumstances, he had no option. As far as he could, he had kept faith with the Soviets. But caught in a dilemma he'd said, Frank figured, either too much or too little. The world wasn't entirely populated with fools—it would soon be seen what the real question was. Evasion only destroyed credibility—and that's what it was, evasion. He had the latest report to the Soviet president on his knee, and a fair idea of its contents. Whatever else, it wouldn't be evasive.

But Arcasso was in no hurry to read it. He let his mind wander, considering the personalities involved in this nightmare.

Funny how wrong you could be about a guy. Alvin Malin, first-class at his job, had buckled at the knees at the first sight of a Xeno photograph: He wasn't just shocked, he was terrified out of his skull. Malin had faced many bad men—gangsters, terrorists—men willing, even anxious, to die for a cause. Once he'd carried a bomb from the second floor of the UN building, a long, slow, nerve-tearing walk down to the entrance and across the plaza, put the device with steady hands in a nest of hastily placed sandbags—and lost a lot of hair and half his clothes when it exploded thirty seconds later. In that sort of situation he had ice-cold courage—but not in the face of Xeno.

At the meeting the President had told Malin to take a look at the situation in Nash County. Arcasso saw the blood drain from Alvin's face and understood the terror in the FBI man's mind; he'd seen it happen in combat pilots, men who could only take so much. Arcasso got in ahead of Malin, saying he wanted to go. Maybe the President, for all his worries, had perception too, for he had agreed quickly.

So Frank would be off at first light by helo. Meanwhile there was the report. He thought of another man who'd surprised him, the author of this Xeno update, the secretary of state. Now there was a hard, cool brain: unmoved by Xeno and not deeply interested in the ICARUS concept, he concentrated on the use he could make of both. Everybody else might be in disarray, but not that cold, impeccably dressed figure. What with the shock news from the northeastern states, Malin's near-collapse, the pressure of time, and presidential hesitation, the meeting had been not far short of chaotic—until Lord got moving. He had the report ready; only the latest details needed insertion. He met little opposition. He knew what he wanted; the rest of the committee was much more concerned with fighting Xeno than sending reports to the goddam Russians.

Frank's wife interrupted his thoughts, bringing him a large rye on the rocks. That was the one good thing about the crisis: At least he'd been able to tell his wife his part in it, sweeping away her suspicions. Right now she was contrite, playing the part of a dutiful wife the way she'd seen it in some movie, forcing him into the role of heavy. With all he had on his mind, it annoyed and at the same time amused him. Hell, it wouldn't last. The next scene would come in the morning; then she'd be the stern Roman matron, seeing her lord off to war. If he got back in one piece, he'd be knee-deep in emotion for the movie's final scene.

He took the drink without a word, playing his part. Maybe that was the hell of marriage, knowing your partner inside out. But suppose he didn't come back— what then? She and the kids would get by; he was worth more dead than alive, and there'd be a pension.

He skimmed through the factual part of Lord's report, the apology for the "unilateral presidential announcement," and the reasons for that action. No one could point a finger at it, all good solid stuff; then came the real meat:

4. *Historical*

4-1-0. The return of the airplanes above mentioned is an established fact.

4-2-0. The arrival of Xeno via those aircraft is an established fact.

4-3-0. Xeno successfully parasitizes humans, and as the latest events prove (2-3-2), it finds humans an adequate food source and earth conditions viable for its life form. These too are established facts.

Arcasso smiled grimly, sipping his drink. No one could deny anything there. He read on.

5. *Xeno*

5-1-0. Larval form. Examination of the single full-grown specimen and the two embryos (See Report Three) proves beyond question this life form is, by earth standards, a sophisticated creature with many unique features, some not understood by our biologists.

5-2-0. Pupal form. A matter of conjecture, assumed to exist because of

5-2-1. The period of inaction/dormancy between the emergence of the larval form and the sudden arrival of the (assumed) adult form, currently at liberty in this country, Germany, and (probably) in the Ukrainian SSR and India.

Arcasso tossed his cigar butt in the direction of an ashtray, grinning mirthlessly, guessing the secretary's drift; there certainly would be no room for evasion in the reader's mind, either, and the Kremlin couldn't ignore the deadpan reference to the Ukraine.

5-3-0. Adult form. So far no specimen has been obtained, but eyewitness reports, including one from an expert biologist, show this form to be derived from the larval form. For example . . .

A long technical analysis followed, relating the larval lung formation to the adult's mode of propulsion and noting the similarity of the toxin in both forms. . . .

In short, it is certain that we are facing a later form of the larval parasite.

6. *Action*

6-1-0. The prime aim is the destruction of all Xenos. This cannot be achieved without more understanding of the creature's anatomy, its strengths and weaknesses. The capture of an adult specimen has the highest priority.

6-2-0. A secondary aim is to devise some protective clothing, to be worn in infected areas. Currently, beekeeper veils are being dispatched to New York State for use by personnel at greatest risk. As in 6-1-0, anti-Xeno protective measures will depend upon a greater understanding of the creature.

7. *Evaluation*

7-1-0. Xeno is of nonearth origin. (See 4-1 thru 5-1.)

7-2-0. It is contrary to all biological knowledge that a creature should spring from nothing to Xeno's present sophisticated state (5-10). Therefore it has developed elsewhere, possibly over millions or, at very least, hundreds of thousands of years, to its present state.

7-3-0. It follows that to survive in our environment, its natural environment cannot be markedly dissimilar to earth's.

"Christ!" said Arcasso softly. "That's really spelling it out!" He drained his glass and glanced at his attentive wife, who quickly refilled his glass. He lit another cigar, tossing the match away. She retrieved it from the carpet without a word.

7-4-0. Given 7-3, it can be assumed Xeno is also a parasite in its natural habitat. What, therefore, does it parasitize? It is evident that its victim—for convenience we call it the "Entity"—has the following features:

7-5-0. It can pluck our aircraft out of our time and space, and return them unharmed, aside from their contamination by Xeno (4-1). It may be argued that the Entity is not necessarily Xeno's host; if so, then we are forced to accept there is more than one Entity. To accept this view would only complicate the problem, and in no way alter the following conclusions:

7-5-1. The Entity has superhuman powers (7-5-0).

7-5-2. The Entity is not ill-disposed to Earth, possibly regarding it as we might regard a bush in a garden. Using the same analogy, our aircraft might be the equivalent of a ladybug, something to be picked up, admired, and carefully replaced, the Entity not understanding—any more than we do—the consequences of that action for the ladybug. Of course, it cannot be ruled out that not all aircraft captured have been returned.

7-5-3. We do not know whether the infection of our aircraft with Xeno is intentional or accidental. If intentional, it is a remarkably clumsy action for an Entity with the powers we know it to possess. Alternatively, if Xeno is an accidental implant, it follows that the Entity has little or no awareness of Xeno, no more than we humans are aware of the myriads of mites and other life forms which exist in and on us in symbiotic relationships.

7-6-0. Of the space-time relationship and the Entity's ability to bridge it, we know nothing and seem unlikely to know more, but the factual evidence we have, and the conclusions we may safely draw, are inescapable. The Entity, by our standards, must be physically immense, for Xeno, which means nothing to It, is lethal to us, and the certainty that Xeno is not lethal to the Entity is confirmed by the self-evident fact that no parasite can exist if it kills its host, for in so doing it seals its own fate.

8. *Conclusion*

8-1-0. In short, the evidence is conclusive: somewhere in space-time, beyond human understanding, exist Entities, immeasurably superior to us, physically and mentally. Depending upon the human individual's beliefs, they may be regarded as the gods of the Ancient Greeks, the angels of the Jewish God, the angels or archangels of the Christian God, or whatever fits any particular theology. But however we may see them in our minds, they *exist*. Again undeniably, they have taken an interest in us. Earth has been found. We must hope and pray that their interest is only passing, that we may be left to work out our own salvation, for by our standards we face a life form unimaginably vast in all respects. We may well be less to these Entities than an anthill is to us, and in their case we have much less power than ants, for while they can reach into our world, we cannot reach theirs.

9-0-0. Your comments are invited.

"The snide bastard!" said Arcasso admiringly.

"Your comments are invited! Fit your dialectical mate-rialism around that!" He dropped the report on the floor, failing to notice copies had also been sent to the Head of State, Ukrainian Soviet Socialist Republic, and Doctor T. Marinskiya. A footnote added that a Russian translation of the report had been included.

Secretary of State Lord had done his best to make sure the impact of his literary bomb was not damp-ened, and had the widest distribution diplomacy al-lowed.

· XXIX ·

At nine A.M. the next day Arcasso's helicopter touched down on Abdera's baseball diamond. Freedman met him, and at the doctor's suggestion the big Sikorsky's rotors were kept running. Their swishing, slapping sound, added to the scream of the air intakes, might give some protection.

Frank clambered out and dropped clumsily to the ground; the helo door shut instantly. Arcasso was wearing—again on Freedman's advice—a combat suit and steel helmet. But in spite of that, and the quiver-ing bulk of the helo behind him giving some physical and sonic protection, he felt exposed, vulnerable. Freedman took a chance on the rotors, driving right up to the aircraft. He beckoned to Arcasso through the windshield.

Arcasso opened the door, swung his grip into the back, and got in, all in one swift motion, but it wasn't fast enough for Freedman.

"Shut that door!" he shouted against the roar of the helo. The car jerked, shooting away from the aircraft, bumping and swaying on the uneven surface. Once clear, Freedman stopped, turned the car off, and leaned back, his hands grasping the wheel, watching the now ascending copter. To Arcasso he seemed a lot older and very tired.

"Why have you come, Frank?"

Arcasso felt a little surprised at the question, but explained that the President thought it a good idea. Freedman hardly appeared to be listening, but it was evident he'd heard. "So you're the President's reporter." He laughed shortly. "You'll have plenty to tell him!"

Both men were silent as the copter thundered over their heads, its wash rocking the car. Freedman watched it disappear over the line of trees, then started the car and drove towards the park entrance, saying nothing.

It was another fine morning; dew glistened on every bush, and the trees were the clear fresh green of spring. Frank stared out. What a beautiful day to go fishing or walking! It seemed incredible that he could not even open the window, that he had to stay in that steel-and-glass box on wheels. He felt pretty silly about the helmet, too.

Turning out of the ball park, Freedman drove slowly down a dirt road, passing a few houses scattered among the trees, which were mostly scrub pine. Frank eyed the scene carefully. It wasn't the classiest residential area, but it really wasn't so bad. With slight variations there were hundreds of thousands like it. But he soon noted one difference: no people. He mentioned it to Freedman.

"What'd you expect?" snapped Freedman. "And I'll be amazed if you see any birds."

Arcasso stayed silent. A few seconds later he jumped when the car phone bleeped.

"Freedman." He listened with that same detachment

Frank had noted earlier, but his eyes were never still. "Is she dead? Yes . . . okay." He replaced the receiver. "That's another—the fifth this morning." He did his best to sound calm, but Arcasso noted he had accelerated and had begun to drive almost recklessly.

"You mean the fifth *today*? Already?" Arcasso was shaken.

"The fifth I've heard about. There are bound to be others—I only get those in my area. It'll be worse up around the hospital, I guess."

"My God—we've gotta do something!" exclaimed Frank.

Charitably, Freedman let that remark pass. "We're doing all we can think of. The local station's broadcasting warnings every ten minutes, telling folks to stay indoors. The school's closed—in fact all schools are closed clear across the county. But that's not stopping some lunatics. Imagine—one woman let her little son play out in the back yard! He was the first today." Mark's face twisted into the semblance of a grin. "Trouble is, the fewer targets we present, the higher probability there is of available targets being struck."

Freedman swung the car around a corner; a short street lay ahead. There were fewer trees, more houses. A figure lay sprawled on the sidewalk, a spilled shopping basket and a purse nearby.

"Hey!" exclaimed Frank. Thinking Freedman had not noticed, he grabbed his arm, yelling, "Hey—that woman!"

Freedman shook his arm free. "I know. Mrs. Kellerman. She was the second one this morning."

Frank screwed round in his seat, staring at the shapeless bundle. "Jesus Christ! You can't just leave her!"

"Why not?" Freedman tried to sound indifferent. "She'd dead. I checked on my way out to meet you."

Arcasso's mind reeled. "But you can't just leave her there! What are you going to do?"

"Right now, nothing. She'll b. picked up tonight." He dismissed the subject. "When we get to my office, I'll go like hell for the door. You slide over to my side and come out the same way—and make sure you slam the car door. Okay?"

Arcasso nodded dumbly. This was much worse than he's expected. This was America, 1984? It was impossible; surely he'd wake up in a moment.

Swinging the car into his driveway, Freedman gave a long blast on the horn and stopped about ten yards from his office door. He reached down behind his seat, donned a strange headgear, letting down a veil which covered his face and neck. He looked so silly, Frank lost all self-consciousness about his helmet. The shrouded head turned towards him. "You ready? Leave your bag."

"Okay," said Frank huskily. "Any time."

"And don't fool around in the entrance. Straight in. Someone else'll shut the door." Freedman dived out of the car, leaping for the door. Arcasso saw no more; he was for too busy sliding across the bench seat, then out, running for his life, kicking the car door shut behind him. It was no more than ten yards, but it seemed like the longest distance he'd ever covered. He shot in and slammed the door, breathing heavily.

Brigadier Arcasso tried to appear calm, but there was sweat on his brow as he removed his helmet with his good hand. Freedman, cursing quietly to himself, was still battling with the beekeeper's hat and veil. The entrance seemed to Frank to be very crowded; in fact, there were only two others, Jaimie as doorman, and Maisie the receptionist, trying to help Mark.

Frank saw one change in Mark's office; one wall was covered with roadmaps, taped together and showing practically all the northeastern states. Red pins were scattered, but the greatest concentration was in Nash County. Frank did not need to ask what they represented. "I get the red markers, but what's the significance of the black arrows?"

Freedman stopped filling his pipe. "Wind direction."

"Yeah," said Frank slowly, "that could be significant."

"Damned right it is," retorted Mark. "Just study the attack locations for a moment—notice something? There's scarcely one attack upwind. My guess is that Xeno jets when it has to, glides when it doesn't. If so, the trend must be downwind, and with this present high-pressure system, which could persist for days, the real high risk areas are New Jersey and New York."

"Have you told Malin?"

"Of course." Freedman puffed rapidly, "And I've told Civil Defense in Albany."

"Hell, I'd forgotten Civil Defense. Have they done anything yet?"

"Hardly had much time. They hope to have a command post set up here today." He smiled thinly. "They asked me to take over as town boss; I refused. Someone else can do the paperwork; so long as he does as I tell him, he'll do fine." He returned to the map. "Frank, you're the military man; what's your answer to this one? I've come to the conclusion Xeno is basically arboreal."

"What's that?"

"Arboreal? A tree dweller. I have several reasons for thinking that—and don't waste time asking me what they are. If I'm right, and if the wind theory is right, then here"—he tapped the map with his pipe—"in this wooded area is where I'd expect to come across some of them—at night."

"How d'you propose to catch one?"

"Christ—I'm a doctor!" cried Mark savagely. "You're the goddam soldier!" He stabbed at the map again. "I'm telling you I think this is a high-probability area; some of the larvae could have made it in there from the hospital, and the wind could have brought more across town as they hatched—and remember, they could still be hatching!"

Frank lit a cigar, appraising the map. Jaimie came in with coffee. "I've got the new after-dark office hours being broadcast right now, Mark."

"Good. You'd better get some rest this afternoon. I'd like you to take the weight tonight."

"Sure."

His tone made Mark look up sharply. "Something on your mind?"

Jaimie nodded. "There have been another two strikes up at the hospital."

Freedman sighed. "Okay. Mark 'em up." Jaimie's manner alerted him, his tone changed sharply. "That's not all, is it?"

Jaimie shook his head. "I'm sorry, Mark. Slim Lewis was one of the victims. Seems there was this woman who'd been hit as she got out of her car. He went out to help."

"The stupid bastard!" cried Freedman in anguish. "Just the sort of thing he would do!" He glared at Jaimie. "At least we can learn from him—let's get some value out of his death! We've lost a damned good doctor, for nothing! So no false heroics, Jaimie." For a moment he stared blankly at his desk, then he sighed again and looked at Arcasso. "Well, have you got any ideas?"

"Yeah, one. Gas."

"What sort of gas?"

"I'm no authority, but we'll rustle up some experts

damn soon. How about hydrocyanic gas? That'd kill everything stone-dead."

"We'd have to be very confident about the wind direction holding."

Frank shrugged. "Sure, but there's risks in everything."

"It's an idea, Frank," said Freedman, "I'd be grateful if you checked it out. See if you can find a nonlethal gas. A live specimen would be worth ten dead."

Frank reached for a phone. "You'll get your strike tonight."

Even the most rabid enemy of the United States cannot deny the Union one virtue: America has repeatedly shown near-genius in its ability to get up and go, once it has seen the need to do so, and to do whatever is necessary in a big way. Detractors say it is just Yank money talking—overlooking the fact that the wealth was created by Yankee drive, plus good natural resources and that touch of luck every human enterprise must have to succeed.

Of course, the results have not always been happy, but by any standards the record is impressive. Starting with the recovery from the trauma of the Civil War, the nation became one of the world's top two industrial powers within a generation. The States made Allied victory certain in two world wars. In the space race, the first U.S. satellite was a pathetic attempt to keep up with the Soviets, who already had Sputnik One aloft, a bleeping monster fifty times bigger. That was in 1958; by 1968 the story was very different. In another sphere, the U.S. had no intelligence agency at all until 1940, and the CIA was not formed until 1947.

Arcasso's phone call set in motion another fast reaction.

By late afternoon Abdera's ball park was a sorry mess. Helicopters, dropping in from late morning on, dug holes in the grass; their engines blasted foliage; and heavy trucks left deep tracks everywhere.

First came a signal section and control team flown in from Fort Detrick, Maryland. They emerged from their copter in full biological warfare suits and masks. These eerie figures quickly set up a tent and a radio link back to base, then distributed radio sets and protective suits to the Civil Defense HQ and to Freedman's office in a requisitioned truck. Civil Defense requisitioned more trucks, and a further supply of suits and a radio was sent out to Nash County Hospital.

Another copter brought in the biological warfare experts and a cargo of gas, spray equipment, and more tents.

Then came two more copters, one as escort, for the second aircraft contained another, very different gas in red-painted cylinders buried deep in foam rubber inside hermetically sealed steel containers. Even so, it was unloaded with great care, placed in an isolated tent, and watched over by an armed guard. The cylinders held a broad-spectrum nerve gas, every bit as deadly as Xeno's. If the first gas failed, it would be used.

Still another copter brought in Air Force photographers, a work detail with floodlights, batteries, and flagged marker posts. Finally there arrived an Army support group, complete with food, drink, chemical closets, and more tents. Their officer made his mark when he warned all personnel over a bullhorn that if caught short, they should urinate in their trousers; under no circumstances was the male organ to be exposed. A biological warfare expert enjoyed telling the officer he'd better take time out to examine his suit; he'd find it catered to such a situation.

Brigadier Arcasso (as advised by the Fort Detrick leader) had overall charge of the operation. Sweating in their suits, he, Freedman, and the BW colonel supervised the marking of the danger area, all three alert for any change in the wind. They were updated on their personal radios by local control with the latest USAF meteorological forecasts.

Beyond the target area, monitoring teams set up their sensors. Locals were warned to stay clear of one road that would be closed at dusk.

The target was a small wood of perhaps four or five acres on the downward slope of the southern side of Abdera's rim, a spot noted for adulterous sighs and urgent coupling at this time of day. But no lovers, however pressing their needs, were in the wood that evening. Freedman insisted that no close approach should be made to the area before nightfall.

The trio stood on the ridge, each thinking of his part in the impending operation. The colonel prayed that the incapacitant would do the job; this funny little doctor, who seemed to carry a lot of weight, assured him that the creature they sought breathed, and on that basis he was quietly confident. Anything that got a lungful of ICX-4 would be out for quite a long count. But if the doctor was wrong—if the nerve gas, never used outside tightly controlled laboratory conditions, had to be used, things could get messy.

Freedman had his worries, but one at least was resolved as they stood in the twilight at the wood's edge.

Arcasso was speaking, his voice muffled by his mask, pointing at something, when Mark's gloved hand sharply gripped his wrist. The gesture was unmistakable; all three froze. Freedman's head, goggle-eyed in the mask, turned slightly, listening.

A few tense seconds and all three heard it, a high-pitched sound, quickly growing louder. Mark pointed, his arm tracking around swiftly to follow a black shape gliding, rapidly losing speed, heading for the trees, its deadly day completed. Perhaps it saw the men, for with one sharp rip of sound it disappeared into the wood at incredible speed. The three humans remained motionless, two of them shaken by the sudden reality of Xeno, until then something they'd only heard about, an abstraction. Freedman, who had now seen more of Xeno than anyone—and lived—shivered. Slowly, with infinite care, they edged back, over and down the ridge, into the growing darkness.

In their car, their masks off, the colonel spoke. "That was it?"

Freedman repressed his excitement. He had been right! "Yes. That was a Xeno—did you notice when the light caught it, the iridescence?"

"Jesus!" said Arcasso, "that thing can sure move when it wants to! Until it switched on its afterburner, I was thinking you might take it with a shotgun, but once it went—" He shrugged, lighting a cigar.

"Okay—we know it's in there—what are we waiting for?"

Freedman shook his head. "We wait, Colonel. There could be more. Give them plenty of time to get settled. Leave it until nine."

The colonel looked at Arcasso, who nodded. "Make it nine; on the dot."

By half past eight all teams were on the starting line, strange figures in suits that made them look more like moonwalkers than anything ever seen in New York State. At ten to nine the thin line of men, gas cylinders

224

on their backs, moved cautiously forward into the brilliant, starlit night.

Freedman and Arcasso were back on the ridge; with them was an Army signaler with a radio backpack. Mark turned, looking down on Abdera Hollow, a nest of twinkling lights half-lost in the trees. Garbage men made their rounds with unusual speed, the mail got delivered, and silent ambulances collected the newly dead. Silence was the keynote; no one spoke above a whisper. The inhabitants transacted essential business as fast as they could, watched by nervous National Guardsmen, whose task was to see that all people were under cover, doors and windows tightly shut, by 9:00 P.M.

At five minutes to zero hour Arcasso and Freedman made their final check on the wind: It held, a soft northwesterly breeze. Both had their face masks off and Arcasso was smoking. It was a cool evening, but both men sweated.

Arcasso took several rapid puffs; they watched the smoke rise, curl, and vanish downwind toward the wood. "Okay, Mark?" Arcasso spoke softly.

"Yes. We'll never have a better chance."

Arcasso glanced at the signaler. "Phase One—go!"

Seconds later, below them, they saw the green light flash back to the line of men waiting by the colonel, who was out in front of his force. The line advanced to within three meters of the woods and stopped, turning on valves.

Arcasso and Freedman donned their masks, watching the spreading white vapor, small clouds that grew and merged into a fog-bank, drifting into the trees. The green light showed again, misty now, flashing a series of dashes. The sprayers advanced up to the trees, raising their lances higher.

It seemed to the men on the ridge that the operation

had no sooner begun than it had ended. A red light deep in the trees waved from side to side and the star-lit white cloud diminished, fading into the wood.

The radio man spoke. "Sir, the colonel says he's finished."

Arcasso frowned; it had lasted a bare five minutes. "Here, gimme that." He took the handset. "Colonel, you confirm Phase One completed?"

"That is affirmative." The tinny voice went on, "I know what you're going to say, but this stuff is highly dispersant; anything breathing only needs one snoot-ful."

"If you say so," said Arcasso. "Haul your men back and rearm with the hard stuff."

"Yes, sir. But let me tell you, it's been snowing birds and I don't know what, but nothing's fallen on me for the last two minutes. My guess is that anything that's going to drop already has."

"Maybe, but you get back with your men. I'm sending in the search line in two minutes." He gave his orders to the radio men and turned to Freedman. "Come on, Mark. This is where we move out."

Suddenly the scene was transformed. Six three-man teams—one man to search, another to handle a flood-light, the third to bear the power pack—began to move, lights on.

"Oh my God," muttered Freedman to himself hurrying after Arcasso, "if Xeno is still in business, it'll think its dawn."

The scene was brighter than any floodlit ball game. Tree trunks threw eerie black shadows in the silent, still wood. Not even a moth gleamed in the light.

Methodically the teams edged forward. All searchers had been briefed to report anything the size of a small bird that they did not recognize. They were hardly into the trees when a man called out. Freedman ran to him; one glance, and he had a hard time keeping his temper. "No, soldier," he shouted through his mask, "that's a bat!" He ran quickly back to the center of the line, treading with great care, amazed at the number of birds and other creatures, including three raccoons and two black snakes, that were lying helplessly in the fresh spring grass.

The search took a great deal longer than the spray operation. There were several false alarms; and Freedman, sweating and tired inside his suit, checked each one, running awkwardly, hampered by the specimen container he carried.

And then the man who had found the bat called out again; although his voice was muffled by the mask, the difference in his tone was recognizable. Fatigue left Freedman as he ran.

"Where?"

The soldier pointed. "I nearly stepped on it, sir!"

Panting, he unslung his specimen can, but before he could move, Arcasso—who was beside him—spoke. "Hold it, Mark. You're sure that's it?"

Freedman nodded, still getting his breath back.

"Good work," said Arcasso to the soldier. "Go get the other men on search detail; I want them to see what they're looking for. And tell their teams to stay right where they are until the searchers rejoin." He forced himself to look closely; to do so sickened him, but if the men had to do it, so did he. Freedman was obviously very impatient, and that made him think of something else. Screwing up his courage, he said as casually as he could, "Maybe I'd better put it in. Not even Xeno can do much to my tin arm."

Freedman, crouching, looked up. Neither could see the other's face, but Arcasso sensed the doctor smiling. "No. Can't trust that claw of yours with this one—but thanks all the same."

The men arrived and stared dumbly; all started back, alarmed, as Mark took the Xeno by the tail, straightened his body, and, still kneeling, held the creature up. "Take a good look," he commanded. "I'm not going to handle it too much—we can't risk damaging it, but note its size and color. This line here is where the wings have folded, but you don't have to worry about them—I don't expect you'll find one with wings spread—but bear it in mind."

Inside his head, Frank Arcasso was screaming for Freedman to stop, to put the hideous thing out of sight.

At last Mark did so; as it slid into the can, Frank heard its feet or something scrape on the metal. Glad for the mask, he curtly ordered the men back to their stations.

For two more hours the teams scoured the wood, but no more were found. The BW colonel asked Arcasso if he wanted the heavy strike; Arcasso looked at Freedman, who said no. The terrible sight of the devastated wildlife and the state of the one specimen they'd found convinced him they'd gotten the only Xeno in the wood. It was not much of a victory, but at least the first step had been taken.

· XXXI ·

Washington knew of the success before Freedman and Arcasso got back to the office. Jaimie, haggard and on edge, awaited them. Washington had been on the line, he told them—several laboratories wanted the specimen. As the field expert on Xeno, which one did Freedman favor? Brookhaven was the closest.

Freedman, avid for a really good look at Xeno,

turned on Arcasso. He had the greatest respect for Brookhaven, but it wasn't close enough. This Xeno should not be subjected to the hazards of air travel or any other form of transportation. Compared to this specimen, the Mona Lisa was just about as priceless as a postcard of the Empire State Building. Arcasso should tell the President and anyone else that the Xeno had to stay right there in Abdera. If a second specimen was obtained, Brookhaven was welcome to it. But not this one.

Arcasso got through to the White House and proved a good advocate. The President ruled in Freedman's favor, adding that anyone who had anything to contribute "had better haul his ass out to Abdera, and fast." This Doctor Freedman knew more about Xeno than anyone else, and had just proved it.

The high-level chat was lost on Mark. Knowing a neighbor kept tropical fish, he gave swift orders to Civil Defense. Shortly after midnight the bewildered neighbor watched his collection being tipped into buckets and his king-sized aquarium manhandled by soldiers and carried to Freedman's office. The dried-out tank was set up on Freedman's desk, holding a branch of white pine hacked off the nearest tree; the doctor danced impatiently, sweeping papers and everything else onto the floor. Civil Defense had found a sheet of plate glass to cover the tank; Freedman had a hole bored in the glass, big enough to take the nozzle of a gas cylinder, foreseeing Xeno might need to be moved to bigger accommodations.

At one in the morning, still rustling around in his protective suit, he cleared his office except for the BW colonel and one of his men, armed with a gas cylinder. Fully buttoned up in their suits and masks, Freedman unscrewed the can, raised the lid a fraction, listened, then tipped the container slowly into the tank. With the same beastly slithering, scratching sound, the Xeno dropped onto the branch, toppled, and fell, landing on its back on the bottom of the tank. The colonel hardly gave Freedman time to get his arm and the container out of the way as he slid the plate glass top in position.

Freedman tore off his face mask, staring intently at the still figure. "How long d'you think?"

The colonel, his mask off, mopped his face. "Who can say? One, two hours." He too looked at the Xeno, his mouth twisted in disgust. "What a helluva thing. I've never seen anything like it."

"Join the club," replied Freedman dryly.

Arcasso came in; he'd been on the phone in Jaimie's office. Averting his gaze from the tank, he said, "By morning you'll be knee-deep in biologists—so how about calling it a day?"

Freedman shook his head vehemently. "No." Already he regretted not having taken a closer look before putting his prize in the tank.

"Aw, hell, Mark! You're tired—we're all tired. I can't remember when I last ate."

"You want anything else?" said the colonel. "Okay—I'll be off."

"Sure," said Mark absently. "Thanks for all you've done. Maybe we can repeat the operation up by the hospital tomorrow night."

As the colonel and his soldier left, Jaimie came in. "There's nothing else that can't wait. I'd like to get back to Shane. She's lonesome."

"You go, Jaimie—and tell Shane I said not to fear the dark. It's friendly."

Frank dug out a cigar. "You're not going to stare at that damned thing all night, are you?"

"You'll find a bottle in my second drawer," said Freedman. "The glasses are through there, in my bathroom."

Frank sighed and fixed the drinks.

"Frank," said Mark, for once not looking at Xeno, "I want you to know I appreciated your offer to pick that up." He gestured with his glass. "Give it to me straight. Does Xeno—even helpless—scare the hell out of you?"

"I can't even bear to look at it," confessed Frank. "I don't go crazy over spiders or bugs of any sort—few people do—but that thing!" He thought for a moment. "If it literally looked like nothing on earth, I don't think it would be so bad—but it could be a distant cousin to a lobster or a scorpion. And yet it isn't. That skin or whatever it is, and that iridescence—" He shuddered and gulped his drink.

"It's funny," Freedman mused, "but I don't see it that way. I know it's a killer. I lost a good friend today, but I don't feel angry at Xeno. Looking at it there, it amazes me, and in a way I feel sad. I'll do all I can to wipe out every last one of them, but with no ill feelings, just as I know that thing in there would kill me if necessary for its survival."

He drank. "It's no good. I can't explain, but even while Xeno scares me, deep down I can't hate it."

"That's because you're blinded by science," said Frank. "Also you're tired. I know I am."

"Go over to my place. There's a spare bed; Thelma will fix you something to eat. Tell her I'll be back before dawn—I hope."

It sounded a lot more attractive than a bedroll in a tent in the ball park. "She won't mind?"

"Hell, no! You go ahead."

Alone, Mark dragged a chair over, set up his recorder and mike, and settled down to work.

"Description of the first captured adult Xeno. Date—"

He got no further. With a sudden, split-second convulsion Xeno leaped into the air, landing on its feet, facing him.

· XXXII ·

A long way back, a lifetime ago, Freedman had stared in the face of the larval Xeno. Now he faced the adult, happy for the centimeter of plate glass between them.

The caterpillar is the larval form of a butterfly; it then moves into its dormant pupal stage, from which it emerges fantastically transformed, looking nothing like its previous self. Anyone ignorant of the life cycle of a butterfly would never believe that brilliant flitting creature had once been the slow-moving, many-legged caterpillar.

But Xeno was no butterfly. Freedman saw many differences between the two stages. The outline of the adult had existed in the larva in appearance and behavior. Both forms had the same awareness of their environment, the same speed of reaction—and both were killers.

The adult was larger, its color that of a shiny chestnut straight out of the husk. It had four legs: stout, hairy supports, repulsive in their resemblance to a tarantula's, legs spread out like a fly's, each with three joints, powerful, holding the body rigid, parallel to the tank base on which it stood.

The head was still faintly triangular, but the shape no longer stood out, the head merging into the body almost imperceptibly. The flattened forehead sloped sharply back; the eyes, set well apart, giving the Xeno a good field of vision, were bright, intelligent, and golden: black oval pupils with fire-gold irises. He thought of Blake: "Tiger, tiger, burning bright . . ."

But it was not the eyes which gripped Freedman. In the middle of the face the nostrils, closely-spaced, small and round, rhythmically opening and shutting, and below them, above the slack, hideous mouth and the weak receding chin, a short hornlike excrescence, one to one-and-one-half centimeters long.

Man and Xeno were perfectly still, watching each other. Psyching himself up for the effort, Mark lunged forward with his head, stopping just short of the glass.

The Xeno reacted with stupefying speed; Mark only glimpsed the action.

Hardly had his head begun to move than the mouth flashed open and snapped shut, fast as a high-speed camera shutter. He thought he saw the tip of the horn open; then his vision was obscured by a patch, the size of a half-dollar, yellow and viscous, on the glass. Instinctively he'd jerked back, his heart beating faster. If it were not for the glass he'd be dead—the shot would have taken him right between the eyes.

Slowly he got out of his chair and poured himself a badly needed drink. He'd learned something: The horn, not Xeno's mouth, was the weapon.

He raised his glass, and stopped. That nasty looking mouth didn't have to be a mouth at all. Just because it happened to be where one expected to find a mouth . . . Xeno fed on blood, and it wasn't the right equipment for the job. Perhaps it had teeth like a snake, except that instead of pumping out venom, they sucked in blood.

He drank, glancing down at the tank. Xeno had moved around to stay facing him. Freedman took two swift strides around the corner of the aquarium; Xeno still stared at him head on, shifting like lightning. He moved back to the chair and sat, getting the same head-on view. Once more he lunged forward, nearly hitting his head on the glass. Xeno didn't move.

Freedman sat back, vaguely aware that he'd spilled liquor on his suit, once again appalled at the creature's ability to learn, reacting to his first threat, ignoring the second, knowing it was harmless. Of course, it could be it had temporarily exhausted its venom supply, but if so, he'd have expected Xeno to take cover in the pine branch. He exchanged the glass for the microphone and got busy, quietly dictating his observations, watched all the time by the Xeno.

The idea occurred to him suddenly: Did the creature know what was he doing?

He tossed the microphone into his chair and refilled his glass. If he was going to start getting paranoid he'd better quit right now and leave it all to the Brookhaven boys.

He walked up and down, ignoring Xeno. Could the thing be getting to his mind? Hell no! Sure, he was studying a truly strange, unearthly creature, which certainly had a better brain than most creatures, but in human terms it still rated a lot lower than the village idiot. To imagine it had telepathic powers was to belittle himself, to give far too much credit to this horrid thing. Maybe he was just tired, but tired or not, he'd finish his observations. He continued where he had left off, a description of the lobsterlike pincers.

Lobster-type pincers—*unsegmented*? It hardly made sense. They did look very powerful, and the surface seemed to be the same as the rest of the body; it could expand, so its structure was not armored like a scorpion's—in which case it had to have an internal support structure, a skeleton. So the pincers, regardless of how they looked, must be closer to hands, with an internal bone structure.

By three thirty he had finished. Tired, and puzzled

by the many problems his observations raised, he accidentally dropped the microphone. But the noise got no reaction from Xeno, who remained motionless on the tank floor. Mark knew he should go off to bed, but he found it hard to drag himself away. This was—or had been—only Day One of the counterattack. Until they succeeded in wiping out the Xenos, most of the work would have to be done at night. All right, then, he'd started in on the new, temporary schedule.

He would stick around a while longer; maybe doze in a chair, watching now and then.

He switched off most of the lights, leaving only a shaded desk lamp standing on the floor beside his desk, and pulled up an armchair. In the dim light, which came from an unfamiliar angle, and with his desk-top occupied by the tank, the office looked very strange. The light, filtering through the side of the tank, threw an eerie image of the bough of pine onto the ceiling. Freedman leaned back, exhausted.

His watch told him he had slept for several hours when he was awakened by a faint rustling sound. He kept very still. Among the indistinct shadows on the ceiling, another shadow moved slowly.

He glanced sharply at the glass top: Xeno could not escape. The movement stopped, but he forced himself to count to one hundred before he dared move.

Slowly, he raised himself on his hands. Xeno hung on a twig by its front pair of legs, tail downwards. It was definitely sleeping. The eyelids, never before observed, were closed over the terrible eyes.

Gently Freedman lowered himself back into the chair. Everything in nature had a purpose, which could be discovered if the observer had knowledge, perception, and a lot of patience. Freedman thought of two answers; unfortunately, both raised more problems than they solved. The eyelids were brilliant, shining white.

After a time he gave up, his exhausted mind refusing to accept any more. But he felt some satisfaction: He'd learned a great deal in the past few hours. The battle wasn't won—it had hardly begun. But from now on it wouldn't be one-sided.

In the days that followed, the nature of the battle changed. Mankind got organized—especially in the center of infection, Nash County, and the action around Abdera Hollow for a radius of twenty kilometers was a microcosm of the whole battle. Habits changed drastically; people slept by day or at least stayed under cover. After dark they emerged, like cockroaches in a deserted kitchen, and went about their business warily and with unusual speed. And while the township made the best of this disjointed way of life, the BW squads moved out to strike new targets and restrike old ones. They learned fast, refining their techniques; the three-man search teams were abolished in favor of individuals, each carrying his own lamp, power pack, specimen can, and tongs.

The manpower that was saved went to form other squads; overnight BW became a growth industry.

But not only man learned. Xeno showed yet again its remarkable and alarming ability to adapt. With the sharp reduction in human targets, Xeno learned to exploit any weakness or lapse in human vigilance. A window left open, a road accident—Xeno soon understood cars—the human that took a chance, were exploited all too often by the bloodthirsty predators.

The second night's BW operation was conducted in a patch of woods near the hospital, with excellent results: Four Xenos were captured. The jubilant BW colonel threw a small party in the early hours: Freedman, Jaimie, and several biologists (Arcasso, back in Washington, had been right) joined in. Five humans had died in the preceding twenty-four hours, but four Xenos in one strike was a great deal better than the first night.

Washington celebrated, too. With security out the window, the command post became the Icarus Intelligence Center, every scrap of information being fed in by Civil Defense authorities, who acted as local intelligence gathering points in affected areas. The total number of U.S. Xenos could not exceed eighty-seven, all ex-*Papa Kilo* victims; now five were in the bag. So Washington celebrated, but not quite as heartily as Abdera, for already the infected area had grown: Red markers now stood on the maps of Boston, New York City, Newark, and Atlanta. An unconfirmed report suggested a Xeno had gotten as far as Wilkes-Barre, Pennsylvania, and the Louisiana group had clearly split up—New Orleans was now infected as well as Baton Rouge. But with that kind of news coming in, the celebration was somewhat subdued.

With five specimens to study, Freedman's objections to the movement of the first Xeno no longer held. Two of the four were killed for examination, but first they were subjected to various experiments—one was exposed to heat, the other to cold. The first showed no signs of discomfort even at 65 degrees Celsius; the other became torpid at 5 degrees and was dead after thirty minutes at −5 degrees. The survivor was then exposed to a variety of gases, and its reactions were much the same as a human's. Further experimentation was stopped for fear of damaging the specimens. F malin finished off the second. The two dead were transported for further study by biolog went to Brookhaven, the other to Harv

School. The two live specimens were sent to Walter Reed Research.

A week passed; ten more Xenos were taken and quickly dispatched to research centers. At the insistence of the secretary of state one was sent to the USSR. The level of attacks in Nash County fell off dramatically; no more than one or two victims died each day. Man can get used to anything if he has to—and what was the death of one or two people, whatever the cause, compared to the highway accident toll?

Outside of Abdera the feeling was much the same. In New York City hundreds die every day from a variety of causes. What was another guy or two, said some citizens (with no experience of Xeno), even if they were knocked off in this horrifying way? Jesus, you stood a better chance of being murdered on the street than of buying it from this thing. A fair observation; naturally, those who made it considered themselves exempt from attack. Only in the affected areas, around Central Park, for example, did tight pockets of fear exist.

Attacks still happened around Abdera. Freedman believed two Xenos were still operating in the area, but although wooded areas were sprayed again and again, no more Xenos fell out of the trees. He suspected they had adapted and now lived closer to humans. The one way left to track them was by sound, but with windows and doors shut in houses and cars, and people on the street in protective suits, the sharp burst of sound could be easily missed. He felt sure that the Xenos now lived in the town, but even if he was right, they could be holed up in a thousand places. Still, he continued to stare pensively at the small steeple on the church.

On the side, he studied his own specimen. While he observed, no member of his staff, with the exception of Jaimie, dared to go near his office. But the Xeno seldom moved. It never tried to escape. Freedman piped smoke in through the hole in the top, banged the side, flashed lights, shouted, and played sudden bursts of sound on his recorder, but none of this had the slightest effect. He concluded that his subject had learned it could not escape, and had also learned that the antics beyond its prison meant nothing. For days on end it followed the same pattern, sleeping on the pine bough at night, resting on the tank floor by day, its passionless eyes watching its tormentor, giving nothing, asking nothing. All the same, Freedman was learning. Every day he photographed it, wrote up his notes, watched for a change in its appearance. One fact stood out: Xeno did not have to feed every day; and the longer the experiment went on, the more this worried Freedman. There are many creatures that, given the chance, will willingly eat daily, but have the ability to last a very long time without food, especially if they are not expending energy. In spite of Freedman's experiments, the Xeno remained still, shifting only to face him as he moved around the tank. Increasingly, it became a personal battle between him and his prisoner.

Then, two events, one close upon the heels of the other. First, the consolidated report of the biologists at Brookhaven and Harvard was submitted.

The second seemed less significant at the time: His Xeno lost its iridescent sheen.

The report came by the night mail. Freedman's day had been hard; life and death went on in spite of Xeno. He looked at the bulky package without enthusiasm until he turned it over and saw the return address.

Entitled *A Preliminary Report on Xeno* it ran to some three hundred pages of text, drawings, diagrams, photographs, and tables. His wife took one look at his face and the book, canceled her ideas for a civilized evening meal, and returned to the kitchen to make sandwiches.

Freedman read the report from beginning to end without getting out of his chair or touching the sandwiches and milk. Many of the observations in it did not surprise him, but some did. Xeno did not have an internal bone structure: the report held that it was "exo-skeletal," the skin evidently possessing "iso-tensional qualities the mechanics of which are not understood." The mouth was not a mouth at all but an air intake, and the lungs performed a double function, extracting oxygen in a conventional way, but also capable—via strong surrounding muscles—of compressing air sufficiently to provide propulsion. The weapon system worked as he suspected, but the hornlike excrescence contained an inner tube which—the surrounding muscles suggested—allowed Xeno to thrust it with considerable force into its victim. The venom sac held enough for at least six shots.

But it was the section headed "Sexual Characteristics" that really intrigued Freedman. Xeno was hermaphroditic; inside its complex system there existed a penis and testicles as well as a vagina and ovaries.

This came as no blinding shock; many forms of life on earth had that ability, including the human tapeworm. In his long hours of thought, he had considered the possibility, but the lack of evidence had caused him to dismiss it. Now he had to face it: Xeno needed no partner; copulation was an internal process. Any eggs it implanted—there was a detailed description of the oviduct, which was part of the tail—would already be fertilized. The destruction of eighty-six of them would not be enough. The remaining one could restart the cycle.

At last the method by which Xeno spread and its lack of interest in its fellow creatures had been explained. Xeno was not social, for the simple fact that it had no need to be. Every single one had to be hunted down and destroyed. Only one faint ray of hope existed: The report "suspected" the testicles to be immature—a vague observation at best.

But to Freedman the implication was plain: While Xeno was adult, it had not yet reached maturity. Brushing aside his wife's protests, he ran back to his office. Suddenly his specimen's loss of iridescence had taken on a new significance.

His worst fears were confirmed. Xeno, reacting to the light, dropped down from the withering branch and assumed its defensive posture. Freedman ignored it, his gaze fastened on something else.

On the floor of the tank lay a pale, shadowy image of reality, the outline of another Xeno, split precisely down the center of the back. Freedman's gaze shifted from the cast skin to the Xeno, and he noticed that its color and iridescence had been restored. And something else: It was larger.

* * *

One of the most powerful and satisfying experiences known to humans is sex, and Jaimie and Shane had plenty of that.

In basic, earthy terms, Jaimie screwed the hell out of Shane on every possible occasion. Their total absorption with each other cushioned them to a great extent against the horrific events which surrounded them, and in some ways the crisis helped. Jaimie worked from nightfall into the early hours, running the practice almost single-handedly, for Freedman was either tied up with hospital work, busy with anti-Xeno operations, or studying his specimen.

At around 5:00 A.M. Jaimie got back home. He and Shane ate and tumbled joyfully into bed where they stayed for a highly satisfying twelve hours. Sometimes he had to climb into his suit to meet an emergency, but even then the summons always came via the bedside phone. In the altered social conditions of Abdera they could be sure of no unwelcome visitors, no distracting invitations from neighbors. But there was another side to the coin: due to their disrupted life and Shane's slaphappy attitude toward practically everything, she had run out of pills.

Throughout the Western world the implications of Xeno raised the biggest theological storm since the Reformation. From secret Vatican conclaves to banner-carrying protests, factions clashed, argued, and prayed in every country. New creeds evolved overnight and vanished just as quickly, symptoms of the profound doubts and fears of humanity.

Secretary of State Erwin Lord watched the storm's progress as he pressed on with his private offensive. In his cold estimation the religious upheaval would have little long-term effect on the West; what it would do to those who had long denied the existence of God, he had no way of knowing.

He saw to it that copies of the Xeno report were sent to the Soviet State Institution of Science (which also had the Xeno specimen), the president of the USSR, the head of state of the Ukrainian SSR, and Dr. Marinskiya. He could not do more without breaking diplomatic rules, and in doing that much he'd badly bent a few. The Kremlin would be enraged by his action, but they could hardly protest. After all, the Americans weren't trying to spy. They were giving information, not seeking it. Nor could the Soviets point to anything in the report that was even remotely political. It was straightforward and factual; if the reader chose to draw his own conclusions, that was not the Americans' fault.

So the urgent request from the Soviet ambassador for an audience came as no surprise to Lord. The ambassador eloquently conveyed his government's thanks for American cooperation, but "for administrative reasons which the secretary will understand," all future material should be passed to the Soviet embassy for transmission.

Erwin Lord understood perfectly and, having no option, he agreed at once. Incidentally, had His Excellency seen the report? No?

He was sent a copy—and a copy of the secretary of state's earlier report—immediately. Lord was satisfied; he'd expected the Soviet move and felt he'd done well to plant as many bombs as he had.

Unknown to him, he had allies—the two Ukrainian Xenos. Within the USSR, over 99 percent of its citizens were ignorant of the horrific events in the U.S., and no one knew of the existence of Xenos in the Soviet Union except the top men in the Kremlin and Tatyana Marinskiya. With the exception of a couple of doctors and a few nurses who, given the Xeno report, might have guessed, no one in the Ukraine, from the general secretary of the party down, had—officially—the remotest idea of Xeno. The aliens could not have asked for better conditions.

Both operated on the outskirts of Odessa for three weeks before any hint of their existence reached the Ukrainian government in Kiev. The Odessa police and the local KGB, puzzled over the deaths from the beginning but having no explanation, were not anxious to report the incidents to higher authority.

The Xenos chose solitary humans as their victims, mostly farm laborers, road-menders, or other humble early-risers, people whose deaths raised no great stir in any community, capitalist or communist. When the toll reached twenty-five, however, a report had to be made.

The news went from town to oblast and from there to Kiev, and on the way the same considerations applied. No police force, regardless of its political color, likes to appear baffled to its seniors. Another week passed before Kiev HQ admitted they could do no better. So nearly a month elapsed before the premier of the Ukraine Republic, who kept a shortwave radio in his country house and thus had some inkling of Xeno—and the ability to put two and two together—learned of the Odessa crisis. He wasted no time in telling Moscow. By then over fifty were dead.

The news shook the Kremlin, but their difficulties had scarcely begun. The team would be seeking only two creatures—a needle in a haystack would be easier to find. In only one sense was the situation less awful than that which the Americans faced: With no idea of what was going on, the scattered local population had no cause for panic. Relatives of the dead might ask questions of the neighborhood police, but in a country

244

that had been obsessed with security since the days of the Czar, no one pushed too hard.

Moscow toyed briefly with the idea of asking the Americans to send in a hunting team, but soon discarded it for a galaxy of reasons. Instead, Tatyana was ordered south. She alone was chosen because she was already on the inside. Her pleas of inexperience in biology fell on deaf ears. She was told sharply that with her experience in the United States and her access to the American report, she knew more than all the Soviet biologists put together. Her task was to find and report the night locations of the Xenos. That done, Moscow would decide what action would be necessary.

The half-baked operation was doomed from the start, although she came very close to fulfilling her part: close enough to become a victim herself.

Tatyana Ivanovna Marinskiya's death warrant lay in her orders. To avoid comment she would not wear full protective clothing, but "other suitable measures" might be taken. She went about her survey in a trouser suit, gloves, glasses, and a plastic rain hood: a lonely, frightened woman, doing her best in a battered 2CV van, traveling dusty back roads, struggling to understand the maps that showed where the victims had fallen. At night she collapsed exhausted in some sad provincial hotel, seeking refuge in vodka from the erosion of her faith in the party by Xeno—and ICARUS.

On the fourth morning, in a cornfield on the edge of a wood, her search ended. The Xeno's venom went through the plastic hood faster than a red-hot rod through butter.

The Kremlin regarded her death with mixed feelings: Xeno remained at large, but at least the number of those who knew the full story was reduced by one. Still, something had to be done, and the one-person search party had clearly been a mistake.

With Tatyana dead, the top men who knew the full story were isolated by their lofty positions from the mere technicians. There had to be intermediaries. Reluctantly the president and the general secretary admitted the rest of their ICARUS group to the full secret. Through them a biologist and two biological warfare officers of the Red Army were chosen to seek and destroy the Xenos. They had to be told the secret, and thus the death of Tatyana was reduced to a useless sacrifice: it is unlikely anyone considered that point.

To insure full local cooperation, the top men of the Ukrainian SSR were also admitted to the ICARUS circle, which now officially grew to nine. In fact, the number that knew unofficially was a great deal larger. Through Western radio, travelers, and numerous clandestine channels, the news of Xeno spread, losing nothing in the translation. If anything, the gruesome reality of Xeno became more alarming with each telling. From the knowledge of its existence it was a short step to the obvious, inevitable question: Where did it come from—and why? Each repetition of the question was, in effect, an assault on the bastion of Marxist dogma.

At fearful cost, the party had dragged a collection of peoples out of the middle ages and hammered them into a twentieth century superpower—six hundred million people, the vast majority proud of their country. But a surprisingly small percentage felt the same way about the party, which, in 1984, still had only fifteen million members.

Of course, membership was not just a question of filling out a form and paying fifty rubles: it involved hard work, dedication, and the acceptance of an iron discipline. Naturally, some joined for the practical benefits—life could be a great deal better for members, especially in the higher echelons—but the vast majority of the party believed deeply in Marxist-Leninist doctrines as interpreted by the party. The party had a view on everything, from abstract art to petty theft. Its view of religion was exceedingly simple: God did not exist. Man—at least Communist Man—was the measure of all things.

Organized religion had long since ceased to worry the party, and priests seldom figured on the list of state enemies. Far more troublesome were the revisionists, those who tampered with the faith: Trotskyites, Maoists. Compared to these traitors and heretics, the party loved capitalists, and was right to do so—even as the Spanish Inquisition had attacked the heretic, not the heathen, four hundred years earlier. Defense of the faith against subversion has always had top priority. Inevitably, the defense fails in the end, but that has never kept people from trying. Not that the party intelligentsia gave failure a passing thought. They had the one True Faith; once the enemies of the party were overcome, mankind would move on to the sunny meadows of communism. God? Old hat. A device used by rulers to control the people.

But now there was Xeno, a lethal threat to humans, and a deadly, slow-working cancer on an unbending atheistic doctrine.

· XXXIV ·

By August, 1984, forty-eight Xenos had been trapped in the States. Freedman's hunch about the church steeple proved correct: One was caught there, the last in Abdera.

After several tense days, during which no strikes were made by the aliens, Civil Defense declared the township free of Xenos. Not only had none been seen, but the net of microphones spaced over Abdera failed to detect any. To be quite sure, suited soldiers combed the eaves of every building in the township, and all roof spaces were fumigated with sulfur, to drive any lurking specimens into the open.

Even so, the Abderans were reluctant to return to their old way of life. Soldiers might remove their face masks, but soldiers were paid to risk their necks and to obey orders. They were also a bunch of strangers.

But Freedman convinced them by walking the length of Main Street hatless and in his shirtsleeves. On the way back, the Civil Defense boss met him, which was a much braver gesture, for Freedman was banking on more than just the house-to-house search. He'd noted the return of the birds, an observation he quickly passed to the CD boss in their uneasy mid-street conversation. As Mark said, smiling grimly, "If that cardinal over there gives his alarm call, I'll be indoors before it gets airborne."

His advice was repeated on the local radio, and for a time Abderans were the nation's keenest birdwatchers.

Elsewhere in Nash County the battle went on. One or two Xenos were still operating close to the hospital; several kilometers east, two attacks quickly shut the Roosevelt Hyde Park home to visitors. BW strikes in Louisiana had reduced the Xenos in the area to one, but several still terrorized New Jersey—business in Newark froze for two days, and twelve people died in a panic downtown stampede for cover. Two or three were spreading more terror in lower Pennsylvania, and ironically, at least one was active on Brookhaven's doorstep, in Patchogue, central Long Island.

In the same week that Abdera Hollow regained a measure of freedom, Mark allowed his Xeno to be taken to the Walter Reed observation unit. It still appeared to be in good health, although it had not fed for over two months.

Once he had swallowed the initial shock of Shane's announcement, Jaimie philosophically accepted his approaching fatherhood. He became less selfish and took a somewhat more somber view of the future in emulation of his hero, Mark. Shane was as happy as a lark. Xeno was a quickly fading nightmare and had been replaced by a much more interesting question: a boy or a girl? Either way, she was crazy about the idea.

Mark however, had no enthusiasm for anything. With Abdera cleared, his life became routine again. Only a deep sense of foreboding stopped his mind from being overwhelmed by an acute feeling of anticlimax. His unease was reinforced when the Walter Reed unit issued a new report on Xeno. One had been killed and dissected; in the biologists' opinion, the sex organs were now mature. The specimen was also two centimeters longer.

Naturally, Freedman read everything he could lay his hands on concerning Xeno. The ICARUS Intelligence Center sent him copies of everything they received—a great deal, for India and Germany were also reporting their anti-Xeno operations in detail.

He read with great attention the confidential report on the B-17's crew. All had developed cysts which were successfully excised the moment they could be positively identified. After recuperating, they were discharged from the Air Force. All they wanted was to live normal lives and try to forget they were freaks. The Air Force, also keen to forget the incident, tried to help. The men left with thirty years back pay—and no forwarding addresses.

But the crew of *Eager Virgin* was swept from Freedman's thoughts by another report. A small geological expedition to the upper Amazon had practically tripped over the wreckage of an aircraft; as they understood it—there were language problems—the plane had been there for over ten years. They also listened to a garbled tale about a tribe who lived deep in the jungle, who worked by night and slept by day, and were said to worship a white god who was a vampire.

The expedition was ill equipped to investigate further. They examined the wreckage, counted seventeen ant-cleaned skeletons, and noted the engine numbers. Records showed it to be a DC-3, the *Dakota*, which had vanished in Southeast Asia in 1945 with thirty people aboard.

The moment the news of Xeno had broken, all CIA stations worldwide were instructed to watch for any signs of the aliens. The local station was on to the geologists almost before they took their first civilized bath. Two jungle warfare experts went in and made contact with the nocturnal tribe. Their report made incredible reading.

Although the CIA men offered untold riches—a whole crate of whiskey—they were not permitted anywhere near the White God. But their contacts would talk, and as the investigators pieced the story together, they too were less than keen to meet him.

The tribe was a poor lot in all respects. They were true aborigines, wild and shy, with a justified fear of civilized man. Through contact with the DC-3's survivors, they had soon fallen prey to diseases against which they had no resistance. Their primitive culture had no real idea of time. The God may have arrived ten or a hundred years before; perhaps their troubles had begun with an earlier contact—they did not know. The CIA men believed the latter: that the tribe was on the path to extinction before the plane crashed, their will to live sapped, their few skills as hunters and trappers insufficient for survival. Certainly they regarded the White God as a saviour, even if he did have a darker side.

The story had many gaps. The aborigines' primitive language, eked out with signs, seemed to say that God or perhaps Gods had appeared among them from out of the sky, and that the God had his own demon vampires. In time the tribe learned that the God did not like them to walk by day, and those that disobeyed were killed by the demons. Thus the natives adapted, coming to their God only at night. On one point the story was very clear—the tribe obeyed the God and in return his demons hunted for the tribe. At night, the men moved through the jungle, finding the bodies of animals; the choicest parts they offered to the God, and they lived on the rest. Their God was old—none of the women he was offered had borne children, and some had obviously displeased him, for they died quickly at the hands of the demons. But one or two had been acceptable, and the tribe believed the God had rewarded them with the power to walk by day.

The tribe believed that the demons were the children of the God and therefore sacred. After much bargaining, in return for the case of whiskey, the investigators received a sacred object from a reluctant elder.

Smoke-blackened, the skin greasy with handling, its closed eyes gray with filth, it was unquestionably a Xeno, but with one significant difference: It was twice the size of any specimen previously captured.

Late into the night Freedman pondered over the report, the photographs of the giant alien, the maps. The CIA had done its job, verifying the existence of Xenos in the upper Amazon basin; but, as before with ICARUS, the solution to one question only raised a great many more.

He called the ICARUS Intelligence Center and got Arcasso, slightly surprised to find him there at three in the morning. His surprise increased when Frank cut him short before he'd uttered two words.

"Hold it, Mark. The Amazon report—right? Before you start, get this: Fifteen minutes ago we received presidential approval for an all-out attack on that area."

"Frank, for God's sake!" Freedman shouted in alarm. "You've got to stop any damnfool scheme to wipe 'em out! They've been around for years; another week won't make any difference. We need to know a helluva lot more—part of that report is the scariest—"

"Mark—will you listen? I told you that was fifteen minutes ago. Something else has come up since then. Civil Defense Harrisburg has flashed a report from a game warden in upstate Pennsylvania. The guy swears he saw a Xeno on a deer's back! He had a real good look through binoculars, and he's sure."

"What!" cried Freedman. "What happened?"

"That's the crazy part: nothing!"

Freedman was not the only one who realized the possible significance of the deer report; and for those who thought as he did, a new and frightening set of possibilities was introduced.

If the Amazonian Xenos killed animals, it was safe to assume they were seeking an alternative food source. That fact made the news of the deer much more sinister.

Freedman attended an emergency conference at

Walter Reed, but even before he left Abdera, his mind was made up. Obviously only those animals killed for food would be found. If others were used as hosts for Xeno's eggs, they wouldn't be attacked, they'd live.

And suppose the Pennsylvania deer had been implanted? Suppose Xeno was switching from humans to animals because humans were proving difficult to implant?

The conference was unanimous in that view. Hard scientific evidence did not exist—they did not even know what types of animals were being found dead in the Amazon jungle by the natives—but all recognized that this was no time to stand around. The destruction of the remaining Xenos, at any cost, had become vital. Every day that passed increased the threat of a new generation of the aliens, and if they established themselves in wild animals the task would be next to impossible. Freedman said bluntly that he believed a second generation was already on the way; at least, they'd better work on that assumption.

Within the hour the White House had been apprised of this opinion. Immediately warnings went out to India, Germany, and Russia, and the President sent a personal representative to Brazil, his task to convince the Brazilian government that urgent action was necessary to protect not only the aborigines but ultimately the country's entire population.

Living within the jungle envelope, protected from strong winds, the Xenos had not yet spread very far; but as their numbers grew, they would be forced to seek new victims. The tribe should be evacuated and the whole area "neutralized" with a lethal nerve gas. The idea of wiping out all life in an area of about a thousand square miles wasn't attractive. But the alternative was less attractive still; a town like Manaus might suddenly find itself under attack. Given approval, the USAF would do the job.

Freedman spent the night in Washington as Arcasso's guest. Dinner was no sparkling affair, both men cocooned in their own somber thoughts. After the first course Frank's wife gave up trying to make conversation and got the meal over as fast as possible. Mark managed a few polite but unconvincing words as she cleared the table, which she took with a tight little smile.

Frank got up, tossing his napkin on the table.

"C'mon, Mark," he growled, heading for the den. He waved Mark to an armchair and fished out a bottle of bourbon and two glasses. "You want anything with it?" he said, still standing. As old world hospitality, it left a great deal to be desired, but Mark understood.

"No," he said, pulling out his pipe, "but what are you going to drink?"

"Yeah," he said heavily, producing a second bottle. "I know what you mean." He poured two big ones. "Help yourself," he said, putting an end to his duties as host. They drank in silence, like two strangers in a bar, Freedman staring blankly at the photographs of aircraft which covered the fireplace wall.

"You heard about Tatyana?"

Mark nodded. "Malin told me. I'm sorry. Such a waste . . ."

"You certainly are a cold bastard at times!" There was an edge to Arcasso's voice.

Mark took it calmly. "No, I'm a professional bastard. In my work, if you're anything else, you get your heart broken daily. She would have understood."

"Yeah," Arcasso understood also. "She was a great woman, Mark."

They drank, neither needing to admit it was an unspoken toast to Tatyana Ivanovna Marinskiya. For several minutes both men were silent.

"I'll shoot first," said Frank without preamble. "The Brazilians have got the message. We're free to strike as soon as they can get those poor bastards out. Remembering what you said, I've arranged for a couple of biologists to go in with the rescue team. They fly down tomorrow night—you can help with their briefing in the morning."

Freedman nodded, seeming less than excited.

"Now the good news. The Germans have caught both of their Xenos." He laughed shortly. "Trust the krauts to be on the ball!"

Freedman made a weak attempt at a smile as he refilled his glass.

"Hell! It's something, isn't it?"

"Oh, sure, it's something," replied Mark without enthusiasm.

"Sure it's something!" exclaimed Frank. "If the Germans can do it, so can we!"

"Frank," said Mark wearily, "you've been with this ICARUS business longer than anyone, and you know we've always been one step behind the action."

"That seems a bit unfair, Mark. Is it really our fault?"

"I didn't say it was. It's just a fact. Okay, so we learn fast—but not fast enough! With no previous experience to go on, we're bound to be behind. Unfortunately, I've got a sneaky feeling we won't get a second chance."

His pessimism forced Frank into the opposite camp. "Come on, Mark. Believe me, the Brazilian Xenos are as good as dead, and the Germans have ironed out their problem. That's a good start."

"No. You come on, Frank," said Mark gently. "Stop whistling in the dark."

Frank refilled his glass, breathing heavily. "Okay, so you tell me."

"First, those animals the Brazilian group fed on. I don't know if they have deer in that region; somehow I doubt it. I think the victims will turn out to be a species of wild hog. That's the item your biologists have to clarify. Nothing else matters. It's obvious that the Amazonian Xenos have thrived on their diet— remember the size of that specimen. They adapted because there weren't enough humans to go around. My guess is that Xeno can get by on hogs and deer, even if it prefers humans." He peered sharply at Arcasso through the gathering smoke. "How many hogs or wild deer d'you suppose we have in the States?"

Arcasso realized this was a rhetorical question, and remained silent.

"Last year we had sixty-five million hogs! And as for wild deer, you tell me! Get the idea?"

The horrified expression on Frank's face showed that he did. He tried to fight back. "You're guessing, Mark. There's no hard evidence."

"No, there isn't, and by the time we get it, it'll be too late. I'm working on probabilities, trying to stay even with Xeno, trying to keep from falling that one fatal step behind."

Frank considered this for a moment. "But you must have some reason for picking on hogs"—he shifted ground—"and just because this warden says he saw a Xeno on a deer's back—"

Mark cut in. "I said I'm working on probabilities. D'you realize that hogs are physiologically very close to humans? The blood structure is similar to ours." He went on quickly, before Frank could break his train of thought, "I'm convinced that Xeno has a very sophisticated blood-analysis system; without exception, it *always* finds the carotid artery in a human. Okay, that's not analysis, it's detection—and it sure as hell has that ability—but somehow, perhaps through smell, it *knows*, it analyzes. I'm aware of only one case of this so far—a girl in Abdera who had been a host to a Xeno egg was literally examined by a Xeno, but *not* attacked."

"You mean Jaimie's wife?"

Mark frowned at the interruption. "Yes," he said shortly. "I've thought a lot about that incident. It's odd. I don't understand it; maybe the Xeno detected something in her blood, some trace we failed to find which kept it from attacking her, I don't know. All I *do* know is that not one of the *Papa Kilo* passengers became a victim after their return. That proves nothing, and it's irrelevant to the point I'm making. If my theory's right, Xeno's blood-sensor has established that other earthly creatures can support it, as a food source and as a host for its egg. I believe that deer report, and if a deer is suitable, I'm damned sure a hog will be!"

Frank flung his cigar butt savagely into the fireplace. "Okay, okay, so what's your answer?"

"We have to get the facts from the Amazon, fast. Every day counts. If my opinion is confirmed, we have to kill and burn every hog within a hundred kilometers of a Xeno outbreak. We've also got to start hunting down and killing all deer in affected areas in the U.S. Every single last one of the Xenos must be destroyed—and all this *must* be completed before the fall!"

"And if it isn't?"

"Xeno will be established. It's no good snarling, Frank. Your outfit can't go spreading nerve gas

257

around in the States! Every remaining Xeno must have a hunting team assigned to it; give them a personal incentive, say ten thousand bucks for each one caught. That's the first priority. Then your Intelligence Center must produce maps of the affected areas, and the federal government must arrange the destruction of all hogs and deer in those areas. It's the only way!"

"Look, Mark," said Frank soberly, "I'm not saying you're wrong; the chances are you've got this doped out. But think of the problems!" He lit a new cigar. "I'm just an aviator, not a politician—thank Christ! But I've been around this town long enough to see the problems. The hog farmers will raise all kinds of hell, and the conservationists will scream the place down if the Army moves in and starts bumping off the deer—"

"So what? It *has* to be done—I'm certain it's our only hope."

"Sure, you're certain, but there's no hard evidence. Do you imagine all we have to do is say 'Okay, it's Dr. Freedman's hunch, so don't beef if you're put out of business'?"

"I'm not alone, Frank. The Walter Reed group and Harvard agreed."

"Oh, swell!" observed Frank caustically. "The hog farmers will be very impressed!"

"To hell with them!" exclaimed Mark passionately. "If the federal government goes along with what we believe, that's enough. The first duty of government is to govern!"

But events took a new turn, one which neither the Walter Reed group and Freedman nor anyone else had foreseen. Abruptly, the attacks stopped.

·XXXVI·

Another week of a long, hot summer passed, a week of suspense in which not one Xeno attack was reported. By the end of the week human nature had reasserted itself; people in the affected areas began to relax, even as Vesuvians had started rebuilding their homes before the lava had cooled. In Washington, the sharp edge of urgency was momentarily blunted.

The Amazonian operation had been executed with speed and precision. Eighty or ninety of the aborigines now lived in a guarded camp. In spite of their terror, they refused to reveal the location of their White God, and without their help, the search party could have looked forever in that terrain. Even the threat of death from the skies failed to move them. In all probability the idea was only dimly grasped; they rejected it as a matter of no importance. The White God came from the skies with his own devils; he would survive and await their return.

So along with every living creature in the target zone, their god and his faithful followers died within seconds as the killer rain-mist drifted down through the jungle's canopy of leaves. Far worse than the Xeno's venom, the sticky gas droplets had a much longer death-life; any creature entering the area for two or three months would quickly die.

The news the biologists brought back was less hopeful. Freedman's worst fear proved correct: the aborigines' food, the "gift of the god," turned out to be a species of wild hog.

Washington went ahead with plans. No one disagreed with the ideas of the biologists, but the cessation of attacks in the States and the success of the Brazilian strike reduced the tempo from white-hot to red-hot, and allowed the bureaucratic machine to get back in gear. Maps of infested areas were produced, but there was no immediate action. The farmers had to be consulted, compensation terms argued, and attempts had to be made to placate the conservation lobby about the deer.

The bureaucrats took the view that the delay of a week—or maybe two—would make no real difference, but with proper organization, a great deal of disruption could be avoided. After all, an estimated one million hogs would have to be destroyed; the procurement of the killing spray and the fuel needed to burn the carcasses would be a sizable project in itself. As for the deer, was it not better to let the hunters do the killing rather than the Army? That way the "sportsmen" would not be resentful. As long as the operation was completed before the first Xeno egg could hatch, what was the rush?

The Xeno hunting went on. It had been difficult enough when they were active, but now that they were unseen and unheard the task became impossible. Only fifteen or twenty remained, but they were scattered over the whole eastern seaboard from New York to Louisiana. Likely areas were still drenched with the knock-down gas, but nothing was produced. The Intelligence Center, plotting and recording all operations, nursed a growing suspicion that once a zone had been attacked, the Xeno avoided it, moving closer to human habitation where the gas was not used. It was the Abdera experience all over again, but until Xeno tipped its hand, there could be no certainty.

For those close to Freedman, life became difficult. Tense and on edge, he called the Center twice daily, despite Arcasso's repeated assurances that any news would be passed on the moment it came in. In bed, bath, office, or car, he had a radio pouring news into his ear. The fact that he could not say what he was waiting for only increased his agitation. He remained totally convinced—Xeno might be silent and unseen, but it was sure as hell up to something.

He was right.

The girl—once a state champion—swam effortlessly, her goal a raft floating well out in the middle of the lake. Behind her, in the shallows, a spirited game of "keep away" was in progress. No one followed her to the raft.

Reaching the float, she hauled herself out, grateful for the warming sunlight. She took off her cap, shook her hair loose, and for a time looked idly at the scene: the glittering water, the bathers on the distant shore. Her mind wandered, enjoying subconsciously the sensation of being young and healthy on a beautiful day.

She untied the halter-neck of her suit, pulling it down to her waist, and for a time leaned back on her arms, surrendering herself to the sun, her eyes closed. The sharp cry of a bird broke her reverie; a flock of ducks took off, honking discordantly. She turned and stretched out, aware of the sensuous pleasure of the coarse canvas against her breasts. Head resting on arms, she felt the sun and wind caressing her. Lulled by the gentle rocking of the float, she dozed.

A small, gleaming shape detached itself from the top of a tree on the deserted north shore of the lake, launching into a shallow glide. Halfway to its target, it ingested air and emitted a faint burp of sound as it climbed sharply and resumed its fast glide. Close to the raft, it banked, wings glistening in the sun as it made two silent circles.

It touched down on the raft and was still, legs splayed, watching its prey.

It crawled closer to the sleeping figure until it was almost touching one leg. Again it waited, motionless, the terrible golden eyes watching, devoid of expression.

The wings folded back, disappearing against the flanks of the shimmering body. Slowly, its touch as light as the faint breeze, it reached up to her thigh with its forelegs, and paused again. The girl did not move. With infinite care, the Xeno crawled onto her thigh.

The girl stirred. Instantly the Xeno froze and remained still until she lapsed back into sleep. The creature's back arched slightly. The tail curved down below the body until it barely touched the girl's flesh and extruded a tiny spot of clear, numbing fluid. A needlelike ovipositor slid out of its protective sheath in the tail. Pink and moist, it went through the center of the spot of fluid, into the girl's thigh. The Xeno remained still for about five seconds, except for a minute pulsation in the tail. Gently the ovipositor withdrew from the girl's body, back into its own. The tail straightened, and at the same instant the wings spread. With the faintest sound the Xeno lifted into the air, darting away like a giant dragonfly. Once clear of the girl, it took in more air, jetting upwards, flashing back toward shore. Its day's work was complete.

The girl stirred again, rubbing the back of her leg with the other foot. Then she slept again, totally unaware of the alien life within her.

There were many like her.

The significance of Xeno's virtual disappearance did not become apparent until ten days after the attacks ceased. Two youths camping in the Blue Ridge Mountains gave the first news; one, returning to camp with wood for the fire, saw a Xeno on his sleeping buddy's shoulder. It flew off instantly, but the teenager, though badly scared, acted responsibly and quickly got his companion to the nearest doctor. The physician immediately confirmed the presence of a "bite" on the victim's shoulder.

The report shattered the fragile calm in both Washington and Abdera: Now it was clear why the Xenos had stopped attacking. But the truly alarming news was the Xeno's location—it had traveled far beyond the area of its last attack. The area in which the fifteen or twenty Xenos could be implanting humans and animals had now expanded tenfold; the maps of "designated areas" had been rendered completely useless.

All evening Freedman sat alone in his small library, staring at his dated maps, thinking bitterly of the lost time. If only they had struck at once—but they hadn't. Once more, Xeno had kept that one step in front.

Arcasso called at around 9:00 P.M. Mark immediately noticed that his voice was slurred, his responses slow and clumsy—he'd been drinking heavily. Well aware of the significance of the Blue Ridge report, the Walter Reed group had killed and dissected two of their Xenos; in each case four microscopie eggs had been found in the ovipositor track.

Four! Was this a new adaptation of Xeno—or had they always implanted that many? Suppose the later eggs were prevented from growing by changes in the host's blood; suppose the second and subsequent eggs could only grow when the demands of the first had been met and the host's metabolism had been restored to normal?

Shortly before midnight his wife came in to find her

husband clutching a half-empty glass, his eyes filled with despair.

"I know you're worried, dear," she said gently, "but this won't help. Come to bed. It may not seem so bad in the morning."

He managed a faint smile, shaking his head slowly. "No, dear. It'll get worse every day from now on. We've lost. Earth has a new, dreadful life form. We'll fight, but—" He shrugged helplessly.

"Perhaps we deserve it. Perhaps God meant it to happen," she said hesitantly.

Suddenly there were tears in his eyes. "Do you really believe that?" She came to him, knelt at his feet, and took his hands in hers. "Do you *not* believe it?"

He had no answer.

Up on the rim of Abdera Hollow, Jaimie and his wife had been asleep for some time. Suddenly he awoke. The windows were open; a gentle pine-scented breeze moved the parted curtains. Shane was not beside him, but this was no great surprise; she was well into her fourth month of pregnancy, and her frequent trips to the bathroom were now a part of life.

For a time he lay still, waiting for her to return. He dozed, then jerked awake again. Still she had not returned. He raised his head from the pillow, looked toward the bathroom door, and saw no light beneath it. Now fully alert, he sat up. Could she have fallen, or be sleepwalking? Silently, he slid out of bed, fumbling for his robe.

He padded barefooted to the top of the stairs. From somewhere below came a reflected glow of light.

Puzzled, he moved quickly down the staircase. The light came from the kitchen, through the half-open door. He reached it and peered in.

Shane stood by the icebox, half-turned away from him, eating. Even as he saw her, she heard him. She turned sharply, her expression a mixture of fright and guilt.

Blood dripped from the corners of her mouth. In her hand, red with blood, was a piece of raw liver.

For an instant, he was paralyzed with shock. Then the realization hit him with blinding force: This was not the craving of a pregnant woman. Now he knew why the Xeno had not touched her. It was not because of what had happened, but because of what was still to come.

"No!" he screamed. "Oh, God, Shane—no!"

·Epilogue·

Julius Pechall, professor of ancient languages, switched off the projector, suddenly aware of the silence as the faint hum of the micro-reader stopped.

For a time he pondered what he had read. Obviously it had been a thinly disguised novel, written soon after God's Finding. He guessed that one of the characters had been the author—Malin, perhaps? None of them had great depth; the story was the important thing.

What did it matter? The story gave him a few interesting sidelights for his paper—providing he trod carefully on the theology. But aside from that, it made him wonder what the world had been like back in that golden, but very sinful, age. It was a time that seemed so remote, yet little more than one hundred years had elapsed since the God first struck, ending the wicked ways, the fornication.

He prayed at once for absolution. He realized he had been very close to Impure Thought, and even for a researcher, normally granted some leeway, that could be very dangerous. One could be sent south.

He got up, donned his lightweight metallic suit, gloves, and helmet, and adjusted the heating. It was fairly safe in New Washington, Alaska, at this time of the year. But even in the capital of United North

America, with all its defenses, there was no guarantee against the scourges of a vengeful God.

He hurried toward the airlock, reciting to himself the Prayer for Preservation. It would not be wise to be late for the dawn service.

Dell Bestsellers

The Latest Science Fiction And Fantasy From Dell

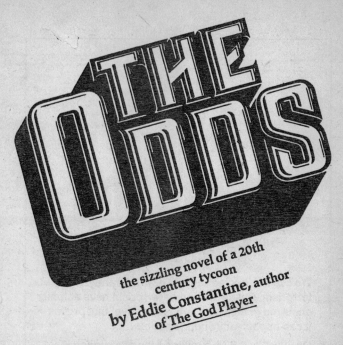

THE ODDS

the sizzling novel of a 20th century tycoon
by Eddie Constantine, author of _The God Player_

In 1939, in Nazi-run France, the penniless young son of a village whore began his odyssey of ambition . . .

Within a decade, Charles de Belmont was one of the richest financiers in the world. He'd loved the most beautiful, the choicest women. And controlled the most powerful—and dangerous—men.

He'd learned to play THE ODDS.

Dell $2.25